Michael Shea wrot[...] 1970s under the [...] stopped writing n[...] Press Secretary, a position he held for a decade. He now combines writing with a wide range of business interests, dividing his time between Edinburgh and London.

Praise for *Spin Doctor*

'Michael Shea knows all about political intrigue and makes fine use of his expertise in *Spin Doctor*, which dashes enjoyably around the corridors of influence. What gives *Spin Doctor* its cutting edge is the fact that Michael Shea has been a spin doctor himself. His fiction bears a disturbing resemblance to fact.'   *Sunday Times*

The British Ambassador

'Michael Shea has produced another first-class thriller in which his experience at the heart of government is put to excellent use.'   *Sunday Telegraph*

State of the Nation

'Michael Shea, who, as a career diplomat and former press secretary to the Queen, has seen more than his share of political intrigue, has struck on a rich new seam: Scotland... and Shea extracts the maximum from a nightmare scenario.'   *The Times*

Berlin Embassy

'A taut, plausible thriller with an intriguing scenario.'
Independent

BY THE SAME AUTHOR

Spin Doctor
The British Ambassador
State of the Nation
The Berlin Embassy

MICHAEL SHEA

SPINOFF

HarperCollins*Publishers*

This novel is entirely a work of fiction.
The names, characters and incidents portrayed in it are
the work of the author's imagination. Any resemblance to
actual persons, living or dead, events or localities is
entirely coincidental.

HarperCollins*Publishers*
77–85 Fulham Palace Road,
Hammersmith, London W6 8JB

www.fireandwater.com

This paperback edition 2000

1 3 5 7 9 8 6 4 2

First published in Great Britain by
HarperCollinsPublishers 1999

Copyright © Michael Shea 1999

The Author asserts the moral right to
be identified as the author of this work

ISBN 0 00 649877 9

Set in Linotron Sabon

Printed and bound in Great Britain by
Clays Ltd, St Ives, plc

All rights reserved. No part of this publication may be
reproduced, stored in a retrieval system, or transmitted,
in any form or by any means, electronic, mechanical,
photocopying, recording or otherwise, without the prior
permission of the publishers.

This book is sold subject to the condition that it shall not,
by way of trade or otherwise, be lent, re-sold, hired out or
otherwise circulated without the publisher's prior consent
in any form of binding or cover other than that in which it
is published and without a similar condition including this
condition being imposed on the subsequent purchaser.

To Mona, Katriona and Ingeborg

'Africa, amongst the continents, will teach it you: that God and the Devil are one.'

Karen Blixen

New and re-emerging infectious diseases
Infectious diseases remain the world's leading cause of death. During the past two decades alone, at least thirty new infectious diseases have appeared. Ebola haemorrhagic fever and bovine spongiform encephalopathy are prominent examples of newcomers. At the same time, older diseases like diphtheria, cholera and tuberculosis are returning vigorously.

The WHO's mission is to strengthen national and international capacity in the surveillance and control of infectious diseases that represent new, emerging, and re-emerging public health problems, including the growing phenomenon of antibiotic resistance. It aims to have a team of experts at the location of an outbreak anywhere in the world within twenty-four hours of being officially notified of it – as happened in the 1995 outbreak of Ebola haemorrhagic fever in Zaire (now the Democratic Republic of Congo) in Africa.

Kisangani, Congo, Sunday 15th May

At last the torrential rain had stopped. A cluster of armed men, some in the drenched and tattered remants of uniforms, huddled by the door of the hut, staring in horror at the young woman as she lay writhing on a filthy palliasse. Two of the soldiers looked no more than children, while the rusted state of their weapons confirmed that they could never have been part of any properly trained fighting force. Each held a piece of cloth over his mouth and nostrils, as if to ward off both the stench and whatever the infection was. They talked nervously to each other, their voices low. If this was only malaria, as they had been assured by their lieutenant, none of them had seen symptoms like this. They knew all about AIDS, but that did not strike people in this way. They were not afraid of death: they had killed too many for that. But guns and machetes were of no avail against fever, so they had all clamoured to move on into the jungle, away from this cursed place. The lieutenant ignored their pleas. His sector commandant had ordered them to bivouac at the village till he returned, and that was that.

One older soldier, more travelled than the rest, suggested to the others that the woman could have dengue fever. He had seen it before. It caused such delirium, he told them. His old grandfather had called it breakbone fever, so severe were the headaches, the backache, the painful limbs. It, like malaria, was mosquito-borne. Sometimes dengue fever caused vast bleeding into the skin, the liver and the brain. After three or four days of hell, there was usually a lull, a temperature-free respite of twenty-four hours or more, then the symptoms returned with a vengeance. Dengue fever was a killer, but if they kept well back, they would be all right.

When his men eventually dispersed to prepare their evening meal, the lieutenant, braver or more caring than the conscripts, carefully approached the young woman with a battered bucket and wet cloth, and, head turned aside, with one hand bathed away some of the sweat from her riddled face and from around the lesions on her neck and breasts. He poured the bucket of water over the rest of her, then he too turned and left her alone.

She was still alive four hours later when the soldiers escorted the doctor to her. He was a white man, more yellow in fact, from years of sweating it out in that tropical inferno. He was a strange man, the doctor, but he was European, and therefore must know the truth. He came dressed in a sweat-stained bush shirt and dirty cotton trousers. In the back of the battered Volvo in which he had arrived sat a nurse of sorts, a nervous African woman in a white coat, who stayed firmly where she was instead of carrying his heavy canvas bag for him. The doctor entered the compound and went ahead of the soldiers towards the hut. He stood alone for a while, staring down at the woman. He noted the strange round wound, high on her forehead. He bent low as if to feel her pulse, but then, on instinct, drew quickly back. He did not need to take her temperature: he knew it was high. He noted the rash, the stink of decaying skin. Then, horridly, he pulled her eyelids roughly open with a sharp stick and stared at the unseeing pupils. There was a strange grey pallor over them that suggested blindness, if not now, soon.

The lieutenant appeared from out of the bush. He came towards the doctor as he was leaving, but hesitated for a moment, nervous at interrupting. Then he steeled himself and asked, in French, if it could possibly be malaria or dengue.

'Neither,' said the doctor. He did not turn, did not look at the soldier. 'You related?' he asked.

'No,' said the African. 'So?'

The doctor appeared not to hear him at first, then gave an imperceptible shrug. 'Have her brought to my hospital,' he said. 'No. Not in my car,' he added quickly. 'I want everyone who's been in close contact with her rounded up, by force if necessary. Keep them isolated here for at least ten days. Tell me immediately if anyone else gets sick.'

The lieutenant's eyes had widened with horror. 'What is it?' he asked.

'I don't . . . Did you go near her too?' the doctor asked.

The lieutenant nodded. Fear of the unknown was the worst of all fears. 'Can you save her?' he breathed. 'Save us?'

Only then did the doctor turn to stare at the African. He shrugged slightly, and the lieutenant guessed the truth. Her gods would be of no avail, and as for the rest of them, only time would tell.

St Philip's Hospital, Central London, Wednesday 18th May

The Medical Board, with special funding from the Department of Health, had excelled itself. The walls were gleaming with new paint; the floors were covered with shining tiles; triple-glazed windows separated the Special Isolation Unit from the outside world. The corridors and offices were similarly divided off from the individual, anti-contagion wards. Row upon row of sparkling disinfection chambers lined one wall, while sealed bags of specially sterilized equipment were stacked neatly on shelves around the central examination room. On hooks by the door hung three-ply overalls with built-in masks which covered the whole head, while below them on the floor, pairs of disposable rubber boots were lined up, which everyone entering the unit was obliged to wear.

Professor Desmond Grant, a senior consultant at St Philip's Hospital, dressed himself carefully in the protective clothing he had been allocated by the staff nurse, and pulled on the double-sheathed gloves. A high profile, acute case had been admitted to intensive care in the Isolation Unit early that same evening. As the director of the world-famous Harman Institute, the professor was principally involved in leading a research project into new variants of CJD, or Creutzfeldt-Jakob disease, the human form of so-called mad cow disease, which rots both the brains and the bodies of its victims. The Institute was also involved in monitoring and treating outbreaks of other rare diseases that occurred from time to time. The professor had been called in from a boring Hampstead dinner party to examine this new admission, and was only given the the patient's background when he arrived at the hospital. The registrar met him personally to tell him that the man, a retired general, was exhibiting disturbing and highly unusual symptoms which had totally baffled the duty medical team.

Professor Grant waited patiently in the corridor outside the private ward until the nursing sister had persuaded the general's distraught wife and daughter, who were almost hysterical at having been made to wear protective face masks before they had been allowed in to see him, to leave him to sleep and to give themselves some rest. From television and from newspapers, Grant already knew a fair amount about the general. Ever since the latter's heroic exploits as a Guards officer in the Falklands, then later in the Gulf and Bosnian wars, General Sir George Haycock MC, DSO, who was always known as General George, had been adept at hitting the headlines. He had held nearly every top post in Britain's armed services, including ex-head of Personnel at the Ministry of Defence and command of Military Intelligence at NATO, and so on. He had retired a couple of years earlier and was now a household name, not for his charity work with the Army Benevolent Fund but because he was such an excellent performer on television and much in demand every time a news and current affairs editor wanted an expert to comment on any story which involved the armed services. He was big, convivial, wise, with sound views on current conflicts all around the globe. Now he had caught something which had totally baffled his own doctors. Because the first symptoms had been memory loss, followed by the rapid breakdown of several of his internal organs, could this be some variant of CJD?

The moment he pulled the protective mask over his face and head and entered the intensive care ward to examine the general, Grant recognized that this could not be CJD as he knew it. He noted the signs of decay, the pustules and rashes which covered the patient's cheeks and forehead, the cracked and broken lips flecked with blood and foam. He saw the strange grey film that lay like a shadow across his eyes and knew that here was something entirely new: new and highly disturbing, even to a man as cool, cautious, and dispassionate as he.

1

Early that Tuesday morning, Lyle Thane bounced into his office, sat down at his desk and stared irritably at the three trays in front of him. The pile in the In-tray was surprisingly small. The Out-tray was empty, waiting greedily for his day's output, while the 'Pending' contents – files, submissions, minutes, Cabinet papers, letters to the PM, to which draft answers needed to be prepared – were stacked a good six inches above the edges of the tray. He disliked Pending trays. He didn't believe in 'pending' anything. He liked action; pending was a weak substitute, but these concerned current problems that demanded advice from ministers or their departments throughout Whitehall. Without that he could do nothing.

While he waited for the morning's post, Thane swung his chair round and stared out through the bomb-proof net curtains, across the clinically neat garden of Number Ten, towards Horseguards, where a squadron of Life Guards was, at that precise moment, parading past on their immaculate mounts. It was too early for guard changing, so perhaps they were rehearsing for some forthcoming State visit. A brief shaft of sunlight on an otherwise bleak May morning glistened on theatrical helmets, breastplates and sparkling harnesses. Bring back Cool Britannia for God's sake, he thought, even if all that inherited pageantry did charge the tills of tourism. He swung his chair back to face into the room, reached into the bottom drawer of his desk, took out a little hand mirror, and surreptitiously examined his face and hair. Not a lock out of place. He practised one of his quick, sincere, smiles. Not bad. A winning look. Carefully replacing the mirror in the drawer, he felt his normal self-esteem gearing up to full swing. He had recently overheard one of his more acerbic colleagues say of him that he had lost all his modesty around the age of three. He hadn't been upset by the remark: why should he be? He had much to be proud of. Why not flaunt it?

Lyle Thane was a small, poised man, no more than five foot five. He held himself four square and erect, and that, plus his carefully immaculate tailoring, made for a good first impression. He knew it. He had a habit of standing well back, giving other people a lot of body space, so he was able to eyeball them without them having to bend to look down at him. He had learnt that technique and many other sharp social habits, without even thinking about them, early on in life; they had always stood him in good stead. He spent a great deal of time on his dress and appearance, including thousands of pounds capping the crazy set of teeth he had been born with. He had locked onto the fact that, in the goldfish bowl of public life, while fashion changed, style remained. That was why his ties and shirts were carefully selected to mirror his bright, modern, but slightly traditional image. Thane was no Londoner, but he had rapidly acquired all the key metropolitan traits, the gloss for the role he had chosen in life. Not even Sarah St Just, his current, highly presentable girlfriend, knew that his shoes were built up to add that extra inch to his stature. Lyle Thane was what he did. Someone in his student days had likened his ambition to that of a Russian commissar. He was perfectly content with that image as well.

He was, after all, at life's peak. With care and some sparky personal spindoctoring, he was unstoppable. He'd reached a career level which was a thousand times higher than his bigoted martinet of an Old Socialist father had ever even aspired to. And he'd got there in just over three decades. How he'd loved scribbling that first, casual, off-hand message home on Downing Street notepaper. It was to do with some social security issue, he remembered. 'May be interested to see the line I've suggested the PM should take,' he wrote in imperious black ink. What he meant was, 'Fuck you, Dad.'

He'd arrived. No doubting that. A few years establishing himself, his ideas, his strategies, here, then Parliament, then upwards. Thank God he'd pulled out of the Foreign Office exam. Thank God he hadn't succumbed to that once-so-attractive research job at Oxford. He was the best. But he was also cautious. He'd learnt much from the mistakes of all those other might-have-beens at the centre of power: no false claims of influence-peddling from him, no lovey-dovey relationships with top journalists, no cronyism. It had often been tempting, especially when the editor of *The Times* himself had called, suggesting he might like an off-the-record lunch with Simon Jenkins. Simon Jenkins: Christ! There was only one area where he wasn't in full control: Sarah St Just. She kept hitting the gossip columns: Dempster, Hickey, the others. Always being featured in *Tatler* and *Jennifer's Diary*. Constantly referred to in the *Sunday Times* It-Girl pieces. Flame-haired, just as he liked them; sensational, passionate, wild, huge sexual appetite, fantastic in bed, almost. A little bit of a problem there: nothing much, but it needed working on. He quickly turned his mind to other, less disturbing things.

He'd always kept his name right out of the news stories. Faceless; behind the scenes. Early fame was a killer. He remembered so many of those other Young Turks, would-be high flyers. God, how they'd fallen. Where were they now? Editors loved too-clever-by-half victims like that. Editors were like the high priests of long ago: they created gods, created devils. They built up some high-flying yuppie on the nursery slopes of politics, garlanded him – it was usually a him – for a day, then came in with some ritual slaughter. The public would have to wait to learn about Lyle Thane. The people he needed now were, quite simply, the top hundred in Britain, London, Westminster, Whitehall, Downing Street. The PM himself, an audience of one, would do. Who else mattered? Peter Morgan, Her Majesty's First Minister, was all the public Thane needed right now. Later it would be different. He would plan it carefully. It was like seduction. Slow, slow, soften up. It always worked. What were those clever lines from Byron about seduction?

> A little she strove, and much repented,
> And whispering 'I will ne'er consent – consented.

Great lines. Great poet. Thane appreciated poetry. He was well read. He knew who to read, whom to have read, whom to let people know he had read. From Burke to JS Mill, to Keynes to all the latest, up to speed, political theorists. He liked Keynes, but that guy had argued that no one ever had a new idea after the age of twenty-nine. Something like that. But Thane was thirty-two, sitting here on life's peak, with bagfuls of new ideas. Only yesterday, for example, the PM had hardly altered the draft of his speech on law, order and benefit fraud. Delivered verbatim, including the light asides – not that benefit fraud was a joking matter. The PM had added just a touch of personal perspective. That was OK. Give Peter Morgan that; he was good, very good on presentation. He'd once let slip his admiration for Groucho Marx's maxim, effectively, if you can fake sincerity, you can fake anything. The media had jumped on it and branded Morgan with the nickname *Mr Sincere*. The Opposition claimed he was poor on facts, poor on substance, worse on strategy, and a disaster when it came to choosing or assessing his fellow Cabinet members. They weren't far off the mark. Except in the PM's choice of his Private Office staff, of course. But what a stage performer Morgan could be. Which was why that man had every single drop of his loyalty. Until he didn't.

Thirty-three next year. Really no new thoughts after that? That was plain, bloody nonsense. Maybe Keynes was rubbish after all. Lyle Thane would always think, create, make possible the impossible. He'd not only give people what they wanted; he'd give them what they never dreamt they wanted. He'd glide effortlessly into the public eye, with eat-your-heart-out-Elizabeth-Hurley Sarah St Just, and what a central casting name that was, at his side. St Margaret's, Westminster wedding? Why not? He'd have to work on his in-bed technique and at the religious bit, as well as sending his cast-off father to charm school before he was fit to be seen in public. He had made up his own personal crash course, rebranding his pedigree as a thoroughbred mix of Cool Britannia and traditional working class values. That was the name of the Thane game. He saw it all so clearly. Personal strategy was everything.

Eleven o'clock. He'd been at his desk since shortly after seven. He preferred it bright and early: prime time to think before phones and meetings took over. He didn't make a thing about his early starts, but made sure, with an occasional quick aside, that people knew. Sarah didn't mind. She'd sleep for another four hours at least, till she started showering and oiling and powdering and dolling up for her It-girl rendezvous with other young ladies who lunched. It was San Lorenzo's in Beauchamp Place today. He'd sneaked a look in her diary. He liked to know where she was, just in case. What a trophy girl she was. What a trophy wife she'd be, if she behaved herself until he was ready for all that. In the meantime, great social life. *Eleven o'clock.* Thane had already had an active four hours. He'd spoken personally to the chairman of British Airways about the PM's worries on transatlantic routing changes, then he'd had a quick word with the Chancellor's private secretary about the briefing for the PM on the way the European Monetary Union negotiations were going. After that, he'd spoken directly to MacCallum, Scotland's First Minister, about the future regulation of television broadcasting north of the border, and put him in the picture with Downing Street's current thinking. MacCallum had been a bit miffed about speaking to a mere underling like Thane; he wanted to speak to the minister responsible. 'By all means,' said Thane, spinning drily, 'but he doesn't really understand what the PM wants, which is why Mr Morgan asked me to ring you direct.' It had worked: MacCallum had got off his high horse and listened. Thane had, lastly, had a word with the British Ambassador in Paris about the forthcoming bilaterals with the French. It was promising to be a tricky summit and he wanted to get the Embassy's views on the line the PM should adopt – and to get a feel for the spin the press office at Number Ten should take if things went wrong.

As he came off the telephone, Daniel Evans, the Press Secretary, bounded into his office to discuss the agenda for the rest of the day. He'd just come from a confidential, way, way off-the-record briefing with the latest editor of the *Observer*. Evans had talked through the approach he was intending to take with Thane beforehand. The two men always got on well, at least Thane thought they did. Evans had an easy-going way about him, but it hid a heart of cold steel. The Press Secretary was a useful man to keep on the right side. He always knew something sensationally indiscreet about someone, and Thane thrived on such gossip. Evans was from the valleys, a tough ex-rugby player who would mutter imprecations in Welsh when outraged by some press story or other. The Downing Street political correspondents all respected him, or feared him. He had a particular dislike of the tabloids, but managed to conceal it except when they went over the top on some ministerial sex or bribes scandal. Then Evans would hit hard, not only directly, but by ensuring that the editors knew he was displeased. It was all right for an editor to declare publicly that he was staying loyal to his lobby correspondent, but if that lobby correspondent was put beyond the pale on a longterm basis, and Evans was very capable of that, then he wasn't much use as a lobby correspondent. In the end, 'Daniel the Press' had the whip hand. The other great thing about Daniel was that he was quick to take a point. He and Thane had a way of getting to the same conclusion, hitting a solution, at the same time. They clicked. They weren't close friends – Thane had none for a start – but they knew the overarching agenda and were prepared to work together to achieve it.

An hour later, around midday, in his tight, pre-planned schedule, Thane had a brief and less than satisfactory encounter with that Grand Old Man of Spindoctoring, Sir Mark Ivor. Dinosaur. Busted his flush years ago, after Thatcher, Major, et al. Yet according to gossip, the old guy still earnt more than just a golden crust from those top industrialists and others who believed he still had influence. No worries. No harm. No competition. Just that one odd little shaft of irritation. Sir Mark Ivor, early sixties, grey-haired, distinguished, avuncular. A fraction off-hand when he eventually arrived. Trouble was, he knew the previous generation. Knew Dad even, one of the Old Labour, key constituency workers, he said. Must check that out. More crucial, knew the PM's dad, and, most important of all, the PM's mum, which was why the boss had agreed to give him a full half-hour. The PM's mum had been quite a starlet in her day: whoopee lady. *Who's Who* relationships, especially who had actually bedded whom in those heady, flower-power days, would be fun investigating, given a little help from the DNA boyos with their devastatingly revealing scientific techniques.

In retrospect, Thane had quite seriously disliked the way Sir Mark had wandered into his office, as if it was still familiar territory. No warmth. Quite distant, actually. No appreciation, no recognition of the new team pulling the current levers of power. His time-of-day exchange had been just OK: 'Nice to meet you.' No substance. No revelations. Most worrying of all, no requests. None. No favours sought. That was a bit lese-majesty or something. He had been sitting there, waiting to be lobbied by Sir Mark. He was a Number One New Achiever. He existed to broker influence. Who the hell did Sir Mark bloody Ivor, 'Hello, and precisely who are you?' he'd asked, think he bloody well was?

Thane would have been more than a little surprised by the answer to his unspoken question. Sir Mark was quite clear who he was these days. He was above such things. On his way out of Downing Street almost an hour and a half later, he might have been seen actually yawning. He yawned a lot now. Age had been good to him. He'd worn well. He ate Young Turks like Lyle Thane for breakfast. Except nowadays he didn't even bother doing that. And as for the current Prime Minister, despite the title he held, Peter Morgan was a nobody through and through.

Under that half-inch veneer – nothing. At one moment the man had actually dried up, as if he'd lost the plot, the thread of his own arguments. But what did any of it really matter any more? Sir Mark was rich; not mega-rich, but rich enough. He could, after all, only sleep in one bed at a time, eat only three meals a day, be driven by one chauffeur in only one car. He had all the luxuries he needed: town apartment with as many modern and ancient paintings as the walls could bear, cottage with every mod con tucked away in the Highlands, and, his latest acquisition, a walled *gîte* in a small village some twenty miles from Montpellier airport. He was a happy man, despite the pacemaker. His motto, engraved on a plaque above his desk, echoed the poet Landor: 'I strove with none, for none was worth my strife.' This wasn't a rehearsal for life any more: this was it, and he was enjoying it.

Sir Mark yawned again, and when he got back to his flat in Victoria, remained in a drowsy, contemplative mood for quite some time. How things had changed at Number Ten. He could remember the days of Harold Wilson. Now there was a real schemer. Wilson had once said of public relations that it was 'organized lying'. How well Harold, the past master, had known that. Sir Mark also recalled how Edward Heath, and Alex Douglas-Home, and Uncle Jim Callaghan and so on, had handled things, quite apart from the Lady herself and her grey successor. They'd all known how to run that particular shop. He'd been in and out of Number Ten so often in those heady days that he was considered a full-time member of staff, invited to express his views on everything and everyone, as they came to value his judgment, his ability to sense danger, his articulateness, his skill in sizing up a problem succinctly. He was the man for all seasons, with the solutions rather than the problems, the adviser who saw the wood rather than the trees.

In the early days it had largely been presentational advice he had offered: a bit of PR here, a touch on the tiller there, to help a Prime Ministerial press officer handle that day's media crisis. Then things had shifted. He'd become a figure in his own right, not out of choice but increasingly because of the things he was known to have fixed behind the scenes. In broadsheet parlance, he'd become the 'Modern Machiavelli'. Then they'd nicknamed him 'The Spindoctor', long before the word was in common usage. He'd more or less invented the term, then had watched it being taken over by others like Peter Mandelson, turned around, rediscovered, rebranded, as if what was now called spindoctoring was so very different from the past. Yet it was different. In those high-powered days, all he did was to help present arguments in such a determining way that the resulting decisions became inevitable. Now, in the new Britain, even after Mandelson had fallen, the spindoctors ruled. What they said went. Every backbench MP, every junior minister, had to clear everything before they said anything. They were not allowed to be interviewed by the national media unless they got permission from the Central Control Freaks first, and could be trusted to stay in line. That was the difference between then and now. These were the days of the Thought Police, an age in which what Claire Short had called manipulation by the 'creatures of the dark' had arrived.

It would have been an exaggeration to suggest that Ivor was concerned by all this. He knew that, sooner or later, there would be another U-turn and democracy would prevail. He'd watched the trend with a certain relaxed detachment, though that detachment became frayed from time to time when he felt himself alienated by the pure mediocrity of those who had come to power. He had attended a recent reception on the terrace of the House of Commons, and had been taken aback when he realized that he knew almost no one there. He sensed that many recognized him, though doubtless they wrote him off as a figure of the past, a has-been, a Neanderthal. Let them. He'd shrugged inwardly. Men and events moved on. The graveyards, to misquote Talleyrand, were full of indispensable men and women. The opponents of his own past were disappearing one by one. Only yesterday, old Lord Pink had died. He'd read his obituary with something approaching pleasure. Pink had once been the most feared and venomous of all the Fleet Street media proprietors.

Princes, prime ministers, politicians, and captains of industry had trembled in his presence. He had been able to make or break a reputation in a flash, and never baulked at doing so. The last time Sir Mark had seen him, he'd turned into a shambling old buffoon, lost in a cloud of senility. Now he was gone, and page after page of the newspapers were full of adulation and praise for a man they had universally hated when he had been part of their culture. He remembered his own battles with Lord Pink: he'd never come across someone quite so openly motivated by financial greed and, it was said, by a hugely deviant sexual appetite.

Ivor only occasionally regretted the times when he could pick up the phone to any editor at any time of the day or night, and place a story, tweak an attitude, polish an editorial. He, like the late Lord Pink, had changed many events, but it had only been in later years, when his name had appeared too often in the papers, that he felt his influence begin to wane. That was life. It had been time to move on, anyway. Now, when he manipulated, when he influenced events, he did it by manipulating others. In that way Sir Mark, though he would have indignantly denied it, was not so unlike young Lyle Thane, sitting there with his bulging ego in his precariously spinning seat at Number Ten, Downing Street.

Someone on television had once asked Sir Mark whether he was the man who had spawned the modern breed of media manipulator. He had avoided answering the question directly. Deep down, he believed he had two distinct advantages over today's hard young spindoctors: he had experience, but, more importantly, he knew where the bodies were buried. Some of the young might patronize him, but he still kept a rough check on who was going where. He sat on a quango or two, and if he didn't know them, those transient pushers and pullers on the levers of power, he knew where many of them came from. He knew more than a few secrets from a long-forgotten past that could be pulled out of the closet as and when needed. But why bother? He who had worked with the great and the good was not as trim as he once had been. His goals in life now largely related to staying fit in body and mind for as long as possible. Little else mattered.

So why then had he been elated by taking up the summons to Number Ten that day? Was it pride, was it vanity, was it a lust after things that were no more? It was none of those. Peter Morgan was, quite simply, doing what so many of his predecessors had done when they approached Sir Mark. He had been searching for dispassionate advice on a whole range of topical political issues from someone who wasn't on the make, no longer had axes to grind, was not looking for prime ministerial patronage. Like his greater predecessors, Prime Minister Morgan had revealed himself as isolated and alone, alone with the buck that had always to stop on his desk; alone, and for a few moments strangely silent, as if he had already lost the plot. In that ivory tower, anyone would value the advice, the judgment, the guru-like qualities, of a man like Sir Mark Ivor.

Back in Downing Street, deep under that exasperatingly clever and, yes, often charming, exterior, Lyle Thane felt unsettled. He had a theory that, in life, most people had something to be ashamed of. Everyone had, at heart, one thing he or she desperately wanted to hide from somebody else, one secret to keep hidden. Fear of exposure, coupled with hidden guilt, ruled many lives, conjured up many hideous dreams, fuelled many a lie. Fear of discovery could strike terror in the most controlled heart. Even in his short life in politics he had seen cover-ups fail, time after time, in British and American public life. The Clinton business was only the most long drawn out, embarrassing and foolish of many. Once something shameful was embarked upon, it was only a matter of waiting for the eventual exposure. You were never secure behind a lie. Thane believed that if he went unexpectedly up to most individuals and said: 'I know the truth about you,' they might laugh, but, if they even remotely believed him, they would also tremble. If that man or woman was in a position of power, given that all major political events were seen through the prism of the personalities involved, such a remark could so easily deprive them of their ability to function properly in the future. A tiny slip, a small financial indiscretion, a casual affair, an unthought-out denial, could bring devastation in its wake. Too often the cover-up was a worse crime than the crime itself.

In the meantime he was required to be on duty at the Downing Street reception that evening. His job was to meet, greet, and, more importantly, single out and bring up to the PM, those whom it would be useful, for strategic or policy reasons, to soften up with his well-oiled chat. They'd already had the pop stars in, the luvvies, the actors, the arts administrators. They'd done the teachers. They'd entertained the leaders of the Welsh and the Scottish assemblies, and had poured the best champagne the PM's hospitality budget could afford into the captains and the kings of industry, commerce and finance. Tonight it was the turn of the sciences and the medical professions.

It was all to do with lobbying. Too often that practice had been vilified. There was all the difference in the world between the single-issue pressure groups, like the nurses or the farmers, pushing their views or campaigning for higher pay or more money in subsidies, and those largely discredited commercial lobby companies, staffed by bright young researchers who had worked for various parties in the last election, who would eagerly pursue any cause if the fee was high enough. But lobbying had too often been seen as a one-way route, outsiders trying to get at, or persuade, the government of the day. In practice, it was often the other way round: from the inside out. Governments needed the support of various interest groups so that their policies went through with as much public support and acclaim as possible.

Thane was ready for anything that evening. A disarming smile playing on his lips, he swung into action, meeting and greeting many an eminent scientist, surgeon, physicist and physician, who filed in to shake hands with the PM and his wife, Janet, as they stood in the receiving line by the door alongside the Minister of Health. Thane was there to lead them on, to be fed and offered drink. Later there would be a speech of welcome from Peter

Morgan, which, Thane knew, would promise all things to all men in the name of research and of the health of the nation. He knew because he had written it. Otherwise it was just another reception, another day like any other.

But no day is ever quite like another. He deliberately picked out Professor Desmond Grant's name from the guestlist and advanced on him. Public health was always a big issue, and Thane's private agenda was to get to know all the key players. He'd carefully read the briefs provided by the Department of Health and knew that the professor, who was the director of the team at the Harman Institute, was pre-eminent, at the very forefront of his profession. He was as good as anyone at the Government's own secret biological research and scientific defence establishment at Porton Down, and was seen as the great white hope for those who were suffering or might sometime suffer not only from some new variant of CJD, but also from one or other of the hitherto unknown viruses and bugs which, from time to time, emerged to infect the populace. Helped by a hysterical media which fed the fears of the great British public, there were always new diseases turning up which threatened to put even the AIDS epidemic into the shade. Thane had picked up quite a lot of background on Professor Grant's work, so, introducing himself, his all-embracing smile on full display, he was able to ask a number of well-informed questions about the Institute and its current research. The professor was flattered and surprised that this diminutive man knew so much. He began with a standard reply, but Thane thrived on facts: he wanted to know. He hadn't got where he had by indulging in pointless small talk.

'Are you top medical scientists really so worried about these new viruses, professor? Or is it all got up by a sensation-seeking media?' Thane asked.

'The media will always hype it up,' replied Grant. 'Usually the wrong story at the wrong time.'

'There's nothing out there to lose sleep over?'

'Quite the contrary.' The professor shook his head. 'There's a hell of a lot that even we experts can't begin to guess at. Known infections, like AIDS, are the easy bit. It's the unexpected that should terrify us all.' As he spoke, Grant's mind strayed to the puzzle of the general and his baffling illness.

'Fascinating. But world shattering?' Thane asked.

'Viruses are the champion killers in the Darwinian scheme of things,' responded the professor. 'They're often very simple organisms, composed of few genes. We all carry lots of them, most of which are benign. It's the new, lethal, ones, moving quickly from host to host, that we're on constant watch for. If your immune system can't cope with them, you're dead.'

'I remember,' said Thane. 'Post-Columbus; smallpox was brought by Europeans to the Americas and wiped out most of the indigenous peoples, didn't it?'

'Exactly,' the professor nodded. 'One day, a virus will come along that's very clever: like AIDS, smallpox, or the plague, it'll shape our history.'

'Surely medical science is way ahead of . . .' Thane's voice tailed off. He'd noticed the PM was coming in their direction. It would be a good opportunity to push Grant forward and show off a bit of the learning he'd picked up in the last few moments.

'Sadly it's not. Science is inadequate. We can't be ahead of some virus if we've never come across it before. How, for example, can we conquer one that suddenly, inexplicably, transfers from animals to humans? Think how quickly meningitis can prove fatal if it's not dealt with immediately. It kills within days, hours, minutes, yet we've known about it for ages. So a new virus . . .'

'Thought that was the stuff of science fiction.'

'You thought wrong, Mr Thane,' said the professor, turning to greet the Prime Minister who was bearing down on him, hand outstretched and an oh-so-genuine smile stamped firmly across his face.

*   *   *

When, some three quarters of an hour later, the PM stood up to address his guests, he began, in the best tradition of any politician, by flattering them and praising their role at the cutting edge of science and medicine.

'In my parents' days,' he said, 'indeed, in my own youth, the major danger to mankind came from the hideous prospect of war, particularly nuclear war. Now the real threat to our planet comes, not from some future Armageddon, but from mankind's carelessness. This has led to global warming and the consequent devastation being done to our environment. You don't need me to tell you about greenhouse gases, the damage that's been done to the ozone layer, deforestation and so on, all of which have, undoubtedly, contributed to the increased ferocity of natural disasters. Look at the recent catastrophic storms that have laid waste so much of the Caribbean and Central America.

'We . . . You, ladies and gentlemen,' the PM paused, arm raised theatrically to emphasize his point, 'have made so many outstanding scientific discoveries, particularly in the fields of medical research, gene therapy, transplant surgery and a whole range of other biological and pharmaceutical advances. Many of us mere politicians forget the huge dangers that lie in wait as well. Churchill, once asked what he most feared, replied: 'The unknown – the unexpected.' You are there to foresee, guard against, the 'unexpected'. I have read the WHO reports; I have seen the worrying conclusions of our own medical working parties. I am impressed by the sterling work carried out, for example, by Professor Grant's team at the Harman Institute, to name but one outstanding laboratory.' Thane, who, in the intervening period, had added that short phrase to the PM's speech, turned to watch the effect on Professor Grant as the PM continued: 'There are the dangers of old diseases like TB, cholera, malaria, yellow fever, reasserting themselves in ever more aggressive forms. New viruses and infections are being cultivated in the higher temperatures that are being recorded around the world. These, taken together, make the threat of nuclear disaster pale into insignificance. I realize only too well, ladies and gentlemen, that the greatest threat to humanity, to the future of civilization as we know it, is nature itself.'

When, after a few more minutes of platitudes, the Prime Minister ended his remarks with a general promise of more government funding and a toast to the experts gathered in Downing Street that evening, the applause from those present was fulsome.

'If he'd really fund us properly,' said Professor Grant to Thane who had come up to him to say goodbye, 'if he really believed there was a threat . . .'

'He does, professor. I assure you, he does,' responded Thane, his natural self-certainty asserting itself. Even he hesitated to reveal that he had written the whole speech, that the PM had seen it only minutes before he delivered it. 'His sentiments entirely. Believe me, professor, Mr Morgan knows how crucial your work at the Institute is.'

'I believe you, Mr Thane. Of course I do,' responded Professor Grant, formally shaking his hand in farewell as he spoke. Lyle Thane stood and watched as the professor left the reception. The young man was an expert in his subject: he too could spot insincerity when he heard it.

Millbank, Central London, Tuesday 24th May

At that precise time, a conversation was taking place in a sixth-floor office in an anonymous building in Millbank. The first speaker was a man; the second a woman.

'The general: we've seen all the medical reports. We don't like it. Not one bit.'

'I bet not, sir. Nor me.'

'So? What action are your people taking?'

'Usual checks: WHO and so on. Urgent. Running all the tests.'

'And you?'
'Identifying key players: experts on new viruses, just in case.'
'And?'
'And? And, I think we've hit some serious good luck.'

2

Dr Harper Guthrie, a battered suitcase in each over-large hand, struggled through the crowd that thronged the Arrivals gate. Mid-forties, tall, stooping, gangling, with unco-ordinated limbs which didn't seem to work the way they should, he had a pleasant, lived-in face, additionally crumpled though it now was by him not having slept at all well on the transatlantic flight. He was, he openly admitted to his friends, somewhat accident prone, so the fact that both his suitcases had actually arrived on the same flight as himself, was a happy bonus. Guthrie failed to make a telling first impression. He had a head of close-cropped fair hair and frameless spectacles for distant vision, which helped to define the image of a brilliant, but absent-minded, American scientist. Much of that was a guise; he was well able to handle himself in any professional conflict and he could switch on the sparkle as needed. Those who did not get to know him thought him slightly boring, someone who lived for his work. Those – usually women – who got to second base found him, with his boyish but world-weary style, quite attractive, though it usually led them to want to mother him. It was not mothers that interested him. He liked his sex, and perhaps because women thought him no threat he got it surprisingly often. In his modest way, Guthrie knew how to make women happy. If they were intelligent, he would appear to be after their bodies; if they were bimbos, he flattered their minds.

Guthrie's childhood had never been leavened by misfortune.

There was no grit in the oyster factor to force him to strive for anything that was not, both by circumstance and by his intellect, handed to him on a plate. He was taken for granted by his family and friends, growing up unobtrusively in a small town close to Boston, Massachusetts, where his family's background was heavily academic. Both his parents were science teachers and young Harper followed steadily in their wake.

As he grew up he did well at the local school, and, in his final year, won several important prizes in chemistry and biology. It was an easy step from there to one of New England's better known medical schools where he continued to harvest high scores all along the way. Good medical qualifications behind him, twenty-six-year-old Harper Guthrie embarked on his research degree, and, sometime halfway through the pursuit of his doctorate, met and became engaged to a girl who announced, shortly before the wedding, that she had changed her mind and had now decided to marry someone else. No small blow to his self-esteem, while this set him back in his relationships with the opposite sex, it ensured, in the decade that followed, that his career progressed rapidly upwards. He soon abandoned any wish to come face to face with real patients, and instead became an acknowledged expert in the field of viral research. He was the published author of a growing number of well-received research papers on how viruses mutated, moved from one host body to another, and how they could be harnessed or destroyed. He was in demand at conferences and seminars on the subject, though he was happiest when well buried in his laboratory. About that time, appropriately enough, some friendly colleague had nicknamed him 'Bugbuster', and the term had stuck. It certainly defined his interest in determining ways of controlling what he considered mankind's greatest enemies, but this fascination tended to spill over into his private life as well. When he fussed over little things like personal hygiene, the cleanliness of his apartment, or the careful handling and preparation of food, it was because he saw potential infection lurking everywhere. And in that he was not far from the truth.

Outsiders wondered what Guthrie could possibly have done to gain such a high professional reputation or why he landed and held down such good jobs. One reason was that he had inherited from his parents what he defined as the Protestant work ethic, which meant working hard and not taking any time off. He chained himself to his computer and laboratory workbench, and this might have continued indefinitely had not one recent event dictated otherwise. It followed his being accepted for a major research post at a well-endowed campus on the outskirts of Boston. In his early forties and uncluttered by matrimony, he met a woman some twenty years younger than himself, with whom he became involved. Unfortunately however, the young lady was one of the sophomore students, and a spirit of high-minded political correctness currently ruled all sections of the university. It was therefore firmly suggested to him that it would be opportune, first of all, to break off the relationship immediately, which he did with some ease because it was going nowhere. Secondly, because of the strident distress expressed by the student's parents and the suggestion by certain members of the faculty that potential corporate donors might not be best pleased were the affair to become public, Guthrie was ordered to go into exile for a period, to give things time to cool down. Thus his long-delayed intention to take a sabbatical year to write up his research on new viral strains was brought into sharp reality.

His love life apart, Dr Guthrie tended to crash into people's lives, then exit apologetically, leaving lots of debris behind but himself relatively unscathed. His main weakness, along with a fastidious approach to the threat from diseases lurking round every corner, was his constant conflict with the little things in life, of which his first exposure to Scotland was typical. More alert people would have moved on rapidly.

'Hey! Big Man! Dinna adjust your mind . . .' the speaker, a small, red-haired man in shiny blue shellsuit and battered trainers, was barely coherent. The zip of his top was undone, revealing a T-shirt with the slogan 'I'm a Health Hazard' on it. Guthrie had already grasped the reassuring fact that health seemed a major preoccupation of the British. As he had waited for his suitcases to emerge, he had noted, in the airport book-shop, that nearly all the newspapers and magazines seemed to be running health stories with genetically altered food the current favourite topic.

'Excuse me . . . ?' Guthrie paused and stared down at the man in front of him. He was certainly being a hazard to his own health: alcohol and the cigarette dangling from his mouth were seeing to that. Guthrie could not but pause, since the man was blocking the way to the exit and the sign leading to 'Taxis'.

'. . . a fault in reality here,' the drunk stumbled and laughed.

'You OK?' asked Guthrie cautiously, looking around for another door. Behind him, his fellow-travellers were bunching up, also trying to pass.

'Bloody marvellous. A've just missed ma plane.'

'Excuse me,' Guthrie repeated. 'Can I . . . ?' Tired after the delayed flight, his normal equanimity was becoming strained.

'Wife and the kids on their way to Teneriffe and A've bloody missed it.' The man, oblivious to the blockage he was causing, was in a mood to chat.

'Sad.'

'Sad? No way! Bloody marvellous. A've been celebrating. A week o' freedom and here's a' the spending money.' The man clapped a heavily tattooed hand to his wallet pocket, staggered back a pace, and stared up at Guthrie. 'Hey? You a Yank? You sound like an effing Yank.'

'American. Now . . . if you'd excuse me, sir, I must . . . a cab.'

'Yank, eh? Well, well. Too bad,' said the man sympathetically, lurching to one side and slapping Guthrie on the shoulder as he tried to pass. 'Well, welcome to Bonnie Scotland, sir. Would you like to share a welcoming drunk – drink, A mean?' he shouted at him.

In a corner, by the baggage control desk, a brisk young man

who had been carefully watching Guthrie's progress started to move forward as if to remonstrate with the drunk, then checked himself. He was out of uniform now, and that was not why he was there. In any case Guthrie, with remarkable agility, had bypassed the little Scot and was now leading the escape of the other travellers through the exit doors and out into a damp Scottish night. As he left, the young man spoke urgently into a mobile phone.

Damp was an inappropriate word. It was raining, not with a purposeful New England downpour, but with a fine, mist-like spray that, with special cunning, found a way to penetrate the crevice between his battered canvas hat and the turned-up collar of his raincoat. Pausing in the partial shelter by the revolving doors of the airport terminal, he looked around for the cab rank. His hesitation allowed a dozen other people to push ahead of him. Slipping on the wet pavement he inadvertently stepped in front of a large-chested lady who was towing a yapping, blue-rinsed poodle on a lead. A porter with a mound of luggage on his barrow accompanied her.

'There's a queue,' she declared indignantly.

'Queue?' Guthrie asked, temporarily confused by the unfamiliar word. It was French for 'tail', he remembered.

'You speak English?' she demanded.

'Yes . . . I . . . er . . .'

'There's a *queue*,' the woman gestured angrily at the other waiting travellers.

'Oh, a line. Yes. Sorry.' Guthrie obediently fell into place behind her, placed his suitcases on the wet slabs, pulled his hat brim down and his coat collar up, and patiently waited his turn. There were, he reckoned, twelve people ahead of him; but there seemed to be a sufficient number of cabs. He should be OK.

He was wrong. All the cabs bore away their passengers, including the huge lady, whose cases, in a fit of charity, he helped the porter load into the back, to be nipped in the hand by her ungrateful dog for his pains. He'd have to look and see if the skin had been broken; Britain had a good record on rabies but one couldn't be too careful.

No further cabs appeared. Behind him, a family – father, mother, a much older woman, and two screaming children, were engaged in a mini civil war. Just then a further taxi arrived, he loaded his suitcases into the trunk – the driver referred to it as the boot – and settled thankfully into the comparative dryness of the passenger seat.

'Effing awful night. Where to?' The driver looked enquiringly at him in the rear-view mirror.

Yeah? Where had he put that address? He rummaged in his pockets. The taxi driver revved his engine impatiently, but remained stationary.

Another of those small, familiar panics in Guthrie's life began to grip him. Why was everything so difficult? Why was he so cold and wet? In his research laboratory back home, everything was meticulous. Each item, each specimen, was carefully coded and where it should be. He liked security. Too often he found the outside world an alien place, without order, without reason, without solution. *Brilliant eccentric*, someone had once written of him. He hadn't minded the brilliant bit, but eccentric he was not. He just liked things clean and tidy, the way things were in nature, except when they were not. His mind strayed to think about that for a moment: wasn't it the odd things, the strange and unexpected blips of nature, the way things jumped from one species to another, that had always fascinated him?

Aware of the increasingly hostile glare from the driver, he pulled himself back to reality. Where the hell was that piece of paper? Eventually he found the envelope with the treasured information lurking inside his spent airline ticket.

'Thirty, Union Road,' he declared, pushing away a fluffy toy dog that was dangling from the rear window at a level that caused it to bang constantly against the back of his head.

'You sure?' asked the cab driver, restrained surprise registering in his voice.

'What it says,' Guthrie confirmed, carefully examining the paper once again.

'You look more like a Balmoral, a Sheraton, or a Holiday Inn at the least.'

'I look like . . . ?'

'Here on holiday?' Taciturnity had given way to aggressive sociability, as the cab driver crunched gears and, death-defyingly, plunged from the airport slip-road onto a motorway heavy with late-evening traffic.

'No, work. Research . . . Medical faculty,' responded Guthrie helpfully, wincing involuntarily as he fought off the impression from the back that there was no one in the driving seat. Oh yes: left-hand drive.

'First time in Scotland?'

''Fraid so.'

'Weather's bleedin' awful.'

'Sure it'll improve.'

'No way will it. Always bleedin' awful . . .' The driver paused as, blaring his horn, he flashed his lights intemperately at some slow driver hogging the fast lane. 'Fuckin' idiot . . . Sure you meant Union Road?'

'Sure.'

Against the lights of the oncoming traffic Guthrie saw the cab driver's involuntary shoulder shrug. 'No accounting for tastes.'

Guthrie struggled to interpret the driver's phrase. 'Not an upmarket area?' he asked.

'Say that again. Union Road, eh?' The cab driver gave a laugh, the guttural sound triggering a tingle of unease down the length of Guthrie's spine. He recognized a fresh indicator of future panic.

'I asked for budget accommodation. A bed is just a bed. The faculty arranged it. I like to spend my money on food. Lots of nice clean restaurants around, won't there be?' he prompted hopefully.

'Buying a car, are you?' came the response. Guthrie was to gather that the standard answer to any question in Scotland was another question.

'No.'

'A chippy, close to.'

'Please?'

'Fish and chips.'

'Ah, a fish restaurant. That'll be great. Anyway, I've arranged to have my evening meal . . . part of the package.'

'A doctor, are you?' the driver asked after a pause.

'Sort of.'

'Sort of?' came the prompt.

'Don't practise. No patients. Research . . .'

'Bugs?'

'Right.'

'Nasty ones about. See this?' The driver passed back a copy of that day's *Sun* newspaper. The screaming headline read, *Flesh-eating Superbug Horror Kills in Minutes*.

Guthrie took the paper and glanced at it. 'Over the top, but yes, that kind of thing.'

'Scary,' said the driver, lapsing into silence. Maybe he was worried about cross-infection from his passenger contaminating the cab. Guthrie had come across that reaction before in his line of work. It was rather like being a mortuary attendant.

Silence reigned for the rest of the twenty-minute journey. Guthrie, alone with his thoughts, stared out into the dark, inhospitable night, trying to make out features through the steamed up windows of the cab. It was a fruitless task. He would be glad to get to a warm room, fresh food, unpack a little, then a good night's sleep. There was no reason for him to turn and look round to where a dark car, with two occupants in it, was tailing close behind them.

After some time, his cab pulled up by a black recess in a stone-built, soot-encrusted apartment building. A yellow streetlight cast a far from sufficient glow on wet paving slabs scarred with disgusting gobbets of old chewing gum. A mangey, collarless dog, the only sign of life, slunk past and out of sight. Fifty yards back down the street, the dark car had also glided to a stop.

'You sure this is it?' asked Guthrie, ramming his hat further down over his ears and easing himself out of the taxi into the night. The fine rain had, if anything, become more sneakily pervasive.

'Am I a cab driver these thirty years?' came the dismissive response.

'Of course.'

'Fifteen fifty, you owe.'

Guthrie got the next step right. He'd been nervously keeping an eye on the meter and had the unfamiliar money ready. 'Seventeen pounds. Keep the change.'

'Thanks,' said the cab driver, mollified, the tip inspiring him to help Guthrie with his cases to the entrance, over which a faintly painted '30' could be seen. The driver peered into the gloom. 'You're lucky. There's light up that close.'

'Close?'

'Aye. Up the close. *That* close,' the man gestured as if to an idiot.

'Ah, yes . . . That close . . .' A common entranceway, Guthrie recalled.

'Mind your bags now,' said the driver helpfully, as he returned to his cab, got in, and splashed off into the night.

'Mind . . . ?' Guthrie pondered briefly, then, seizing both cases he made off purposefully up the dark entranceway.

Further up the street one of the men watching from the parked car turned to the other, shook his head, and said, 'Poor bugger doesn't deserve what's coming to him.' The other nodded in silent agreement.

A faint light illuminated the stone-flagged common stairway sufficiently for Guthrie to be able to marvel at its graffiti-daubed walls. A strong blend of urine and carbolic took him back to the smells of the lavatories at his junior school. Unlike his own clinically spotless apartment block, this must be a breeding ground for the most traditional of nineteenth-century germs. A new virus wouldn't stand a chance here. As if to reinforce this judgment, despite the lateness of the hour, an elderly woman was washing the bottom flight of stairs, or, rather, was wetting them with a grey sudless liquid with the help of an equally grey, wooden-handled mop. It would be difficult to invent a more perfect instrument for the transfer of whatever bugs existed, from one step to the other.

Round another bend of the stair, he came face to face with a courting couple. This was no brief romantic flirt, judging from the way the blonde's skirt was riding high.

'Sorry,' he said lamely as he pushed past, eyes firmly fixed on the graffiti, where, he noted, there was no escape from sex. The 'f' and 'c' words abounded under graphic anatomical pastel drawings of the act he had, despite his efforts to avoid it, just witnessed.

Two further breathless floors up, he stood thankfully outside a black painted door on which a shining brass plate announced the name 'Murray'. He pressed the bell. After a full minute's wait he heard the sound of locks being undone, then the door opened to reveal Mrs Agnes Murray, his landlady, hair in curlers, dressing gown wrapped inadequately around her substantial girth, incongruous fluffy pink slippers on her feet.

'Harper Guthrie,' he said, smiling and extending his hand. 'Glad to be here.'

His hand was ignored and the two acid words, 'You're late,' singularly failed to convey any warmth of welcome. At first he felt he had stumbled on the Murray home at some tragic moment. Perhaps a relative had just passed away. It was none of these things. Mrs Agnes Murray was to prove a mean-spirited dragon, whose face carried a look of permanently sculpted disapproval. The frigid image was maintained as he was shown down a featureless passageway into a room, walls hung with grey wallpaper, curtains equally dull and faded which scarcely closed in the middle, and, for a carpet, a threadbare rug. In such an atmosphere, any dustmites would probably die of hypothermia.

'Your friends saw it. Thought it would suit you well,' said Mrs Murray firmly.

Guthrie presumed she must be talking about someone from the faculty; he had no friends here. In any case, he was preoccupied by the sight of the dismal bed, guessing at its lumpy arctic secrets which any self-respecting bed-lice would reject. He scarcely noticed the noise of plumbing which echoed through the large and small pipes with which the walls of his room were liberally festooned; that would be a pleasure to be experienced in the watches of the night.

He unpacked a little, then went in search of Mrs Murray. She had remained standing four square in the hallway, awaiting anything resembling a complaint. There was the small question of food, he stammered: some bread and cheese, perhaps? The temperature was turned down further, then, with considerable reluctance, he was handed the keys to the front door with the admonition not to lose them and grudgingly informed that within a minute's walk he would find both a take-away pizza parlour and a fish and chip shop. Extracting a scarf and a pair of gloves from one of his suitcases, a short time later he ventured back into the friendless night.

After a few minutes' wandering he located the fish and chip shop. It was warm and steaming inside and, given his hunger, the smell of frying was welcoming. He lined up behind two urchins who should have been in bed long since, who whiled their time waiting by kicking each other with their Doc Martens and swigging from cans of industrial lager. Eventually, reaching the glass-fronted counter, he ordered the least revolting of the objects displayed, and was only a little startled to have them served to him, crystalized with salt and dripping with vinegar, wrapped in swathes of steaming newspaper, and also doubtless containing, he mused, interesting batches of listeria, e-coli or worse. It was a bad beginning.

Across the street, two pairs of eyes again watched Harper Guthrie from a parked car. One man, his voice low, turned to the other and muttered the thought that the other had also been asking himself. 'If he's one of America's greatest men of science, God help us all.'

It was a minor media sensation. The Sunday broadsheets rivalled the tabloids in their coverage. Talking heads appeared one after another on the television screen. Fellow peers, neighbours, mistresses, those who knew him and those who claimed to have known him, all offered their views, their wild suspicions, their theories about Lord Rumbold's disappearance. There was always going to be a lot of press coverage when he died. He'd had such a picaresque, tumultuous career. World traveller, almost-made-it politician, life peer, former diplomat, spy, wickedly acerbic contributor to the weekly magazines, man about town, flirt, breaker of women's hearts. A great British eccentric to some, an out and out bounder to others. And now he'd vanished. There were no obituaries, no wreaths; there was no funeral, no grave. The media love a mystery: they had one here. There appeared to be no motive for his disappearance. He was no Lord Lucan, running from a botched murder. He was no bankrupt. He did not need to flee from some sexual scandal: the tabloids trawled the gutters and sewers looking for evidence of just that and found none. In any event, he had survived many decades of often well-justified innuendo and gossip, so why should he feel the need for flight now? There was no substantiated suggestion of foul play.

If he had not fled, where was he? Had he dropped dead in some culvert somewhere? Had he lost his memory, or had he taken off to one of the old familiar places that people disappear to – South Africa, South America, Thailand – when they become tired of the life they lead? Did he have a secret love nest in some ultima Thule, some end of the earth? Given his age – he was in his late sixties – the most mundane explanation won out in the end, even among the most imaginative of conspiracy theorists. He had wandered off and died and his body would be found in the course of time. Yet an inch by inch police search of all his known haunts, and the woods and hills of the estate surrounding his ancestral pile at Athelstane, even the dredging of the little loch half a mile away, revealed no clues. The kidnap theorists also had their run, but the family, through their Edinburgh lawyers, firmly ruled that out. He was rich, but not that rich, and in the absence of any ransom demand that last balloon of suspicion was also punctured.

Days passed. There were sightings from Bournemouth to Rio. There were stories of frictions among the members of the family he had left behind. Despite some low-key protests, first the media and then the police quietly put their files away. They could easily be disinterred if a body was found later or if the family, hungry to share his estate, went to the courts to have him declared legally dead. And that was all, except for a small paragraph in a local paper, the result of some clever checking by a junior reporter. It read as follows:

> The untypical way in which all his staff were instructed by the family to take their holidays in the very week that he disappeared – chauffeur, secretary, housekeeper, butler, even his gardener, was odd. In the past they had scheduled their vacations for when he himself was abroad or staying with friends. It was widely believed that he intended to stay at White's, his London club, for the duration, yet he never turned up there. More oddly, in the days preceding his disappearance, while the facts are hard to confirm, he appears to have sold off a substantial holding of stocks and shares and a minor Old Master at Christies, the family insisting that all the proceeds were paid in cash. At a modest estimate, something close to half a million pounds was realized . . .

The Harman Institute, East London, Monday 30th May

Behind the high security fence, the arc lights, the bars and the hermetically sealed windows, the Harman Institute's Acute Viral

36

Research Facility had every external appearance of a prison. It had begun life between the wars as an East End fever hospital, but most of the buildings in the complex had, over the years, been altered and modernized for its new role as one of Britain's key research centres into the threat from naturally occurring or deliberately targeted, bacteriological agents and deadly viruses of one sort or another. An adjunct to the Government's Porton Down network set up in the First World War to counter German toxic gas attacks, it also conducted secret research into a range of diseases which still had no known antidote. As a result, security was absolute. There were many electronic locks and doors to negotiate before one reached the central laboratory where Professor Desmond Grant and his top flight team of medical scientists and lab technicians worked. Nothing was left to chance. Sterilization of everything going in and out was paramount. Of the many bacteria and viruses that were stored, studied, isolated, and experimented on in that complex, many were relatively harmless, but some were so deadly, so immune to any known treatment, that they had to be handled with extreme caution. It was here that one team was working, for example, on controlling a strain of bacterium that continued to threaten patients in hospital wards throughout the world: methicillin-resistant staphylococcus aureus, colloquially known as 'superstaph', was a bug difficult to treat with any known antibiotic.

In a separate high-risk area, thousands of samples of appendixes and tonsils were being routinely screened for new variant CJD, under the general supervision of the Chief Medical Officer of Health, as part of a Government-funded programme which was trying to find ways to diagnose the disease in a patient before its more visible symptoms began to show themselves. Another key team of lab technicians scrutinized such samples for traces of the rogue protein prion, that might, if isolated and correctly applied, eventually save the lives of millions, either as a preventative measure or an antidote. It was a never-ending game of hide and seek with nature. Among the treatable and the known, Professor Grant and his colleagues were made all too well aware, on an almost daily basis, that nature seemed fully resolved to keep ahead of them. New and ever more virulent strains of virus appeared or evolved all the time, to defeat any medical treatment currently known to man. As soon as one virus or bacterium was conquered, another emerged to take its place, as if to give medical science a continuing sense of its own inadequacy. What personally fascinated Professor Grant most of all was not just the bug or virus, but also the ways it found of transmitting itself from person to person, or, since many seemed to leap from species to species, from animal to human. Ever since the days of Lord Lister and his experiments at Edinburgh in the second half of the nineteenth century which were aimed at defeating gangrene through developing various antiseptics, the medical profession had been alert to the extreme dangers of cross-infection. These modern viruses were proving even more diligent than the old microbes in finding ways to breed and spread, through people breathing the same air, being carried by mosquitoes, fleas and their animal hosts, or through direct bodily contact, the food chain, and in other hidden and unexpected ways. Most critical of all, because some viruses had such radically different incubation periods, it was often impossible for medical science to predict where the next epidemic might lie hidden or when it would strike.

When Professor Grant, outwardly austere and emotionless, was admitted through the double-screen doors early that morning, he was greeted by his assistant, Dr Rebecca Stevenson, with the blunt news: 'The patient died at seven this morning.' Dr Stevenson, an attractive if somewhat forbidding thirty-something single woman, knew her boss well: he would, deep down, be as upset as she was by what he would consider to be a defeat. The professor knew which patient she was talking about. He had last seen General George late the previous evening in the isolation room at the Institute, to which he had been rapidly transferred from St Philip's Hospital the day before, when the professor had recognized that he was dealing with something quite extraordinary and potentially very dangerous indeed. He had realized then that it could only be a matter of hours until the general's dreadful agony, and that of his family, would be over. It had been less than two weeks since his first admission to hospital, during which time they had been totally unable to isolate any antidote or identify any drug that might have saved him. Grant recalled how he had questioned the general's weeping wife about the first time she had noticed that anything might be wrong.

It had been at a meeting of the charity committee in the village hall, near their country home. The general had suddenly stopped in mid-sentence. For a moment his wife and the others around the table had wondered if he'd had a stroke, but then, suddenly, he came to and carried on as if nothing untoward had happened. A friend had taken her aside and told her that it was nothing to worry about. But the next day the general had complained about not being able to read *The Times*, then he went into a brief coma again, and she had first noticed the strange grey pallor over his eyes and that an ugly rash had suddenly erupted around his neck and mouth. From then on it had been a horrifying downhill descent to its dreadful conclusion.

Professor Grant continued to show little emotion though privately he felt a sudden feeling of inadequacy. 'You've taken a full set of samples?' he asked softly.

'Of course, professor.' Dr Stevenson handed him the file of medical notes. He turned towards her and nodded. 'Ensured that the family have no contact with the body, that disposal is in the special bodybags, that cremation is at scale five?' he asked, knowing what her answer would be. He glanced down at his notes on the case as he spoke: so much about it was unusual and unexpected. Many more tests would be needed before the full truth was known. Well staffed though the Institute was, there were still huge gaps in their knowledge of all the varieties of mutant viruses, one of which, at a guess, must be the cause of the general's death. 'I take it,' he went on, 'that you're closely monitoring the family, watching anyone who might have been in recent contact . . .'

Dr Stevenson nodded. She had worked with viruses long enough to know that the phrase 'playing with death' was no hyperbole in their dangerous lives. 'All that's complete or under way,' she confirmed. 'We've removed all the specimens and swabs. They're in the high security refrigerators.'

'The press spokesman's saying?' asked the professor, pulling on a pair of sterile rubber gloves.

'That's emerging as a particularly sensitive issue. Someone's just arrived at the Institute's press office. From the Ministry of Defence. Wants to talk to you personally.'

Ten minutes later, the professor, accompanied by Dr Stevenson, emerged from the high security area to meet his visitor. The man, a trim, precise figure, with a peculiarly tense way of speaking, was vague about what he did. 'Ministry of Defence, Public Relations,' he muttered, but his message was clear enough.

'Look at it this way, professor. Army general dies of mystery illness. Has been involved in Intelligence work. Had strong views about Gulf War Syndrome being entirely psychological. Quite a fuss. Remember? You – we – can't say what he died of. Doesn't look at all good. Not for you, professor, nor for the Institute.'

'What're you saying?' Grant stifled his irritation at the implied threat.

'You're worried. Must be.'

'Certainly. I don't like the unknown. So?'

'So, with the agreement of his wife and family, we're going to have to be . . . er . . . economical with the truth. About how he died. Just till we know, of course. Doesn't look smart otherwise,' the man repeated.

'You're not remotely suggesting that Gulf War Syndrome could in any way . . . ?'

'Certainly not. Doesn't exist. Government enquiries have confirmed that. Nontheless, just in case something odd . . .' The stranger smiled politely. 'You don't mind if we get a second opinion, do you? On the death?'

'No. I suppose . . . but who?'

'We have someone in mind. Knew you'd understand, professor.' The man smiled another tight-lipped smile, turned and left.

Professor Grant had always been a great believer in the truth, but as far as the press was concerned, his visitor was undoubtedly right. If the media got hold of the idea that some new virus had emerged which had killed off one of Britain's best-known generals, the headline writers would go wild. Clearly the Institute had to identify precisely what it was and how it might be contained before the full story broke.

Returning to the secure area to examine the photographs and latest samples and cultures that the hyper-efficient Dr Stevenson and other members of his research team had set out for him on the long white laboratory table, Grant remained deeply puzzled by the slides. They clearly showed the strange grey sheen over the eyes, the skin eruptions, the stages of putrefaction of the brain, liver and kidneys. What a hellish conjunction of symptoms it had proved to be.

They had a huge database to refer to and a short time thereafter, his team, under Dr Stevenson's guidance, having merged all the symptoms and blood tests into the computer, came up with one possible answer: it was a bug most of them had never even heard of.

'If you're right and this is, by any chance, Virus ZD198, who's done any recent work on it?' Professor Grant asked Dr Stevenson, when he had examined the provisional results. He looked hard at her as if seeing her for the first time. She was a tall, dark girl, with large intelligent eyes; she had several degrees and was, he suspected, even brighter than him.

'When I hit on this as a possibility over the weekend,' she replied, 'I scanned the websites for any relevant research papers: went through all the medical journals and the entire histopathology press. Most advanced reports on vectors and incubation times for Virus ZD198 are by Rankin and Guthrie.'

'I remember: California and Boston, aren't they?' asked the professor. As a practising consultant as well as a researcher, he had to depend on his junior staff to keep him up to date on the latest details in the medical press.

'Yes. Rankin works out of Santa Barbara,' said Rebecca.

'And . . . ?' asked the professor, watching her, knowing there was more to come. Behind the heavy glasses and tied-back hair an attractive woman was constantly trying to get out. He'd always felt she was one step ahead of any game, with her own very personal agenda. But what mattered most to him was that she was very good at her job.

'Did a quick bit of non-medical research, professor. Amazing coincidence.' She smiled efficiently. 'Guthrie, you'll recall, is Dr Harper Guthrie who, very fortunately, has just been awarded a temporary secondment to the Edinburgh Specialist Unit, with funding from the national CJD surveillance people up there. How about that?' She looked pleased with herself.

For once Professor Grant showed a flicker of emotion. He was almost as impressed as if she had just isolated a new virus. 'Edinburgh. Goodness . . . He's not going to join that idiot MacArthur's team, is he?' he asked.

''Fraid so, sir.'

'MacArthur's so jealous of everything we're doing, it's criminal. He won't let someone of Guthrie's stature talk to us. He's computer illiterate and proud of it. Wouldn't know a new virus if it came up and shook his hand,' Grant growled.

Dr Stevenson laughed at her boss's unusual outburst. 'I foresaw that, professor.'

'Foresaw?'

'I have a few contacts in Edinburgh.'

'And?'

'Very helpful. They've tracked him down. I know where he's staying.'

'Well done. But how do we get him down here, and out of his deal with MacArthur?'

'I have an idea, professor. Give me a little time,' Dr Stevenson said cautiously, then she suddenly grinned. Professor Grant's casual reaction to this news disguised a particularly alert sense of mood. He hadn't needed someone from the Ministry of Defence to tell him that the Institute would be faced with a serious crisis if the virus wasn't identified or if it started to spread. Given the time factor, having Dr Guthrie's expertise to call on would be a great asset. And as for Dr Stevenson's detective work, not for the first time in their years of working together Grant wondered about what drove her. Not that he let it show – his face remained as inscrutable as ever.

The Theatre Royal, Drury Lane, Monday 30th May

Illness is no respector of rank. The famous and unknown can share precisely the same fate, and a possible second victim of the new virus was an oddly random choice. The first signs of trouble meant nothing to anyone. As the final curtain fell, the backstage hands spoke in shocked whispers. Disaster had been averted, but only just. Ralph Rowland had never fluffed a line in his life, had never dried up on stage. He was the performer *par excellence*. He was the grand old man whom every aspiring young actor tried to emulate. He could and had invented a thousand characters. He had held many an audience spellbound with his roles drawn from Shakespeare to the most avant garde playwrights. His voice was astonishing for its range, its gravitas, its hyperbole. He was head and shoulders above almost anyone of his ilk on the British stage.

And yet tonight he had faltered. He missed a line, then another. There had been a long pause, but fortunately it happened at a point in the play which was full of meaningful pauses, and the bubbling Stephanie Bartlett, his partner in that scene, had been able to pick up and run with the next lines of dialogue, so that no one in the audience noticed a thing. But backstage they noticed all right. The strangest thing of all was that Ralph Rowland did not mention it, did not admit to having fluffed anything, nor to having missed his lines, nor to having departed in any way from his well known perfection.

He said not a thing about it. It was as if he had noticed nothing. No one dared tell him to the contrary. Only his dresser noticed a faint grey pallor that lay across the usually brightest of bright blue eyes, and heard the great man bemoan the sudden rash he had developed on his cheeks and around his neck. Perhaps he was allergic to that new make-up colour he had been using; perhaps his skin was reacting to something in it. His dresser promised to throw it out and return to using the old familiar greasepaint.

3

The telephone in the World Health Organization's makeshift regional office in Kisangani seldom rang. It took a long time before Clegg Hurley, its American deputy head, answered it. It was a local call for a start and they were particularly rare, since the telephone exchange, inherited from a distant colonial past, had been vandalized by the rebels, and the automatic network was in terminal decline. It was much easier to ring New York by satellite than to get a call through to Kinshasa, or the other side of town for that matter. Runners – messenger boys – were the quickest method of local communication. He recognized the caller's name, of course. He'd deliberately steered clear of Dr Banquier since he'd arrived; his predecessor had warned him what he was like. That said, the doctor's message could not be ignored, for staff at the regional office were meant to keep a running tally of all cases of notifiable diseases. 'Notifiable' meant death-delivering ones, that could spread with huge rapidity: cholera, yellow fever, dengue fever, tuberculosis, and some strains of hepatitis. The few remaining doctors in the area were obliged to report to the office direct, or via the Congolese Ministry of Health. Each day Hurley would go through the list and see if anything interesting had turned up. Hurley was listed and only paid as deputy head. In fact he had been in sole charge for months, ever since his Pakistani boss had been flown out suffering from depression. Hurley had sympathized. It was that sort of a place.

Clegg Hurley was an unimposing thirty-five-year-old, with

sandy hair and a scruffy beard. He had freckles and a skin texture that hated the heat, that hated the 110 degrees in the shade, that hated the rainy season which this year seemed to have gone on for ever, that hated the packs of insects that homed in on every part of his vulnerable body. His was not a complexion that tanned like a film star's; his went blotchy and red. If he did not cover up, even in the most dense jungle, he would burn, burn, burn. Africa in close-up had proven hideously different from the picture his youthful idealism had imagined. From a distance, how exciting and romantic it had seemed. Hurley had longed to go, explore, travel across deserts and through the rainforests, and watch the breakers thundering on sandy shores fringed by tossing palm trees. The images in his mind had been of happy Africans sitting outside their mud and straw huts, of missionaries and nuns in their schoolrooms, of capital cities, bustling and vibrant, where street markets overflowed with an abundance of exotic products. The devil came with the detail; the devil came with knowledge and experience. Africa, particularly this viciously devastated part of it, with one hundred per cent humidity, was something different. Banished were the romanticized images, gone were the sanitized wildlife television documentaries. Remembered now was grim news footage of famine and civil war, of ethnic atrocities, of one tribe massacring another. This Africa was a deep green hell. All around was riot and revolution. Death by bullet, machete, or simple starvation, was more common than death by disease. Much of that reality had changed little since Joseph Conrad's time. Each country in this great swathe of sub-Saharan Africa seemed to want to compete in a wild retreat into the heart of darkness once again. Colonial rule had had many defects: British, German, French, Belgian. But the white man had never been more brutal than those who ruled or fought over this Africa now. Hurley knew it was politically incorrect to say so, but what else defined such a return to the primitive?

By any standards, Kisangani itself was a dreadful place, a city in ruins. Hardly a building remained undamaged. Almost all the infrastructure had gone: everything lootable had been taken over the past few years by one armed group or another. Thousands upon thousands from indigenous and invading tribal armies had been slaughtered in and around the town. Only the little people, the Pygmies, had proven small and agile enough to escape most of the fighting, by fleeing with all their native craft into the depths of the deepest, most impenetrable, jungle. There were occasional signs of a better life returning. The survivors had to exist. Primitive market stalls had appeared at occasional street corners, then the braver expats started coming back too, lured by the diamonds in the abandoned mines. This time they came well armed and prepared, and set up their own stockades, barbed-wire fortresses, powered by their own generators, supplied by their helicopters. Then came the aid missions, then the WHO, to try to re-create a little patch of civilization amid the surrounding chaos.

Yes, Clegg Hurley had once liked the thought of Africa. Among the brightest medical administrators in one of North America's top hospitals, he had resigned one day on an apparent whim, and had given up a reasonable income and a wonderful job to join the WHO and save the world. All too soon, he had been despatched by his new boss in New York, the dreadful Dr Boekamper, to this hell of hells. Here, civilization had packed its bags and left long since. Thank God he had only signed on for a year. Here he was alone with his fears, and these fears were legion. He hated the insects, particularly spiders, and this part of Africa was one of the greatest breeding grounds for both. He hated the humidity, he hated never having a shirt that stayed dry on him for more than two or three minutes. He hated the long nights of crackling and hissing that came from the dense jungle that constantly encroached both on the office and on his corrugated iron-roofed house, that few minutes' walk away along a dark and fearful pathway.

Clegg Hurley was an administrator, a statistician, not a doctor. So much of his daily workload was a matter of recording the guesswork sent in by overworked and undertrained medical staff in the field. Lacking enough skilled members of the profession and without decent facilities to allow anything other than the most rudimentary laboratory tests of what disease was what, particularly since so many of those infected died long before they could be properly examined, he knew his monthly surveys were faulty to say the least. He consequently tried to concentrate on the rare, the difficult, the outbreaks of virulent fevers which might conceivably spread to other more civilized parts of the world with devastating effect. On paper he had many other duties, but with the continuing civil war in the east, and the periodic massacres of one tribe by another over by the Uganda border, most of the clinics, hospitals, and rural medical centres whose standards he was also supposed to be monitoring, could no longer be described as such. They were so run down, so devoid of most resources or medicines, that they lacked even the most basic facilities for tropical hygiene. Some of the non-governmental organizations which had bravely managed to return were better: the Oxfam and the Save the Children Fund clinics had imported modern methods and resources. Otherwise, so-called health care was a shambolic mess and he was sick to the teeth with it. His latest bid for help, supporting a request from the current Congolese Junta, had been for urgently needed medicines from WHO stock. It had resulted in one old Dakota flying in with crates of almost-past-their-sell-by-date medicines and vaccinations, which might have helped a few victims had there been anyone around to administer them. How could the medical services be expected to cope when most of their qualified African staff had long since been killed, or kidnapped to serve with the government or the rebel armies?

Most of the messages from New York he had dealt with that morning were routine – requests for the latest demographic death statistics, life expectancy rates and so on, as if there were any government statistics worth sending. That his girlfriend who had spent the last three months out here working for a German charity, had upped sticks and left two days earlier to return to Munich to finish her doctorate, had added to his woes. She'd been fun and it had made life bearable for a bit. Ever since his university days he'd been in favour of world compassion, which was why, after all, he was working for the WHO in the first place. But today, like most days recently, he'd woken up wondering why the hell he had given up so much. He'd wanted to save the world, but was this world worth saving?

On top of it all, the one or two qualified doctors he had come across, including a handful of Westerners, had alcohol problems or behaviour patterns that were more suspect than any he had ever come across in his life. He'd found most of them decidedly odd, but his *bête noir* was the reclusive Belgian, Dr Raoul Banquier, who ran his so-called School of Tropical Medicine two hours north of the town. He was reputed to top the lot in terms of dubious behaviour. Hurley's predecessor had had his own pet theory as to why Banquier was working out there, and it was not a savoury story. It was even rumoured that there was a warrant out for him back in his home country. That, among other things, was why Clegg Hurley was so distant, so unwelcoming, so reluctant to take seriously what the caller told him.

When the phone call came, the American was already halfway through a particularly bad day. The heat was intense, there had been a hole in the mosquito net over his bed last night which he hadn't noticed in time, and so he was covered in bites, particularly around the ankles. On top of all that, his so-called secretary was off sick once again, and he had a pile of faxes and e-mail messages from Boekamper to respond to on his own. How the hell was he meant to do what he had to do in this sweating hell-hole without some decent backup?

The conversation was brief and not particularly friendly. 'You found what?' Hurley asked. The line was bad and the Belgian's English was far from perfect.

'A case . . . I believe . . . of surge fever. The patient, a woman, died. I am ringing to report it.'

'Thank you,' said Hurley, scrabbling for his list of diseases. Surge fever meant nothing to him. 'Any other cases?' he asked automatically.

'Don't know.'

'Don't know? Can't you find out?'

'No way. Not with all the fighting around here. Impossible.'

'Couldn't you try?'

'Come, see for yourself,' said the voice angrily. 'Then maybe you'll understand what I mean.'

At the other end of the line, the Belgian slammed down the telephone in anger. 'Idiot American bureaucrat,' he growled. Banquier normally prided himself on his emotionless approach – compassion and sympathy were not strong points in his make-up; they got in the way of clinical judgments. But right now, as he looked down at his hands, he saw that they were shaking. He reached up to a bookshelf behind his desk and took down a half-full bottle of whisky, wrenched the cork out and took a slug of the stuff. It was only mid-morning, but God he needed it. Right now he was sure of only one thing: he'd been a fool to have the woman patient brought here. Engrained on his mind was one terrible medical fact: the first ever recorded case of AIDS had been here in Zaire – the Congo. A single, very sick man, way back in 1959, had died of the HIV virus. It had probably smouldered away for some decades before that, perhaps in some primitive village deep in the jungle. Till then it had been what was called a dead-end infection: killing its host and itself before it had time to travel far. And now this.

Banquier had at once recognized what it could be. He should have acted as he had on the last occasions he had come across this so-called surge fever. Two, three times before, was it? He should have left the jungle to do what it did so efficiently and act as a natural *cordon sanitaire*. This time, despite the huge personal dangers of disinterring his past, he had obediently reported to the WHO office what he thought he had identified. He was already bitterly regretting his action. Now he would have to face the consequences.

Central Edinburgh, Tuesday 31st May

Harper Guthrie's desiccated old grandfather had, on one unpleasant occasion, reputedly looked down at the feckless youngster who had just broken a window with his ball, and had quoted an old American Indian saying that, in the right wind, even turkeys fly. Fortune had provided such fair breezes, and while he appeared something of an absent-minded figure as far as the everyday details of life were concerned, Guthrie had been blessed with a remarkably clear and incisive brain. He might seem uncertain and lost, but, in the end, he always reached the correct conclusion. One of these decisions had been to settle in quietly over the weekend following his arrival in Edinburgh, to recover from jet lag, and to find time to adjust his body to the vagaries of the Scottish diet. He had tried to telephone his new boss, Professor MacArthur, but was told he was off fishing, so Guthrie had plenty of time to adjust his mind and to prepare for whatever new demands he was about to face.

Around six each morning so far he had been wakened by a cacophony that, were he musically informed, he might have confused with the atonality of something by Stockhausen or Birtwhistle. Every pipe in the tenement seemed to pass through his room, as their liquids, driven along snakes-and-ladders plumbing with a monstrous gurgling and burbling, fought their ways to many destinations. The first morning had been typical: the noise drove him early from his steel-framed bed. Despite it being almost summer by his book, it was still bitterly cold, so he quickly dug a dressing gown and towel out of his suitcase and emerged into the corridor to identify the bathroom he had been allocated.

He was used to having a shower to sluice away unwanted body grime, but there was none to be had in this place. He would have to make do with keeping close company with his own dirt in a hot, soapy bath. But the fluids flowing through the pipes in

51

his bedroom did not extend to hot water being directed into the large, lime-encrusted tub. After fighting with the verdigris engrained on the chrome taps, he managed to obtain a trickle, then panicked when a sudden scalding gush of hot water poured forth. The other tap was corroded solid and he had to transfer cold water from the basin in a plastic bowl he found underneath. Then, feeling that he had already completed a day's hard work, and having identified a sliver of white as his allocated soap ration, he sunk half-contentedly into the steaming water. His relaxed reverie seemed to have lasted only a few seconds when he heard a bang on the door and the stentorian voice of Mrs Murray announcing: 'Your breakfast's ready. It willna' keep, y'know, Mr Guthrie.'

Reluctantly he dragged himself from the water and, hastily drying himself, repaired to his bedroom, dressed, and, without shaving, made his way to the dining room, or parlour, as Mrs Murray had described it, where he sat down at the solitary place laid at the well-polished table. An empty plate was already in front of him, with, beyond that, a steaming pot containing a grey slush. Cold, limp toast, a very wet fried egg, and a microscopic slice of butter, completed the meal. As he took his place and unfolded a paper napkin, decorated inappropriately with Christmas holly designs, Mrs Murray appeared bearing a huge china teapot.

'Tea,' she said. It was statement rather than enquiry.

'Coffee?' he began.

'Tea,' she said firmly as she poured the heavily brewed contents into his cup.

'Porridge,' she added, helpfully pointing to the grey concoction. 'And fresh milk. You'll no be wanting sugar.' Again it was not a subject for further discussion. He asked for his egg to be cooked further; he had come across many cases of salmonella poisoning in the past. It was ungraciously returned to him later, baked to a rigid yellow consistency.

'Scotland's wake-up cereal,' Guthrie thought to himself as he bravely spooned out some of the oatmeal into his plate and splashed cold milk over it. In perspective, perhaps it was the stiff whisky nightcap he'd taken before bed the night before which caused his nausea. Perhaps it was fear of Mrs Murray's wrath if he did not eat the stone-hard egg in front of him. Whatever, the result was the same; he consumed the majority of the porridge, then just made it out of the dining room and down the hall to the bathroom, where he was briefly and violently ill. E-coli it might not be, but that instant purging made him feel more prepared to confront the challenges of the new day.

The following Tuesday morning it was as if a sodden grey blanket had been lifted from the city. The skies were blue, the air invigorating and the pavements glistened in the sunlight. He stepped readily out of the close, clutching a battered leather folder containing the correspondence he had had with Professor MacArthur. With the help of a street plan, he made his way on foot round the back of Edinburgh Castle, towards a group of blackened buildings of a variety of civic styles where, with little further difficulty, he discovered both the faculty he was looking for and the familiar name pinned on a door.

'Dr Guthrie? What a surprise.' As he was shown into the room by a bird-like secretary, the overbearing figure of Professor MacArthur emerged to greet him from behind a massive, paper-laden desk. MacArthur, a legend in his own mind and a figure of ridicule in the eyes of most of his scientific contemporaries, possessed forensic abilities that failed to reach his own opinion of them. Dressed in an ancient three-piece suit of heavy country tweed, and a paisley pattern tie and mauve shirt that were inappropriately colour-coded, the air in his office was filled with medically dangerous pipe smoke.

Well enough trained for a previous generation of scientific research, MacArthur was not a believer in many modern methods of disease identification and control, but he had key friends in the Government, and his unit continued to receive substantial official funding as a result. Little of real value had emerged from its work in recent years, which the professor put down not to his own outmoded approach, but to peer-group jealousy, in particular that emanating from the Harman Institute in the person of Professor Desmond Grant. He did Grant an unrecognized injustice: the latter barely recognized MacArthur's recent research work as deserving of any comment, since he believed it to be of such low calibre.

'Great to be here, professor,' Guthrie beamed pleasantly. 'Not too much of a surprise I hope.'

'Surprise. Yes. Do sit down. Coffee?' The professor gestured grandly in the direction of a huge leather armchair, the horsehair stuffing of which spewed from various venerable cracks.

'Surprise?' Guthrie echoed. 'You were expecting me?'

'Of course we were expecting you.'

'Then?' queried Guthrie.

'We were not expecting you *now*.' The professor emphasized the final word.

'I have your arrival date firmly in my diary. The thirteenth of June.'

'I sent a subsequent message,' Guthrie protested. He rummaged in his leather folder, located the document and presented it triumphantly.

Professor MacArthur deigned to look at it, then waved it away. 'Odd,' he said, 'small confusion somewhere. Point is: you're here. A lot to be done. People will want to talk to you about your work.' He spoke more to himself than to Guthrie. 'Settled in, have you? When did you arrive?' The professor went through belated motions of being polite. 'Found some digs?'

'Digs?' Guthrie looked blank. He was a medical man, not an archaeologist.

'Digs, yes. Accommodation. Found rooms? A flat, perhaps?'

'A Mrs Murray . . .' Guthrie started lamely.

'Mrs Murray. Ah, yes, I'd forgotten.' The professor's voice dropped appreciably. 'Bit frugal, but, if you like that sort of thing . . .'

'Your office arranged it,' Guthrie grunted unhappily.

'Did we? Right, well I hope you'll be comfortable there.'

'I don't think I will.'

'Oh, dear.' The professor briskly examined his watch. 'Oh dear,' he repeated. 'My lecture. Nice meeting you. I'll get Zenna, my secretary, to sort out all the administrative stuff for you and find you a quiet place to work. Till tomorrow, then. Must fly . . .' With that, the professor sped from the room, leaving Guthrie alone with his thoughts.

Some time later he found himself ensconced in what might be termed a cranny, in a remote corner of a pharmacology lab. It was scarcely a match for his immaculate research facility back home, with its computers, its rows of indexed files, its banks of bound books, articles and offprints, but it allowed him just enough space to park his laptop, so he did not complain. His view, through a partly leaded window, was of the corner of a municipal car park which appeared to be the meeting place for the local winos, and, on top of everything, there was a constant heavy background noise caused, Zenna explained, by jackhammers or, as she called them, pneumatic drills, all to do with 'the modernization programme'.

A normally even-minded individual, over the next few hours Guthrie was hit by a whole gamut of mood swings as he faced up to the gritty realities of modern Scotland. Where was the proud nation he had read about? Talent and industry had travelled widely overseas over the last two hundred years. What had been left behind? These superficial thoughts were overtaken by events. Accessing his e-mail, he found he was much in demand. Among a lot of correspondence from the States was a message from a Dr Rebecca Stevenson of the Harman Institute, urging him to contact her as soon as possible. Its director, Professor Grant, was keen to talk to him urgently about his research findings on Virus ZD198. One isolated case had been identified in London: it was baffling them. Where could it have emerged from, he was asked? Guthrie did not need to access the historical data, since he clearly recalled that it had been several years since the last outbreak, also an isolated one, of a mercenary soldier, an ex-US marine, who had spent some time fighting with rebel forces in the Congo.

Since then the disease had, to the best of his knowledge, been dormant.

He sent a holding reply. He would respond in full as soon as possible. From memory he gave Dr Stevenson references as to where she would be able to access the information about the last outbreak. On the face of it her case did seem odd, he added. The virus was extremely difficult to transmit. It tended to kill people very quickly, within days or hours. This somewhat longer gestation period suggested a mutation, a spinoff version of the real thing. He would think hard about that, look up his previous research and come back to her as soon as possible.

4

Clegg Hurley's house was a palace in comparison with every-thing else in the neighbourhood. Two storeys, walls bullet-scarred but otherwise relatively intact after the civil war; a fine verandah and plenty of space to entertain had there been anyone to entertain; well-barred windows, particularly on the upper floor; a staircase with, at the top, another grille, so that night-time marauders could be kept at bay in this modern for-tified castle. A local staff of two looked after him relatively well, while good air conditioning – the essential of essentials – made his bedroom and study reasonably habitable. Only there, in those two rooms, and in his office of course, did he feel safe from all his fears of Africa.

That morning he was brave and forced himself to walk to work. Though it was less than two hundred metres from his house to the WHO's office, and the sector was relatively secure at the moment, he usually drove, particularly if it was raining, since they had issued him with an almost new four-wheel-drive Land Rover. It wasn't that he'd ever even seen a snake, and the local people had given him little trouble since he'd arrived. Most of them looked too under-nourished to be threatening, though the ill-disciplined teenage guards who slouched about the place with their AK47s swinging aggressively at their hips were a constant worry. He'd been reassured by a visiting military attaché from one of the Western embassies that most of their guns didn't work, they were so rusted and uncared for, but the young soldiers all had well-sharpened machetes swinging from their belts too.

It was a degree or two cooler that morning, and he arrived at the office in less of a sweat than normal. He unlocked the door and let himself in since, as usual, he was well ahead of the local staff. He switched up the air conditioning to full blast, and settled down to read through the e-mails and faxes that had come in overnight. There was nothing that couldn't wait, except for an urgent response from that bastard Boekamper in New York. Boekamper was his line boss, and the instruction was unequivocal. He was ordered to go and see the Belgian, Dr Banquier, immediately, and report back with the fullest details of both victim and virus which the man had reported on in his telephone call the previous day. If it really was a case of surge fever, which was listed more prosaically as virus ZD198 by the WHO, Boekamper warned that alarm bells would start ringing all round the world.

Hurley went to his filing cabinet to remind himself of what precisely Banquier had reported. The local African name, translated into English as surge fever, was so called because of the convulsions the victims suffered in the terminal stages of the disease. Banquier had been far from precise about how he had identified it: something about having come across a few other cases in the distant past, in villages deep in the jungle, where the victims died before any proper tests could be carried out. Hurley had made a file note that the doctor had been remarkably unforthcoming about the whole thing, so much so that he had wondered whether to even bother reporting the call to the New York office. Now it seemed to have stirred up a bit of a hornet's nest. Inaction would have been a wiser course, but it was too late now.

Trips up country were not Hurley's favourite occupation. When he went anywhere, he had been firmly instructed to take at least one armed guard and a local staff member with him. He did not need to be told. He was no hero. He scratched nervously at his mosquito bites, pulled on his bush jacket and went out of his office to find a guard, a technical assistant and a driver who would take him to find the reclusive Dr Banquier. As it happened, no one was available. He shrugged. Too bad: he wasn't going on his own. There was no particular rush; it could easily wait another twenty-four hours.

10 Downing Street, London, Thursday 2nd June

It was over in a few seconds. Lyle Thane caught Daniel Evans's eye as the press secretary turned his head away to hide his discomfiture. They were halfway through the regular mid-morning briefing meeting with the Prime Minister when it happened. They had been talking about fitting in the parliamentary programme with a heavy schedule of future overseas trips, to Washington, to Tokyo, to Beijing. Maybe China would have to be postponed until the latest civil unrest had sorted itself out.

Then it happened. The two men waited, embarrassed by Peter Morgan's unusually lengthy pause. Normally the PM was too glib; words flowed rapidly and easily; sentences came well formulated. If his remarks sometimes sounded a little sterile, that was the way with professional politicians like him, who wanted to avoid saying anything that might cause controversy unless it was carefully planned by the spindoctors first. Peter Morgan could have been chosen by Hollywood's Central Casting for the job of British Prime Minister. He was polished, persuasive, and a good looker. That had always served him particularly well with the female vote. One of his spindoctors had referred to it as the 'halo effect': if you looked the part then people thought you were also wise, considerate, understanding, and a great leader of men. Little did they know.

Peter Morgan was blandness personified, but he smiled sincerely and chose his ties well, or at least Janet, his wife, did. He was a man for all occasions. He read his lines with feeling, was attentive to the briefs his civil servants put in front of him, knew how to hedge answers to difficult questions, and had a great way of giving responses when an answer did not fit. He would have made a great actor, so well did he play the part. Peter Morgan sailed through life, always expecting the car door to be opened for him, the chair to be pulled back ready at the table, the papers to be neatly flagged up, the right voice to be whispering in his ear. Some people called him an automaton. He was, and a highly efficient one too.

This definitely wasn't planned. Thank God Winston Rogerson wasn't present as he often was at these mid-morning briefings. He'd have made a thing out of it, whatever 'it' was. The Deputy PM was incapable of keeping anything quiet, and even at the best of times could turn the most banal event into a front-page headline. Rogerson was nothing if not compulsive. He was not a bad fellow, but to be fair to him, which Lyle Thane seldom was, Rogerson would have been more at ease living in the obscurity of some local pub, for which nature had clearly designed him. He saw himself as the voice of the man in the street, good at saying things that were full of workaday common sense. That was a dangerous attribute in political life; common sense seldom matched practical and financial feasibility. The other trouble with Rogerson was that he was always opening his mouth and putting his foot in it by talking about things that even he should have realized were way beyond his competence. Deputy Prime Ministers, Thane believed, should be chosen for their ability to do the dull boring stuff, read the briefs which the PM had no time to read, make the speeches that no one of any importance would listen to, mouth the platitudes that were the everyday bread and butter of politics. But unfortunately Rogerson came from a wing of the Party which, the Whips had persuaded the PM, needed to be pacified. Thus all the dangers implicit in his non-job were constantly lurking in the undergrowth. For all those reasons, it was a blessing that Rogerson wasn't there when it happened: the PM's few seconds' pause, that empty look, with no apologies, no embarrassment, no apparent realization that anything untoward had happened. Then Peter Morgan had swiftly clicked back to reality and gone on with what he was saying, with all his usual panache and aplomb. So what was there to worry about?

The Edinburgh Shuttle, Thursday 2nd June

Sir Mark eased himself gently into an aisle seat on the 1600 hours flight to Edinburgh. All around him was bustle as his fellow commuters stowed their briefcases and struggled to fasten their safety belts. The plane was full. Just as he was looking forward to closing his eyes and dozing for the duration of the flight, he spotted an old colleague, Martin Milner, formerly British Ambassador to Washington, whose sudden departure from the Embassy there had caused quite a stir some years previously. Milner and he had kept in intermittent touch since then: they liked each other, were in many ways similar, and had both recently been eased into their sixties at a joint party thrown by a group of mutual friends. Milner was about to sit down a few rows ahead when Ivor waved at him, and, after a certain amount of negotiation, managed to get someone to change seats so that the two friends could sit together.

'What takes you to Edinburgh?' asked Milner.

'Lecture at the university. You?'

'Meeting the Foreign Affairs Committee of the Scottish Parliament,' Milner replied. 'They want my views on opening up a Scottish embassy in Washington. Whether it'd go against the Residual Powers Agreement with Westminster and all that.'

'Would it?' asked Sir Mark.

'On paper, probably. But if the will is there no one will object.'

They settled back in their seats, put away thoughts of catching up on lost sleep, and chatted on in a desultory way. The plane took off, and when an air hostess appeared with a drinks trolley they both ordered whisky 'for old times' sake'. They had sunk many a bottle together in the past. Milner admitted he got fuddled quicker these days, but why not? He wasn't striving any more. He still had his ambitions, but they were things more of mind than of material. He was, he said, mainly bent on avoiding Enoch Powell's gloomy prediction that all successful public figures ended up being sad and lonely at home.

'No way, Enoch, wherever you are now,' Sir Mark smiled.

'You know, Mark,' echoed Milner, 'as I grow older I realize that little in life is important and even that doesn't matter very much.'

Anybody overhearing those two ageing gentlemen, into their second whiskies prised from a reluctant stewardess, might have wondered who they were, or perhaps have recalled some forgotten photograph or incident, or maybe even have been tempted to tap one of them on the shoulder and ask, 'Didn't you used to be somebody?' Towards the end of the flight, when Milner dropped his voice to a whisper, an alert observer might also have been a little curious at what was being said. When voices are raised it usually is about some matter of little import. Whispered conversations are more interesting because, by their very nature, an attempt is being made to withold information from others about something.

'Not all you're doing in Edinburgh?' asked Milner.

'Not quite.' Sir Mark hesitated.

'Telling me more?'

'Strange message yesterday.' Sir Mark half turned in his seat. 'Ever come across Rumbold?'

'The peer who vanished? No. Never.'

'Nor I, but I know his daughter. Hadn't heard from her for ages, then she rang last night out of the blue. Asked if she could come and see me. Urgently. Said she was living just north of Edinburgh. As I was coming up, we've arranged to meet.'

'So?' Milner prompted.

'So, I'm not sure,' Sir Mark hesitated. 'She has something to tell me.'

'About Rumbold?'

'About Rumbold.'

'Why you?' asked Milner, curious despite himself.

'I was the spindoctor, remember?' Sir Mark laughed. 'She hinted he's still alive.'

Their discussion was halted as the plane landed and Milner became more concerned about where he was to meet the driver whom he was expecting to collect him. There were too many people within earshot so, as they disembarked, the two men briefly discussed the political situation. 'Age of political pygmies,' said Milner grandly, struggling into his coat.

'Are you looking back to that golden age when figures like Major and Kinnock strutted the stage?' laughed Sir Mark.

'Each generation deserves its own,' Milner responded softly. 'How d'you think the PM's doing?' he asked as they moved into the terminal building to wait for their bags to come off the carousel.

'Superficially well. With his huge majority, the Opposition seems to have disappeared without trace. The media has deserted even their brightest spokesmen since what they think is no longer news. It's the antis inside the party, like that brute Rogerson, who count. Knives flashing in the Cabinet make exciting copy.'

'I find it difficult to get excited about any of it.' Milner reached down to grab his bag.

'You're jaded, that's all,' joked Sir Mark.

'Maybe. Maybe they're not the same quality.'

'Balls! The quality's still there: just hidden. System works as it always did. Leaders stand waving to the crowds. Make their speeches, go on international visits, pose with presidents and princes, but, as always, it's the people behind the throne, the string-pullers, the strategists, the spindoctors, the think-tank men and women, who make the running. They formulate the decisions which their bosses appear to take.'

'You're still at all that, are you, Mark? Influence greater than power, I remember. Is it still the same?'

'Always has been. Throughout history, the most famous and the most notorious rulers have been manipulated by the string-pullers.' Sir Mark in turn picked up his bag from the carousel.

Milner ventured a last glance at his friend. 'Rumbold? What does his girl really want?'

'My guess? Something nasty's happened to him, and she wants my spindoctoring to present this to an astonished world.'

Camden Town, London, Friday 3rd June

In the cluttered study of his rambling house in Camden Town, Ralph Rowland was decoratively slouched in a large, overstuffed armchair. Beside him, watching him closely, was his agent, Zak Levine, and his housekeeper, Amanda Murphy. Rowland was in full flood, lecturing them both in his usual domineering way on what he thought of last night's new play, about today's actors and actresses, about the deplorable level of State funding for the Arts. Rowland off-stage was a bore, a man solely interested in what he himself said. His attention strayed from this central theme only when the question of money came up, as it always did shortly after Zak Levine arrived.

They turned to talk about the next contract: a Shaw revival. 'Can't they ever give me something new?' bellowed the legend.

'The way Kenny's going to direct it will be very new,' Zak pleaded.

'Asking me to do it in drag, or naked, or something?' asked Rowland, an unpleasant sneer in his voice.

Zak sighed, while Amanda looked the other way. She had put up with a great deal over the years: his insanitary habits, his bullying, his extraordinary ability to put himself first all the time.

Ralph Rowland was in full flow when something distinctly odd happened. He paused, eyes staring, mouth half open, hand poised in mid-air, as if suddenly frozen in time and space. Zak and Amanda looked at him in astonishment, wondering if this was some theatrical gimmick. They waited for a moment or two, then Zak asked, 'You all right, old man?'

There was no response, not a flicker of an eyelid, not a tremble of an arm. It was as if Rowland had become transfixed, yet he still appeared to be breathing normally. Zak wondered aloud whether he'd had a seizure, but the great man's features were alert, his shoulders were still four square. Only in the eyes did they both see something different: a grey pallor had fallen over them, like a diaphanous veil.

Zak stood up quickly. 'Amanda, come, help me move him. We'll call his doctor.' They moved together towards Rowland's chair, but as they did so the actor's body shuddered, then seemed to relax.

He turned to face them, blinked for a moment, then demanded, 'What's the matter with you both? What are you staring at?'

'You all right, Ralph?' Zak asked again anxiously.

'All right?' replied the actor aggressively. 'Course I'm all right. What's the matter with you?' he repeated.

'You ... er ... er ...' Zak began, but Amanda, who was standing close behind him, put out her hand and touched him softly on the shoulder. He stopped. 'Nothing,' he said lamely.

'So, where was I?' said Ralph. 'You put me off my stride you know, Zak. You're bloody irritating. Always doing it. I don't know why I've put up with you all these years. You tend to cut me off in mid-sentence.'

'Sorry Ralph,' said Zak, sighing. It was a sigh not just to do with the usual obnoxiousness of his client, but with a sudden realization that this particular source of income might, one day, suddenly disappear. For there was no doubt whatsoever in Zak Levine's mind that something was decidedly wrong with Ralph Rowland.

Later, much later, as he was leaving the house, Amanda took Zak aside and told him that this was not the first nor the second incident – maybe the fifth over the last few days. She'd tried to broach the subject with her employer, but he seemed not to understand what she was talking about. Amanda had had a mother who suffered from Alzheimer's, she said, but this wasn't Alzheimer's. This was different. These were total black-outs. Rowland had never fallen over, never fainted, never looked particularly different, apart from that strange grey film that seemed to cross his eyes every time it happened.

Zak saw the tears in Amanda's eyes. He had always assumed she must have loved the great man in her own way. Despite himself, despite the hard-hearted career he followed, Zak was moved, and so he put his arm round her shoulder to comfort her.

'It'll be OK,' he said, 'he'll be fine.' But neither of them believed, in their heart of hearts, that this was true.

5

Winston Rogerson had spent most of his fifty-eight years hating his Christian name. He intensely disliked having everyone realize whom his parents had named him after. He was a person in his own right; he was a political animal; he didn't need to reflect a great figure from the past. In any case, the other Winston had been of a very different political complexion; Rogerson had been born a cockney, in Lambeth, and he was proud of it. Rogerson was a man of anger. When people first met him, or saw him on television or at the dispatch box, they would guess that he could become easily aroused. That flushed face, the enlarged red veins in his nose, signalled both a lively temper and many decades of liking for the bottle. A bristling grey moustache suggested further aggression, while his eyes glared accusingly at life from under great bushy eyebrows.

Rogerson was an odd man to be Deputy Prime Minister of the United Kingdom. After all, he came from an army background followed by time in the prison service, where he'd ended up as Governor of Brixton before moving into national politics. His father had also been in the army, and his mother came from military stock, so law and order was deep in his blood. He believed in the State, he believed in authority, he believed in the good regulation of things, which was why, as he told everyone, he was in politics in the first place. In the past, left-wing political opponents had called him a fascist, but he was not that. He was correct, honourable, upright, outspoken, and deeply intolerant of a whole range of social ills in contemporary society. In many other ways he was an outsider in the fast-moving, trendy politics of the new Britain.

No one could question the fact that Winston Rogerson was a thoroughly decent man. His true enemies were few. He was widely seen as doing a reasonably good job. The Prime Minister made a fuss of him from time to time, particularly at Party conferences. The Downing Street staff tried only to employ him as a front man when difficult issues over matters of sleaze or cronyism had to be defended in front of a wider electorate. No one could ever accuse Winston Rogerson of dishonesty. He was a man whom people understood. Though, in the end, he always toed the party line, obeyed the Government whips, and had done so throughout his entire political career, never hitting the headlines over anything scandalous, he was perceived both by the media and the general public as the benevolently cantankerous face of Government. 'Good old Rogerson,' people would say. 'They've pushed him forward to front on this unpopular piece of policy.' Or, 'Now the Minister for Sport's hit the tabloids over his pretty research assistant Rogerson'll be paraded to take the heat out of it. He'll be straight, full of good common sense, understanding, humanity.'

Behind the scenes, however, Rogerson could be both difficult and unpredictable, which was why Lyle Thane and the other Downing Street staff were always wary about what they told him. He had a few close colleagues he'd been to school or college with, or had served with in the army or the prison service. He was loyal to them and they were loyal to him. But he had no close friends. Except for Tina. Tina, his wife, had died the previous year of cancer, and when she had gone, Rogerson had felt a huge emptiness. It was as if a black hole had appeared and, with the help of a whisky bottle, he nearly slipped into it. It was only his military background that stopped him from giving up politics and disappearing into the oblivion of retirement. One other reason that he didn't fall totally apart was largely due to Tina's brother, another military man, a retired army doctor, Colonel Sam Broomfield. Because of the very different lives they had led, the two men did not know each other well, but Tina's death brought them briefly close. The colonel was not an emotional man, but he had been fond enough of his sister, felt sorry for Winston, and had determined to help him as best he could. He felt he owed it to Tina's memory. He consoled Rogerson through a difficult period, talking to him and humouring him. It worked after a fashion, but later the two men drifted apart once again.

Not that Colonel Broomfield, doctor though he was, was the best man to help anyone in a crisis. He was a deeply introverted figure. Not for him the bonhomie of the Mess, nor the bedside manner for the sick. He once revealed to his brother-in-law that he'd always felt a bit apart, both from the army and from other medical professionals. Sometimes people in a mix of careers such as his shone because of their differentiated skills: the sum total of two disciplines made for something greater than they could have achieved in either. Not so with Colonel Broomfield. He was different. He was a loner; at times he even felt himself an outcast. Yet, when he tried, he'd found it easy enough to get by with his curious mix of professions. Other medics tended to say, 'Well, he is an army doctor, isn't he,' while fellow officers branded him as special because he was not a fighting man like themselves. Like his brother-in-law he'd never really had any close friends, and while he'd been briefly married, the details were buried deep in his past. Yet he'd always lived the life of a normal, healthy bachelor in any Mess to which he was posted, since it was demonstrably clear that he had a normal interest in the opposite sex.

As a result of his remoteness, and no one could ever put their finger on what lay behind it nor suggested that he had lacked the necessary qualifications for the jobs he had been assigned to, his superiors had never been totally happy with Colonel Broomfield. He had never transgressed any of the many military or medical rules to which he was subject, but Ministry of Defence personnel records nonetheless branded him as 'a difficult man to know', and 'not particularly sociable'. Beyond that, their specific criticisms were few, but because the system was always uncertain what to do with him, particularly as he advanced from captain to major to full colonel, and because he was unmarried, he was often selected for special missions to difficult places. What that system did not know or recognize, was how much this created a deep feeling of injustice within him, both with the army and with his lot in general.

Colonel Broomfield harboured many other perceived grievances: over his varied postings, over what he believed were the sneering asides of his fellow doctors and officers and, above all, against those who consistently failed to promote him to the top ranks in the army medical service. Had he not always done his work efficiently, never spared himself, never complained? Had he not always gone beyond his duty to help his patients and his army colleagues? Had he ever written one single protest letter at being sent from one hell-hole to the other? Had he ever misbehaved in the Mess, or in the military hospitals, or in the field ambulance stations where he had spent so many years trying to help his fellow men and women? When he reached retirement age, Colonel Broomfield failed to get any more honours or awards from the Ministry of Defence, and so he retired unhappily, to nurse his various grudges in a modest semi-detached house he had bought for himself in the west London borough of Ealing. That he still did not see much of his brother-in-law even though they now lived relatively close to each other, surely was a small factor in the course of history.

Edinburgh, Wednesday 8th June

It took a full week before things came to a head. Until then Harper Guthrie was left in relative peace to adjust to his new surroundings. In his remote corner of the laboratory and in front of his computer screen, he was in full command. But as always with him, little things kept cropping up to play havoc with his life. By the beginning of the week following his arrival, he was so consumed with worry about his cholesterol levels, as he forced down yet another indigestible meal of stew and hard-boiled potatoes, that he summoned up enough courage to tell Mrs Murray, as she pressed him to round off his dinner with some of her home-made steamed dumpling as 'afters', that he intended, as he put it, to 'dine out' in future. Guthrie did not normally play with versions of the truth, but in Mrs Murray's case, he made an exception. He lied. The room was . . . er . . . fine, but he was on a strict, medically-supervised diet. He did not wish to put Mrs Murray to any unnecessary trouble.

'The university assured me . . .' she snarled.

'I'm sure they'll explain,' Guthrie kept his head down.

'There's a lot of explaining to do,' Mrs Murray sniffed, draining her sinuses in emulation of the noises from the pipes in his bedroom. Then she turned and, with the closest thing to a flounce someone of her build could muster, left the 'parlour'. Nothing more was said. If that was her wrath on a mere matter of meals, what would happen when he came to leave? It would, he surmised, have to be a midnight flit, unless he employed the tactic of telling Mrs Murray about the deadly viruses he dealt with daily. That might just reduce her enthusiasm for having him as a tenant.

He had enough activities on his plate at the moment to leave that decision till later. Concurrently he was having to cope with the tensions he found in any contact he had with Professor MacArthur. It began halfway through that Wednesday morning as, in his cramped and noisy corner, he was attempting to build a particular vector model on his computer, when Zenna, MacArthur's secretary, appeared. The boss wanted to see him. He stood up, straightened his tie – he was one of those few scientists around who actually wore a tie – and meekly followed her out of the lab.

The professor was in high spirits. Guthrie noted the breath of whisky in the air though it was barely eleven-thirty, which would account for the professor's rubicund expression.

'Dear boy, how are you? Settled in well? Good!' The man did not wait for a response but turned to the matter in hand. 'Your head of department in Boston, Professor Lanchester, when he wrote about your sabbatical, said you'd be happy to take a seminar or two.'

'No, no,' said Guthrie, wondering what Lanchester had actually said. 'He knows I'm only here to research. Teaching isn't my forte.' His words petered out as he realized that he had totally failed to hold MacArthur's attention. The latter had moved behind his desk to where a large wall-chart was covered, Guthrie could easily make out, with the tell-tale box markings of an academic timetable.

'Let me see. You could help out with the research fellows sypmposium.'

'I don't have my notes.' Guthrie felt himself sinking. He had been steeling himself to ask MacArthur whether he could take a few days off to visit the people at the Harman Institute, but now was obviously not the moment.

'Have them sent over.' Professor MacArthur stood poised over the wall-chart, felt-tip marker in hand. 'Lanchester told me you'd be most obliging. Look, I'll work out a schedule and let you know. Nothing too arduous. We don't want to interfere with your research, do we? A couple of seminars . . . challenges of youth and all that . . . let me see . . .' The felt-tip pen was again poised. Like the biblical handwriting on the wall, he marked out Harper Guthrie's doom.

'But professor,' Guthrie began. 'There never was any question of . . .'

'You're the great expert on disease transmission? Theoretical models and all that?' MacArthur asked, but did not wait for a reply. 'Talk on that. These young people will love it. I don't know one end of a database from another,' he went on. 'Computer illiterate and proud of it. Don't know how you supposedly hyper-intelligent technocrats work without understanding the past. If you're into disease transfer, epidemiology and all that, unless you know what happens in primitive societies how can you be certain what is going to happen in advanced ones? Even the medieval doctors weren't that bad at diagnosing disease.' The professor was warming to his theme. 'They knew the plague when they saw it, you know. Insisted on keeping the sick in charnel houses till they died, then burnt the bodies on pyres. Those sent to collect the corpses used long hooks. Not a pleasant concept, is it? Think of the Four Horsemen of the Apocalypse: wasn't pestilence one of them? Not just an historic concept. Could so easily happen again.'

Guthrie nodded. At last something had been said with which he could agree. He also had a point about primitive societies: he'd plotted on his computer how rapidly AIDS had spread across sub-Saharan Africa.

'Mean it,' said MacArthur, somewhat irritably, as if expecting Guthrie to disagree. 'What'd happen if we had a new plague today? Fear of the unknown. Primitive panic. Mass hysteria. A new unstoppable virus could rule out the future for most of us.'

'What I've always—' Guthrie started to say, looking down at his hands.

'Doesn't bear thinking about,' MacArthur continued. 'Done a lot of reading up on it – as a hobby. History of medical science is fascinating, you know. We ought to teach it to all medical students. Make 'em read Daniel Defoe and Albert Camus on the wider effects of plagues. Give them a sense of perspective. Nothing new under the sun. Rather there's always something new under the sun.'

'Science is always close behind,' Guthrie ventured. Had he felt under less pressure, he might have actually enjoyed this discussion.

'Close, but not close enough,' Professor MacArthur growled. It was the truest thing he had said so far. 'So, you'll take the seminar?'

'But . . .' Guthrie began again.

'Professor Lanchester *assured* me,' Professor MacArthur said, without turning round. He sounded really annoyed now. 'Part of the deal. Reason we agreed to you coming here at such short notice. Visitors can be very time-consuming for us too, you know. Take up valuable scarce resources – laboratory space, my time, all the back-up this great faculty can offer you. So good of you.'

'But . . .' Guthrie made a final attempt to interrupt. Damn Lanchester to hell.

The professor turned and yelled through the open door: 'Zenna! Get Euan Davidson up here. Straightaway. Want him to show . . . er . . . Dr . . . er . . . around.' The interview was at an end.

Dr Euan Davidson did not appear to appreciate the style of his summons and it showed. He was a good head shorter than Harper Guthrie, dark, deep-eyed, impetuous. Guthrie had already heard a little about him. He apparently considered himself something of a ladies' man, a dangerous self-image in an occupation that brought him, as a senior member of the faculty, in close daily contact with numerous impressionable young medics. He had spent much of his working life in the States, but in between that and various marriages, had acquired a reasonably good reputation in the field of public health. Davidson also claimed to be an arch proponent of scientific ethics; he misused his considerable tactical skills in this minefield, and made himself a pain in the neck to many of his colleagues in the process. If he had better qualities, he kept them well concealed, so he was not, therefore, going to be an obvious soulmate for Guthrie.

Davidson arrived with, 'I have better things to do with my time than this,' written all over his face. He shook hands with negative enthusiasm. He complained he had been badly briefed: it was typical of the bloody faculty that nobody had told *him* Guthrie was arriving. It was all most inconvenient. Guthrie apologized, though he felt little requirement so to do, reckoning that there was little likelihood of them having a meeting of minds. They left the professor's rooms and began walking aimlessly along a corridor together.

'Field?' asked Davidson distantly. There was something in his manner which suggested, despite his question, that he knew a great deal about Guthrie already. When Guthrie had politely explained, Davidson appeared dismissive. 'So unfair. You probably have a bigger personal grant for vector research than we have at all our Scottish facilities put together.'

'We're well endowed,' said Guthrie, modestly. 'Heard of the Craigie Foundation?'

'Never. But I wish there were rich benefactors around to help me,' snapped Davidson. 'My research grant is a minus figure. If I economize, I can probably turn in an article of worthwhile research every two years.' Davidson was giving every indication of being a compulsive complainer.

'Good research wins out in the end,' said Guthrie helpfully. 'D'you ever collaborate with Professor Grant's people at the Harman Institute?'

'Grant?' Davidson demonstrated mock rage. 'Don't mention his name here – biggest civil war in the profession.'

'I'd heard. Why?' Guthrie prompted.

Davidson responded by looking at his watch. 'Nearly lunchtime. If you're not doing anything,' he offered grudgingly, 'come to the staff canteen. Food's rotten, service is worse, but it's subsidized. We can talk about Grant without being overheard.'

They walked off briskly together, Davidson gruffly pointing out a few items of interest on the way, only brightening up when a pretty student passed them. She greeted Davidson with a wink. 'One of my better protegées,' he said, turning and staring after her, largely in the direction of her legs. 'Talented young lady,' he continued. Guthrie wondered at the use of the word *talented*; well-endowed would have suited her better. When they reached the canteen, Davidson steered Guthrie straight to the bar. 'Quick one, if you don't mind. Can't get through a whole afternoon of bloody tutorials without a large jar of anaesthetic.'

Guthrie was not used to drinking at lunchtime, but opted to play along. In the event they both downed a pint and, in the process, Davidson appeared to warm up.

'Married?' he asked.

'No,' responded Guthrie.

'Better, isn't it? I've been married, ... more than once,' Davidson volunteered, looking hard at him. 'Temptation comes one's way so frequently,' he added.

'So I'm told,' said Guthrie disingenuously. It was early days to start swapping home truths.

'Seen much of the town yet? Nightlife?'

'Went to a pub on my first night – noisy place – for a quick nightcap.'

'Which?'

'Called the Bonnie Charlie, I think.'

'My God. Bit downmarket for the likes of you.'

'Yes.'

'Now, wait a minute. You don't mean . . . ?' Davidson paused and appeared to reflect for a moment. 'I know the Bonnie Charlie. Along Union Road, isn't it? That means the office has put you up with old Ma Murray. They keep bloody doing it.'

'What d'you mean?' asked Guthrie. 'Yes, I'm staying with Mrs Murray. Not pleasant, I can tell you.'

'I bet. The reject from hell, one of last year's visiting professors called her. Never met the lady, but with her reputation, I'll keep it that way.' Davidson suddenly looked amused. They moved from bar to cafeteria where, picking up a tray from a pile, Guthrie followed his new-found colleague to the food counter, above which someone had, complete with spelling mistake, triumphantly written: 'We do no serve genetically modified food'. The only good thing about the lunch, modified or not, was that it was indeed remarkably cheap, though having eaten it he agreed with Davidson that it deserved to be given away free. Later they sat talking over a cup of coffee. Davidson's sole topic of conversation still seemed to be the range of talent available in his final year class. 'They don't come to learn, most of them. They come to grow up, and breed, like bugs.'

Guthrie pretended to be shocked. 'The pursuit of knowledge . . .' he began, with only a trace of a smile.

'The pursuit of what? F— that for a lark. University is for living it up before they have to settle down and start earning a living. Most of them do the minimum, only read the *Sun* or *Sunday Sport*, then scrape up a pass at the last moment so as not to annoy mummy and daddy. Couch potatoes on legs, they are. Do I blame them? In the economic climate we have at the moment, even a first or a PhD doesn't guarantee you a job. Lowest common denominator – *dumbing down*, that's the phrase, isn't it? Why bother?' he repeated. 'Feel like a brandy?' he asked, hopefully.

Guthrie looked at his watch; it was nearly three o'clock. Didn't anyone do any work around here? 'I'll leave it this time,' he ventured, then: 'So tell me about relations with Grant and the Harman Institute.'

'How much d'you know about that?' asked Davidson. A sudden sharp note had entered his voice. Guthrie assumed it must be to do with the rivalry between the two organizations.

'Reputation only,' he replied cautiously, wondering why he chose not to mention his message about ZD198 from Dr Rebecca Stevenson.

'Dangerous to know.' Davidson was looking hard at him. 'Suppose I'd better get over to the department. I'll have half a dozen of those winging bastards waiting around to read their plagiarized so-called papers to me.'

'Subject?'

'Immunology. Public health. Disease control in Third World settings. Mainly African casework. Stirring stuff.' Davidson scowled, then brightened. 'I've just remembered: it's Wednesday. That means that girl . . .' Davidson paused. Again there was that hard, almost steely look. 'Look,' he said. 'Got an admission to make.'

When it came, Guthrie could not have been more surprised. Hardly changing his jaded tone of voice, Davidson suddenly drawled: 'Actually, know all about you already. Apologies for the performance, but I've got to earn my crust here.'

'I don't understand. What are you . . . ?' Guthrie was taken aback.

'Friends in London. They briefed me. Been keeping an eye on you. Wanted me to try you out . . .'

Guthrie waited, saying nothing. He felt confused.

'Bit of play-acting till now, I'm afraid. Sorry.'

'Sorry? I don't understand.'

'No, you wouldn't. Look, it's like this: that thing that's come up, in your field, at the Harman Institute.'

'What are you talking about?'

'You know exactly what I'm talking about. Your speciality: Virus ZD198, that's what. Very senior army general died of it. That set the cat among the pigeons.' Davidson was watching Guthrie, waiting for any reaction. 'They've maybe got another case now.'

'How d'you know?' Guthrie was bewildered. What game was Davidson playing and for whom?

'My job to know. Know exactly when you arrived, what you've been doing. No, don't say anything. We were slow. My chums in London didn't tell me. They didn't even know you were coming over. Of course they didn't know it was definitely an outbreak of ZD198. Now we – they – need your help.'

'Why didn't Professor Grant just ring and ask me, or is Professor MacArthur bugging my telephone? Surely it's not such a great secret!' Guthrie burst out. He was irritated by Davidson and still didn't understand what he was getting at.

Davidson laughed. He'd been warned about Guthrie's apparent naïvety, 'Quite right,' he said. 'But there's a lot more to it than that.'

'What?'

'Let *me* ask you: *what*? What's the single oddest thing about your ZD198?'

'It's rare because it kills its host, the person it infects, and therefore itself, before it can move on to a new victim. Dead-end virus.'

'Exactly. So?'

'So what?'

'So how precisely did our general get it?'

'I don't know. I haven't seen all the facts.'

'Exactly. Nor do we: nor, by the way, do the germ warfare experts at the Pentagon. Everyone's getting very excited. And . . . and want to know.'

'The Pentagon? How do they . . . ? Where do I come in?'

'My friends would like you to transfer to the Harman. As I said, London was slow off the mark. They should never have let you come here to Edinburgh. MacArthur will burst a blood vessel when he knows where you've gone, but I'll do my best to patch things up. We mustn't have a public fuss.'

'I was going there in any case,' volunteered Guthrie. Davidson hadn't commented on his economy with the truth about receiving Dr Stevenson's e-mails. Perhaps, if he knew that too, he was used to people behaving in that way.

'I know that too, Harper,' Davidson eerily echoed his thoughts. 'Dr Stevenson – clever lady, she is. I'm going to make it easier for you to join them, that's all. Then, when you get there, perhaps we could keep in close touch?'

'Why should I?'

'Because it matters, that's why. It could affect British, and American, security.'

Guthrie stared hard at Davidson. 'Exactly who are you working for?' he asked.

'Professor MacArthur, of course,' Davidson was smiling.

'And?'

'Science knows no boundaries, Harper. You know that. Rest assured, the Brits and Americans are at one on this.'

'Why? Why so important?'

'You've guessed why already, Harper. I bet you have, haven't you?'

Guthrie looked away. He realized slowly why the authorities in London and Washington would be very interested, with their secret research into germ warfare, if like him they had even begun to suspect that Virus ZD198 might have been deliberately targeted.

6

Near Kisangani, Congo, Wednesday 8th June

In the event, Clegg Hurley was struck low with a nasty bout of amoebic dysentery, and was, despite ever more frantic messages from Boekamper in New York, incapable of moving from his bed for several days. There was no one else around who could go in his place, and Dr Banquier was either ignoring or did not get his messages to come down to see him. On Wednesday, though he was still very weak, Hurley pulled himself from his sickbed and made the long-delayed journey. It took about two hours to reach the so-called School of Medicine. Up a long, deeply rutted track, the cluster of buildings was set in a compound in a jungle clearing, surrounded by a rusting, barbed-wire fence. The unattended gate was open, and at first there appeared to be no sign of life. Then his armed guard pointed out a couple of local women washing themselves and their clothes at a tap to one side of the main building, a run-down, two-storey affair with a corrugated iron roof that had not seen paint in years. They stared at the new arrivals, then scuttled out of sight as soon as the truck pulled up.

Hurley climbed out and looked around him. The guard and his medical assistant got out too and stood nervously behind him. There was an uneasy feel to the place, as if they were being watched. The sign on the fence announcing *École de Médecin Tropicale*, was hardly legible, the letters bleached by a relentless sun. Leaving his two colleagues where they were, Hurley left the truck and went and knocked on a door marked

'Reception'. It gave against his fist. He pushed on inside and walked through an abandoned office until he reached a small lecture theatre where he found, slumped in a broken wicker-work armchair, a European man of about fifty. Dressed in a dirty white coat, he was staring through the bars of a cage at a pair of mating monkeys and barely moved even when Hurley came up behind him.

'With you in a minute,' the man said in French. He did not look round, but waited until the marmosets had finished with their play, and then and only then, half turned in his chair and looked up at the visitor. His face brightened perceptibly. 'Oh, hello,' he said. 'Sorry. Thought it was one of my students.' He pushed himself to his feet and put out a reluctant hand. 'Sorry,' he repeated. 'Wasn't expecting visitors. Were you meant to be coming here today?' he asked.

Hurley stood back a pace, noting the stains on the man's once-white medical coat. At a guess he had neither shaved nor washed for days. 'I'm looking for Dr Banquier,' Hurley said in English.

'You just found him,' the man replied, also in English. ''Fraid this place is a bit, how you say, run down. Since rebels came through. They loot everything worth taking. And I been sick,' added Banquier, apologetically.

Hurley could sympathize. He was feeling far from steady himself, but Banquier's bloodshot eyes, deepset and sallow, were framed in a gaunt face that had been baked by the constant heat to an unhealthy yellow. Christ, he thought to himself, if I stay here too long I'll end up looking like that.

'You British?' asked Banquier.

'American,' replied Hurley. 'From Chicago,' he added unnecessarily.

'My English not so good,' said the doctor. 'It better when my Englishman friend here. We talk a lot. And drank . . .' he laughed.

'English? Here?'

'Yes. Doctor too. Army. Had field hospital, Western charity,

81

deal with victims of the war. 'Oasis of sanity in mad world, he say,' the Belgian was vague. 'He gone now. Nice have someone to talk to,' he added wistfully. Again Hurley knew how he felt.

Hurley then explained that he was from the WHO office in town. 'We spoke last week,' he added, 'on the telephone.'

Banquier looked startled, then worried. ''Course. I remember: surge fever. So, what I can do for you?'

'About that virus,' said Hurley. 'Headquarters urgently want more information about the outbreak. Did you keep any samples, any body tissue?'

Banquier laughed. 'Samples, here? *Merde*, but you are joking. I had the body burnt as soon I knew what it was. Samples, body tissue . . . *mon Dieu*. Who would have taken them?' He laughed again, and Hurley shuddered despite himself.

'I'm not a doctor,' said Hurley. 'I don't know much about the technicalities.' He looked down at the printout of the e-mail he had received from Dr Boekamper which had arrived that very morning. 'I gather someone's identified a case with similar symptoms somewhere in Britain,' he explained. 'A man has died of it. The WHO have given the virus, your surge fever, an index number: ZD198. They're concerned; worried in case it breaks out, escalates, somewhere else.'

'Breaks out? If is really surge fever no can break out,' said Banquier firmly. 'Unless mutated, or . . .'

'Or what?' asked Hurley, puzzled.

'Don't know,' said Banquier slowly.

Despite his imperfect English, Banquier explained the background logically and clearly, and Hurley had no difficulty in carefully noting down everything he was told. The doctor began by describing the few isolated cases he'd come across some years earlier. They'd all been one-off victims, in remote tribal villages. The symptoms, as far as he could recall, were always the same: memory blanks, fits which then corrected themselves, with the victims not realizing that anything was wrong with them. Then came the rashes, the gradual rotting of the skin and body tissue, the smell, and the strange grey pallor, like a veil, which spread over the eyes. The last stage which gave surge fever its local name, came with the near-epileptic seizures, the spasms of extreme pain that, in one case, Banquier explained without a flicker of emotion, had led a passing soldier to shoot the male victim to put him out of his misery. Hurley shuddered and asked how long ago the other cases had been.

'Four, five years ago. Can't remember. Until woman last month.'

'A long gap,' said Hurley.

'Like I say,' Banquier responded, 'virus needs help to travel.'

'Like what?' asked Hurley.

'Broken skin. Must come through broken skin. A wound, something like that.'

'The woman?'

'Had big cut in forehead. I think she unbalanced, mad, *folle*. I seen it before.'

'What have you seen?'

'Round incision in forehead. Primitive trepanation, I guess, but sure I am right. Witch doctor; traditional healer. Hole drilled into her skull, to let demon out.' Banquier paused. 'But it let demon in instead. You like a drink?' he asked, without pausing. Banquier laughed again and suddenly Clegg Hurley felt very sick indeed.

Central London, Thursday 9th June

It was becoming a habit when he first woke up in the morning. Lyle Thane lay still, collecting his thoughts for the day ahead, the reassuringly naked body of Sarah St Just sleeping easily by his side. He hoped she hadn't been too disappointed with his performance last night: he hadn't felt up to it; he was tired; he shouldn't have drunk so much. For a moment he was worried. Was something going wrong with his potency, his libido? Was it Sarah? What more was he looking for from her? From elsewhere? He sat up and pushed away these brief doubts. Today it was a new day. He was in charge: the mover, the shaker, the manipulator, the hidden hand, the man the Prime Minister was coming to trust more than anyone else. He looked upwards at the mirror suspended from the ceiling above the bed. Even with the curtains closed, he could see himself quite clearly.

'You're consumed more by your image than your performance,' Sarah had actually laughed at him only last night. He hadn't liked that, but had forced a smile.

'I'm not.'

'You are. I'm always catching you looking at your reflection in shop windows, or stopping to comb your hair at the entrance to a restaurant, or wherever we are.'

'I don't.'

'You do. Look how many mirrors you have here in your flat. Then there's that dreadful one. That's real kinky.' She had pointed up at the huge one he was looking at now, which reflected all the actions of the naked bodies on the double bed below.

'You like that too,' he responded. They had both turned to look upwards and watch their reflected passions. It was indeed exciting.

'You're right,' she had breathed contentedly at last. As for him: well, no matter. Maybe it was just a brief aberration.

The first thing Thane did on arriving at his Downing Street office each morning was to check the diary printout. He carefully monitored every moment of the Prime Minister's day. Information was power. His career progress depended on his knowledge of each detail. The PM was having an easy ride at the moment; the official Opposition were nowhere to be seen, and his enemies in his own party had been knocked into a corner to lick their wounds. Even Winston Rogerson was staying in line. The PM was riding high in the public opinion polls as well. Not even the Whips could come up with any seedy personal secrets about wayward ministers which the tabloid press might hit on and kick around. Right now, even the spindoctors could relax. The image of a highly successful Prime Minister leading a disciplined Government against a background of a country and an economy that was on a boom, was unshakable. Peter Morgan had, just the other day, deliberately echoed a phrase from another age that 'you've never had it so good'. It was a daring thing to say, but the broadsheets picked it up and ran with it and even the sharpest media critics could find little evidence to gainsay it. But Thane knew: when everything is riding so high, from then on, the only direction in politics is down. No one expected the slide to start for a while yet, nor quickly. His closest staffers could hardly be blamed for not foreseeing the unexpected.

It happened again when Thane was alone with the Prime Minister and Daniel Evans, his Press Secretary. They were polishing up the line he was to take in the forthcoming interview with Joe Tinker of ITV: a long, in-depth piece, about current national and international affairs, a detailed review of the Prime Minister's strategic thinking. How did Peter Morgan see Britain in the first decade of this new millennium? The whole spin was to build up the great international statesman image. Morgan was no mere Party political leader. He was way above such things these days. As a world leader, few could rival him, with the flawed idiots currently in the seats of power in both Washington and the Kremlin. It was upwards and onwards time. Then it happened once more. Evans and Thane were concentrating intently on how the PM said he saw the interview developing on Europe, when the man dried up, just like the first time. He froze for fifteen, twenty, thirty seconds. His shocked assistants both stood and moved quickly towards him. Daniel reached forward to touch his shoulder. 'You OK, Prime Minister?' His voice revealed how horrified he was. The PM, who had been sitting at his desk facing them, stayed rock still, eyes open, staring ahead, hand outstretched towards the desk as if in rictus.

'What the hell . . . ?' Daniel stuttered.

Thane went up behind him and stared closely at the PM. 'No idea. Some sort of . . .' He hesitated to say anything dramatic, like using the word *stroke*, because – since otherwise he looked so perfectly normal – the Prime Minister might hear him. 'You all right, sir?' he echoed Daniel's words.

Still there was no answer. The PM was locked rigid, like a statue. 'I'll go call Dr Taylor,' said Daniel, moving towards the door.

'No, wait. Think first. We've got to keep the lid tight on this. Give him a moment or two,' Thane insisted, with more confidence than he felt.

'Look at his eyes! What's the matter with his eyes?' Daniel started to say, but then it was all over, just as it had begun. The Prime Minister let his hand sink slowly to the desktop, blinked once or twice as if unsure of where he was, then turned to stare at them. It was as if nothing whatsoever had happened.

'You all right, Prime Minister?' asked Daniel. He should have said nothing.

'All right? What do you mean, all right?' the Prime Minister responded crossly. 'Come on. How d'you see the Europe slant, Daniel? Will Tinker be fair? Get a grip. Something the matter with you, is there?'

Daniel looked away, embarrassed. 'No, sir,' he stumbled. 'We're talking through the Europe line on the Tinker interview.'

'I know that's what we're doing, for Chrissake! Why the hell d'you think we're all sitting here? Are you cracking up, Daniel? Want time off, or something?' The PM was being unusually irritable and aggressive.

Thane sat back, listened, thought hard and said nothing. Shortly after that, the meeting ended uneasily. The PM said he had some urgent private calls to make. The two staffers could go. They felt him staring hostilely after them as they left the room.

Once outside the Prime Minister's study, the two men slipped into a corner of the press office briefing room. 'Jeez, what the effing hell was that?' Daniel asked. 'Scary, or what?' He was shaking, more as a result of the PM's anger than anything else.

'Real issue's what do we do about it?' said Thane, coolly.

'Ask Mrs Morgan. Or his doctor?' Daniel suggested.

'Think it through slowly. No point in confronting the PM himself. He didn't realize anything went wrong. Real spooky,' agreed Thane.

'So? Cabinet Secretary?' Daniel suggested.

'No, not yet. Say nothing to no one.'

'His doctor, Taylor, has to know.'

Thane almost shouted. 'No, Daniel! In any case, Taylor's a buffoon. It was probably a momentary glitch. It'll sort itself.'

'That's the second time . . . What if he's suffering from some brain–' Daniel broke off and looked nervously at his watch. 'He's got a bunch of major public engagements coming up.'

'A few hours more isn't going to make much difference. If it happens again, of course . . . we'll, er . . .' Thane spoke with a degree of resolution which he did not feel. 'I promise you, Daniel, then we'll tell people. 'Till then, musn't let a whisper out that there's anything wrong. Rogerson would leap into his chair at the slightest sign we'd got a problem. Then we'd all be out like a shot.'

'Some things are more important,' began Daniel, looking hard at the younger man.

Thane put on his steely look. 'Like what?' he said aggressively.

'Like the PM's health.'

'What's more important, Daniel, for God's sake: him, or the health of the nation?'

The Harman Institute, East London, Thursday 9th June

He made a half-hearted effort to see Professor MacArthur, but was curtly told that he was busy, so a relieved but nervous Dr Guthrie caught the four o'clock GNER train from Edinburgh to King's Cross. Much to his delight, since he never expected his travel arrangements to work smoothly, an official car was waiting at the station to take him direct to the Harman Institute. From what Dr Stevenson had already told him, he knew in general terms what they expected of him, and was beginning to realize how critical it was all becoming. He was accomplished at tracking the effects of highly toxic infections and virulent bugs of one sort or another, but his was mainly a theoretical approach; he created laboratory models showing how they travelled between hosts, between individuals, on the screen of his high-powered computer. Guthrie liked computers. They were safe, compelling, hygienic, didn't answer back, and when they were in a good mood, usually came up with the answers he was looking for. They were so much more intriguing and less demanding than real people. People and their illnesses had a tendency to get in the way of the theory; he had found that time and time again.

He'd also heard a certain amount about Professor Grant, had read most of his scientific papers, and had, generally speaking, been impressed by them. Grant had written some compelling stuff on deliberate biological infection which he had found particularly interesting since the time, years ago, when he had been drafted in to help the forensic unit of the New York Health Department. A number of local Bronx residents had been taken seriously ill. He'd come up with the most obvious solution: from his research he quickly proved that it had to have been deliberately spread by a local retailer who had a grudge against some of his customers. The health department officials, blinded by the constraints of their own research, had been looking everywhere else for clues: clues in the drains, the water, in nature. They had never once looked for a malicious reason for one of the biggest incidents of mass poisoning to hit that great city in decades.

Guthrie had also learnt that Grant, while neither pedestrian nor obscure, tended to be over-cautious in coming to rapid conclusions. Once, several years ago, the professor had stuck his neck out and expressed doubts, given the current flimsy evidence, about there being any likely link between CJD and its relationship with BSE. He had soon been proven very wrong indeed. Grant's opinion had been printed in the *Lancet* and it stood there to haunt him for the rest of time. The professor had learnt one lesson from that: he was not going to be proven mistaken again as the result of coming to a conclusion too quickly. Nothing he now said or wrote about was so definitive, so dogmatic, that people could, at some future point, say, 'There: Grant's got it wrong again.' The professor was caution personified, which was why, despite that one past slip-up, he was widely consulted and used by the Department of Health. When Government ministers or civil servants were looking for someone to stand up and say 'More research is needed,' or, 'We need more time to pursue,' or, 'It is too early for a definitive view,' on some new food, drug, or epidemic scare, they turned to Professor Grant. For that reason alone, Guthrie was worried about how well they would work together.

Dr Stevenson, Grant's efficiently incisive assistant, already shared that concern. She in turn knew a surprising amount about Guthrie and his reputation for walking into problems. That initial judgment was reinforced as, restraining a smile, she watched him struggle clumsily through the revolving glass tube which was the high security, sterile admission door, into the research lab itself. As she went forward to greet him, she noted the crushed shirt, the clumsy walk, the huge hands. When she took him through to meet Professor Grant, the latter immaculate as always in his well-laundered lab coat, she sensed the unspoken disapproval. Guthrie was not his type and Rebecca knew that if the meeting didn't work out in scientific terms, then she could be criticized for having gone ahead and invited him down to the Institute in the first place. That was Grant's way: she knew how meticulous he was in everything he did. By contrast, Guthrie was a desperately chaotic-looking figure to find operating in such a precise field, though his published work on vectors was unquestionably brilliant.

Minor irritations followed. The professor offered Guthrie a cup of tea but the latter asked for coffee. That was always an inconvenience in a laboratory where coffee had been banned ever since Grant had publicly taken on the instant coffee industry over some of its genetically engineered content. A flicker of disapproval crossed Grant's features as he characteristically despatched his assistant, high-grade scientist that she was, to prepare the unpopular brew in the little kitchenette to the rear of the laboratory.

By the time Dr Stevenson returned, things were a little more relaxed. Guthrie and Grant were seated opposite each other at a laboratory bench and had turned to the business in hand. The professor was summarizing his reasons for believing that the cause of the general's death was almost certainly Virus ZD198. The mystery was how and where he could have caught it. All other known cases of the disease were now several years old; each one, as far as British and WHO records showed, had had some direct link with central Africa. But the general hadn't been to Africa in nearly ten years, and hadn't even left Britain in the previous six months, and that was far too long an incubation period. He had to have picked it up live in Britain. Guthrie responded by reviewing for them the details of all the back-case studies he knew about, describing how he had plotted the circumstances of each one against a model he had built on his database. The vector, the transmission agent, maybe another person, would not, Guthrie believed, have necessarily been affected themselves. The two men agreed that there could of course have been other cases of Virus ZD198 which had gone unreported, because of wrong diagnoses by doctors, by regional medical authorities, or by hospitals with no previous experience of the disease. Apart from Dr Guthrie confirming beyond all doubt that it was ZD198, it was difficult to see what more could be done. Despite Guthrie's quiet suspicions, 'Some freak of nature: a one-off accident,' was their initial, joint conclusion.

As Dr Stevenson listened to Guthrie talking, she understood why he might sometimes prove to be his own worst enemy. He tended to stray off course by explaining things that both she and the professor were all too familiar with. As if he was lecturing to first-year medical students, he briefly digressed with a history of the research into the transmission of malaria. They all knew about the long-held historical belief that it was caught from bad air, or from infected water. Guthrie then turned to talk at length about how he had built a dynamic model to explain the spread of bubonic plague, a disease largely carried by rats or mice. Just as the professor started throwing barely concealed looks of frustration at his assistant as if to ask why they were wasting their time on him, the American hit them with a crucial insight.

'I can't prove it yet, professor,' said Guthrie almost casually, 'but my guess is that we'll find your patient died because two different factors came in close conjunction. One bug destroyed the body's immune system, the other, Virus ZD198, was lying dormant in him or somehow came in for the kill.' He paused reflectively. 'Put it this way: remember those weirdo cult followers in Japan who went around poisoning everyone? Of itself, the venom they used was pretty harmless, but the deranged scientist behind it first of all destroyed his victims' immune system, then, when the chosen individuals drank the poison in their tea, only they died, while the rest were hardly affected. As I remember, it took the police and medics ages to find out how what had happened had happened.' He looked up at them both and smiled unexpectedly.

'What you're saying, Dr Guthrie, is that you believe the virus could be out there, carried by a lot of people, just waiting until . . .' Rebecca Stevenson conjectured.

'Possibly,' Guthrie responded. 'I know you at the Harman Institute have been working for a long time on the range of viruses which most of us carry in our systems. You know the majority stay sleeping unless the body's immune system takes a nosedive.'

There was a long pause. Grant nodded approvingly, waiting for Guthrie to continue. Nothing came. Guthrie was staring at his hands, then he began examining his fingernails. Dr Stevenson started to say something, then checked herself.

Eventually, Grant filled the silence. 'On that basis,' he began, 'we should check all the general's contacts for traces of the virus, then see if there could have been outbreaks of less deadly variants of it, without anyone realizing it. The Institute has collated evidence of several non-fatal bugs going around recently, where a local GP or hospital has thought that they were dealing first with a severe case of flu, then some new strain of viral meningitis. We perhaps need to look back at each of these outbreaks to search for any common connection.'

'A question,' said Guthrie, nodding.

'Yes, what?' The professor looked mildly irritated.

'The gestation period?'

'We've so little to go on. We know of only a handful of these cases. You must have identified more . . .' said the professor slowly. He had gone into defensive mode.

Guthrie took over again. This time he had their full attention. 'In the States I've recently identified a new hybrid virus, not unlike ZD198, where people die within twenty-four hours of anyone noticing they're ill. We traced others who were carriers, like HIV-positive individuals who never contract full-blown AIDS, who were harbouring the virus without contracting the disease. What's always scared me stiff is the possibility of other latent strains, much more devastating, which sit there for months if not years, until one day they hit their full potential. I uncovered another type recently: symptoms like amnesia, short-term memory loss, then collapse of all the brain's functions. We found that the bug had been sitting there dormant, waiting to do its worst. The good news is that it, like a lot of them, is difficult to transmit. You can't just pick the virus up. Yet, that is. But you've both seen how cleverly they mutate to survive. My guess: one day an epidemic of truly global proportions will hit us.'

'We're not quite there yet,' replied Professor Grant, a thin smile playing round his lips. The American was letting his imagination run away with him. 'Back to the vector for this one, Dr Guthrie. What's your guess?'

'Not sure yet,' responded Guthrie vaguely. 'Working on a few possibilities.' He reached into an inside pocket of his jacket, produced a folded sheet of A4 paper, unfolded it and looked at what he had written. 'Yup, some things puzzle,' he said. 'Puzzle me a great deal. I don't see . . .' Guthrie paused and looked up at his two colleagues. 'I just don't see how,' he repeated, 'it hit the general in the way it did.'

Professor Grant was phased for a moment. 'Have you ever examined any patients with –'

'Hell, no,' said Guthrie, interrupting. 'Me, I'm a backroom boy. Do all my work on skin tissue, X-rays, blood samples, via my computer database. I leave the personal pathology to people like you.' He smiled. 'I don't think I have much of a bedside manner. Wouldn't you agree?' he asked. They had no reply to that.

Millbank, Central London, Friday 10th June

In the world of hi-tech eavesdropping, it is seldom totally clear who is listening in to whom. Government Communications Headquarters, known as GCHQ in the UK, along with the NSA in the States, and similar secret monitoring stations in nearly every country in the world, routinely listen in to diplomatic and to foreign telephonic and business communications. It is spying without the spies. Even the most sophisticated encrypted and coded messages and faxes can be unscrambled. Talk almost anywhere and you can be overheard. Nowhere is totally safe from official and unofficial ears.

MI5's Technical Department was responsible for security at all the top secret research establishments in the United Kingdom. The Harman Institute was one of these: indeed it was a top priority target. In conjunction with technicians from GCHQ, they sent in a team every few months to sweep the establishment, looking for listening devices or other electronic eavesdropping equipment. That day they got very excited when they found an extra microchip – it was more complex than that, but that's what they called it – which had been clandestinely inserted into one of the central, high-grade computers. It shouldn't have been there. Without touching it, they worked out what its functions were and who might be accessing the information it was sucking from the supposedly highly secure system. The Americans had been careless: the Technical Department were pretty confident from the outset that only they had had the access or capability to have inserted that extra chip. So what was going on at the Harman that the US desperately wanted to know? If they were so keen, should not the appropriate British agencies keep a close watch on what was going on as well?

The so-called Intelligence Community is a complex and highly confidential web of organizations and relationships. Without question, one of its other most important and secretive parts is the Special Scientific Unit, or SSU. Set up in the latter stages of the Cold War, in an age of nuclear stand-off, it existed to assess the threat from chemical, biological and germ weapons, including the possible use of nerve gases. In the fullest collaboration with the Ministry of Defence's secret establishment at Porton Down, and with the backing of all other parts of the Intelligence Community, it soon began to play a key co-ordinating role in Britain's scientific response strategy. In the war with Hitler's Germany and during the subsequent Cold War with the Soviet Union, both sides had steered clear of using anything so deadly, so uncontrolled, against the other. But having won the Cold War, the West rapidly became fearful of the consequences of the peace. Such devastating, yet relatively inexpensive weapons, falling into the hands of terrorists and those countries which backed them, conjured up a hideous Apocalypse scenario. There were too many régimes which would not care about the world-wide consequences of unleashing germ and bacteriological weapons. Saddam Hussein's nerve gas attacks on the Kurds in northern Iraq might well be seen by history as a tea party in comparison with what could happen.

MI5's Technical Department sent the intelligence about the rogue, probably American, bug at the Harman Institute direct to the SSU. It caused a huge stir. If MI5 were correct, it was a hostile act by the Americans to bug a British scientific establishment. Some people in Government would have been very angry if they had found out, but to take the Americans to task, or reveal to them that the British had uncovered what they were doing, would give away Britain's high-grade expertise in bugging buggers, as the jargon had it. Thus it was that both countries' systems began, automatically, to record what was going on at the Harman Institute. What they were looking for was not even known to these technicians who had placed the listening devices in the first place, since everything operated on a strictly need-to-know basis.

In science as in life, few things happen in isolation. Enquiring minds think alike or move along similar paths. History is littered with controversies over who invented or discovered what first. But Lister and Pasteur, like Baird and Marconi, could, by and large, keep their work under wraps until they were ready to reveal their findings to a wider world. With modern technology such secrecy becomes almost impossible. This monitored investigation was obviously in its early stages. It was an ongoing discussion between a man and a woman who did not know that their every word was being listened in to by those whom they did not even know existed. The female voice came first:

I'm not getting anywhere with David.

You're doing fine. You've identified the gene family member controlling his immune system. Isn't that exciting?

Depends what turns you on.

David should matter to you.

There are other things in life.

Not now there aren't.

So tell me: what am I looking for next?

Any signs of that immune system weakening.
OK. What's the next stage?
As I said, implanting the virus in David.
How long will it take? Will he be in danger?
He's in perpetual danger. You know that.

Less than two hours later, a second conversation was intercepted. This time both voices were male, the first one distinctly American.

How's David shaping up?
There's been a real turnaround. He's keeping ahead fine.
What happened?
You came up trumps as usual, Harper.
Did I?
You suggested this new viral agent. The cell seems to destroy some of the virus, but there's another part of it I can't quite fathom, that keeps pulling away.
Pulling away?
A spinoff. It's keeping ahead of me. Nature testing science all the way through. Like a game. Every time we feel we're getting somewhere, the virus disappears. It finds an escape route. Look! See there on the bottom-left quadrant of the screen. It's like chess. It's gone into spinoff.
I see. D'you play chess?
I did.
We should try some evening. I'll take you on.
OK.
You're more optimistic about David, then?
Optimistic? I suppose so. David's keeping ahead just fine.

The case officer in MI5's Technical Department was not best pleased when the two monitored conversations reached him late that Friday night without any accompanying commentary, particularly when he saw that a copy had also been sent direct to the desk of his head of department, who was notorious for wanting to know everything that was going on in his domain.

The case officer's consequent reaction was a terse message to the SSU duty officer:

URGENT: TOP SECRET

Your message R920/00 to Section H4. Please explain: Who is Harper? Who is David? What is wrong with him? What virus is being discussed? Have there been any recent cases? Are there any defence or security implications? Respond by return.

Message ends.

The SSU duty officer did not bother to look for any more intercepts. The unit had a wide network of trusted agents in every major scientific establishment up and down the country. It should not prove difficult to find the person who knew where to find the answers to MI5's questions. He rang an Edinburgh number and asked for a Dr Euan Davidson.

7

Dr Boekamper made it abundantly clear to Hurley that he was disappointed; he did not consider the first trip to Dr Banquier a success. In retrospect, Hurley agreed. He admitted to himself that it was all because, at that first meeting, he had disliked the Belgian so intensely; he should have extracted more information from him, but could not wait to get away from the school. It was pure gut instinct: never before had he reacted so aversely to anyone quite like that. He saw the Belgian, with his cages of wild animals and run-down wards full of the sick and destitute, as the personification of some hidden evil, so much so that, before he got Boekamper's next message ordering him to see him again, he had already asked WHO Records to make enquiries about the doctor through their Brussels office. Within the day, the information he was looking for came back: Banquier was fully qualified, indeed had a first-class biotechnology degree on top of a range of good Belgian medical qualifications. All that was in perfect order, but the subsequent paragraph suggested that the man had suddenly disappeared from his research institute in Brussels a decade previously, at the height of some unspecified police investigations into unethical medical practices. The report said little more than that, but it made Hurley doubly wary. When he tried to analyse his negative reactions later, Hurley found it difficult to define them. Was it something about the man's hands – they had been too white, too soft for the work he was meant to be doing? In contrast to the lack of attention he gave to his clothes and general cleanliness, his nails had been beautifully manicured.

This time Hurley sent an advance message to say that he was coming. This time the doctor was neatly dressed in a newly laundered medical coat, he had a stethoscope hanging around his neck, and the whole reception area had been cleaned up beyond recognition. When Hurley arrived in his Land Rover, he was saluted at the gates by an African security guard in a smart khaki drill outfit. Even the lecture hall had been spruced up and was now manned by a young black woman in a crisp new nurse's uniform. She actually smiled and offered him a coffee before ushering him into Banquier's presence. The latter stood to greet him, all warmth and handshakes, before leading Hurley through to his private accommodation to the rear. The rooms there were tastefully furnished; in the background, classical music emerged from an impressive array of CD equipment. Recalling the doctor's remarks about having had most of his possessions looted by the rebel army, Hurley wondered what to believe.

Banquier offered him a drink, and when Hurley asked for a beer the doctor personally poured him a glass and one for himself.

'You still interested in my surge fever case, I think? What you call it: ZD198?' asked Dr Banquier in his precise but faulty English.

'Correct. More questions from Headquarters. They want to know what happened to your reports on the earlier cases you mentioned,' Hurley said, watching the other man. Despite the improved environment, there was still something about Banquier's behaviour that continued to unsettle him, particularly the way he kept nervously flicking his tongue over his heavy lips. It was absurd, thought Hurley; no one can be quite so unnerving. The climate was getting to him.

'Records burnt by rebels, long ago,' said the doctor, sipping slowly at his glass.

'D'you remember any more detail? They're keen for anything

at all. Particularly the vector, how ZD198 gets passed on? There's a definite case in the UK. Confirmed. Out of the blue. No one can understand how it happened. The victim had no connection with Africa.'

'No? Odd, I guess. I tell you before: no can break out,' said Dr Banquier, staring hard at his visitor. 'Needs help.'

Hurley watched fascinated as Banquier again licked his lower lip. What was so unnerving about that tiny gesture? 'How d'you know? How are you so sure?' he asked, pulling himself together.

'I know . . . I know, because I tried,' came the chilling reply.

10 Downing Street, London, Wednesday 15th June

Shortly after seven o'clock on the Wednesday morning, the duty policeman who opened the door of Number Ten to Lyle Thane stopped him and whispered urgently in his ear. Thane nodded briskly, thanked the officer, and moved rapidly through towards his office. As he did so, Janet Morgan, the Prime Minister's wife, came rushing down the main staircase two steps at a time. She was still in her dressing gown and had obviously been crying. 'Lyle,' she said, 'thank God you've come. I don't know what . . . I need to talk to somebody.'

'What is it, Mrs Morgan . . . Janet?' He hesitated. He'd never known quite how to address her. She'd always insisted on him using her first name, but he'd felt diffident doing so until now. Mrs Morgan had never been much to look at until the spindoctors and the colour-me-beautiful experts had had their way. Before her triumphal entry into Downing Street, hand in hand with her husband, she'd looked mousey, always seeming to be having a bad hair day. Then the image experts got at her, dressed her, chose her cosmetics, found a new haircut that fitted the odd shape of her head. It wasn't that Janet Morgan was a dunce; no way. Many believed she was far brighter than her husband; she certainly had a mind of her own. Any new-found glitz was abandoned that morning. Newly awakened from her bed, she'd obviously done nothing more than pull the dressing gown round her and thrust her feet into a pair of rather naff slippers. She was at her mousey worst.

'It's Peter. Something's wrong with him,' she blurted out.

Thane at once sensed what could have happened. 'What is it? Flu or something?' he asked, guessing what her response would be.

'Nothing like that. He's had some sort of . . . of fit. Went rigid for a few minutes. I've noticed it once before. I don't know what to do. He doesn't seem to realize, recognize, anything's wrong, so when he comes to and I start talking about him seeing a doctor, he laughs. Or gets angry.'

'I know exactly what you're talking about, Janet,' said Thane, dropping his voice to a whisper. 'I've seen it. Twice. Lasted only a few seconds.'

'You have? God! Why didn't you say?' Janet Morgan stared at him in horror.

'We mustn't let this get out. Who else knows?'

'Only Daniel, though the policeman at the front door seems to realize something's up. That's because I started getting security to call a doctor. Peter stopped me. He went wild.' She stared hard at Thane. 'Why didn't you tell me?' she asked.

'For the same reason you didn't call a doctor. How could we when he doesn't . . .'

'You don't think anybody else knows?' she repeated.

'Never sure of anything in this place. Leaks like a sieve,' Thane replied. 'Where's the PM now?'

'Upstairs. Having his breakfast. Cool as anything.'

'He knows you're down here?'

'Suspect so. He knows something's upset me, but thinks it's my time of life, or tension over the Party rally.'

They stood whispering in the well of the staircase. A cleaning woman, bucket and brush in her hand, looked curiously at them as she passed.

'So? What to do?' Janet Morgan looked at him pleadingly.

'Leave it to me,' said Thane bravely, 'I'll hint to the policeman that it was a small domestic problem, if you don't mind. I'll have to talk to Daniel. Maybe . . . yes, I must tell Eric, too.' Eric Caldwell was the Principal Private Secretary. 'We'll work out a strategy.'

'I don't want it to get out, whatever "it" is,' repeated Janet Morgan forcefully.

'No way,' Thane responded. 'Leave it to me.' He put out his hand and touched her shoulder to reassure her. He wouldn't normally have been so familiar, but she nodded, thanked him, then, drying her eyes with the sleeve of her dressing gown, she walked slowly back upstairs.

An hour later Thane, Daniel Evans and Eric Caldwell closeted themselves in Eric's office. The Press Secretary was more subdued than usual. Gone was his customary banter and bounce. He looked white-faced and tense, though maybe that could also be to do with the after-effects of dining with the Newspaper Society the previous evening, since he was reputed to like a drink or two. Eric Caldwell could not have been more different. One of the brightest men in the civil service, he was the silent, speak when there's something to say, type, and no great looker. He had a huge domed forehead over which the few remaining hairs on his forty-year-old head were carefully combed out in a vain attempt to camouflage the fact that he was almost bald. This somewhat bookish impression was further heightened by the round, schoolboyish glasses he wore perched halfway down a thin, beak-like nose. His lips were thin, his teeth were small, but he had a razor-sharp mind. At that moment, he was swaying backwards and forwards on his long spindly legs, his face expressionless, but Thane could see that even his normally unflappable exterior was beginning to crack.

'You're the pressman. You tell us how you'd spin it if it did break,' Caldwell began quietly.

'Working too hard and late. Interests of the nation. Needs a holiday. Quality time. Everyone does.' Even Evans didn't look impressed by his own suggestion.

'Key thing,' said Thane, 'is not to let it out. I've told fairy stories to the policeman on the door, but –'

'For God's sake, surely we can come up with some better line than that?' Caldwell snapped. 'Minor ailment on the health front, which people can start sympathizing with him over. Use a small story to hide a big one. Didn't John Major have a dental abscess, and the blessed Margaret suffer from carpal tunnel syndrome in her hand?'

The three men looked at each other, sharing their unusual feelings of indecision. It was crisis-management, jobs-on-the-line, time.

'I see one hell of a lot of snags in that,' said Evans. 'For starters, the Prime Minister himself. Fact is, he doesn't recognize he has a problem. By the way,' he added, 'did you notice that nasty rash he's developed on his cheek and neck? Supposing something happens, or someone spots something when he is on a public stage or giving an interview? There's one lined up with Joe Tinker in a couple of days' time. Supposing he freezes on one of them? The story'll be out.'

'Rash? What story, for Christ's sake? Don't start inventing problems, Daniel. Let's think what . . . I have it,' said Caldwell, turning and facing his two colleagues. 'Remember the Double B Plan? The Big Brush Strategy he's always going on about? We pull together a programme around that. The PM going to take time off, to think, to study, to formulate longterm strategic decisions without having to make any public appearances and so on. Thank God Parliament's still in recess.'

'Can you swing that on him?' asked Evans.

'We all put it to him that the time is ripe; we can dream up any number of reasons. Shove that long-draft strategy paper in front of him. Sweep him off to Chequers.' Cardwell paused.

'Think he'll go?' asked Thane.

'If we all push at once. Diary's pretty clear. God, I can't believe we're talking like this. If we were in the White House all this would be being taped,' said Caldwell grimly, skimming through a leatherbound book on his desk. 'Let's see: mainly in-house stuff. Party activists, et cetera. I'll brief Winston Rogerson to take them on.'

'Rogerson, for Christ's sake?' said Thane. 'Keep that bugger right clear.'

'His job, isn't it?'

'He'll smell a rat.'

'Not if we dress it up nicely. Flatter him. Suggest he's being groomed for the succession.'

Thane almost choked at the thought. 'Stuff that for a lark!' he responded.

'Can't cancel Joe Tinker. No way,' said the Press Secretary.

'We'll have to live through that. But kill the rest.' Caldwell was suddenly decisive and firm. 'OK, we're all clear? Message is: the PM wants to give ministers, particularly Rogerson, their heads for a while. He's going off to think big. Capital Think: capital Big.'

The three men stopped talking and turned nervously to face the door as the handle slowly turned. It was the PM's wife. Janet Morgan looked more in control now. She closed the door carefully behind her.

'You've told them?' she asked Thane. He nodded. 'Had to. Upstairs?' he gestured.

'As right as rain. Peter's working on some speech at his desk in the sitting room. Brighter, more sparky than ever.'

'What've you said?'

'Nothing. How can I? How can I persuade someone who doesn't know he's sick, to see a doctor?'

'His next check up?' asked Caldwell.

'He remembers all that stuff himself.' Mrs Morgan gave a worried shrug.

'We've got to get Dr Taylor in to see the PM without him realizing he's being examined. Find some excuse to invite him up for a drink or something.' Thane hesitated. 'What do you think?'

'Good idea,' Mrs Morgan responded, 'but can't one of you talk to Peter direct? Please! I'm worried sick. It's fortunate he doesn't have anything major in the diary today.'

Caldwell again consulted the desk diary. 'Been through that, Mrs Morgan. Minor things. One or two people booked to see him, but we can play around with them.'

'How about building up attention elsewhere to take attention off him? Start a small Balkans War,' Daniel Evans started to joke, then backed off. 'Sorry,' he said.

'Ministers will suspect any diversionary tactic straightaway,' said Thane. 'They hate surprises.'

'Won't it be a surprise if they hear he's taking time off at Chequers?' Mrs Morgan asked.

'We'd have to bring some of them in on it,' Evans hesitated.

'In on what, for Christ's sake?' It was her turn to react angrily. 'You're speaking as if he's bonkers, going senile like Churchill did, or Reagan. This isn't that. Maybe it's some little brain clot which can be sorted out quickly. One of you's got to help me confront Peter. Argue that he should make a clean breast of it. Nothing to be ashamed of or alarmed by. Go public.'

'No way, Janet,' said Caldwell. 'It'd be suicide right now. Think of Rogerson's reaction. Let's talk this through slowly, before we say anything to anyone. Look,' he said, glancing at his watch. 'Sorry, I've got to call the Foreign Secretary urgently about China, on the PM's behalf. Like right now. Have to leave you. Say we meet again in half an hour?'

A few minutes later, Thane was sitting at his desk, a pile of mail in front of him. He'd already glanced half-heartedly at it and through the day's press cuttings, but his mind was racing elsewhere. How could they get some specialist to give the old man the once over? How could they make damned sure no one else found out? If he'd had some sort of a blip, a minor stroke perhaps, it could surely be quietly sorted if they played it cool. Medical ethics; the Hippocratic oath and all that. A specialist would keep the lid on the truth. Things took on a momentum of their own. He was looking at his watch and thinking of getting back together with Evans and Caldwell, when Janet Morgan came rushing downstairs at a gallop and into his room. A Garden Room secretary who'd just arrived for work stared at her in surprise. Then the other two, hearing the noise, rushed in as well and slammed the door behind them.

'Out again. Totally. Eyes open, staring. Gone a funny, faded colour. The doctor, quick!' she shouted at them. Evans had already dialled a number and was talking to someone on the other end of the line.

'For God's sake let's stay cool,' Thane ordered, standing up behind his desk. 'It's no good for the PM, nor for anyone, if we let things leak, . . . until we know what is wrong. Maybe some minor . . .' His voice tailed away as, for once, he ran out of words.

'Right,' said Caldwell. He was trying to regain control. 'We're going to walk quietly into the hall together. Let the staff see us. Chatter, even smile if someone comes past, then upstairs, OK?'

The three men followed quietly behind Janet Morgan, then moved after her into the private flat. The Prime Minister was stretched out on a couch, almost naked, a towel wrapped round his middle, staring at the ceiling.

'He was taking a shower. Stumbled into the room and collapsed. See, he looks almost OK now,' she said, going and sitting beside him. 'He's breathing easily. Oh, my goodness! Look at that rash. I never noticed . . .'

'His eyes,' said Eric Caldwell. 'They're . . .'

'That grey sheen,' Thane's voice had dropped to a whisper.

As they were speaking they heard a noise from outside. Dr Taylor, longterm family friend and GP to the PM, who lived in a small flat at the back of the Tate Gallery, had already arrived. As luck would have it, he'd been getting into his car when Caldwell had got him on his mobile, which accounted for the speed.

'OK, out,' Taylor ordered. 'Everyone except you, Janet.'

Harry Taylor was somebody who expected to be obeyed.

He was a doctor of the old school, an irascible Scot, gritty, salt-of-the-earth, a short-back-and-sides man of stocky build. When he told his patients what to do they did it, and sharpish. How up to date he was with modern medical developments was another matter.

The three staffers stayed their ground. 'We've got to know, Dr Taylor,' said Caldwell. The strain was at last showing on his face. 'Do we call an ambulance?'

'Belt off. Outside. Now,' the doctor growled.

The three men moved out onto the landing and stood whispering nervously to each other. An ambulance screaming into Downing Street would drive every other story off the front pages. After only a few seconds, the door swung open and framed in the doorway was Harry Taylor with, behind him, an apoplectic-looking Prime Minister. He was shouting. 'I don't know what the fuck you are on about, Harry! I'm as right as fucking rain!'

The three staff members winced and moved downstairs as Taylor turned and said, 'OK, Peter. But I want you to have some tests. Today. You've had a funny turn.'

'Never felt better in my life!' yelled Peter Morgan, emerging into the corridor. He stopped when he saw his three bewildered staff, stared quizzically at them for a moment, then, still dressed only in a towel, seized his wife and kissed her theatrically on the lips right in front of them. Then he pulled her inside and slammed the door behind him, with the cry, 'Doesn't a man get any fucking privacy, just because he's Prime Minister?'

Dr Taylor waited a moment, then, putting his fingers to his lips, beckoned the others to follow him downstairs. They gathered in Caldwell's office and shut the door behind them.

'What the hell's the matter?' asked Caldwell. 'We've got to know.'

'Haven't a clue,' said Dr Taylor, with shocking honesty. 'He was lying there, comatose. Suddenly he sat up, blinked, and appeared to be fine. Started shouting abuse at me. Straightaway. Wouldn't even let me take his pulse, or look at that rash. What the hell was I doing? Was I having an affair with Janet, for

Christ's sake.' He made a grimace. 'I hope he was joking,' he added. Nobody smiled.

'OK, doctor. Here's how it's been: it's happened three or four times to our certain knowledge,' said Thane quietly. 'You've got to get him to a specialist, Harry.'

'No press leaks,' added Caldwell.

'You've seen what he's like,' said Taylor. 'He's determined to see no one in the state he's in. Thinks he's as fit as a fiddle.'

'What is it?' asked Daniel.

'I tell you I'll have to consult somebody.' The doctor continued to look as lost as they did. 'Didn't like the eyes; didn't like that rash. I'd like to run some tests.'

'Consult somebody?' asked Caldwell, a worried note in his voice. 'Who are you going to talk to?'

'Don't know.' Taylor suddenly looked tired, as if he knew he was into something well beyond his competence. The three staff stared back at him, each sharing the same thought.

Millbank, Central London, Wednesday 15th June

MI5 had insisted on maximum coverage, which was why the case officer was sitting in a tiny, sound-proof, top-floor office, over-looking the Thames, listening to a tape of two people talking. He was taking notes, though he was still far from sure what it all meant. There were several sections, each recorded, the covering note explained, with a few hours' break in between them.

How's David?
Not at all well.
He was pretty sparky last time.
That was yesterday.
The new gene?
It's taken all right. But he's not picking up. I'm worried.
What're you injecting next?
I'll ask Harper. It's his field.
He's bright, but not practical.

He's got great gut instinct. Spots a solution a mile away.

If you say so.

I do.

And David?

I said: I'm deeply worried. Right now it's touch and go. Anything could happen over the next twenty-four hours.

There was a pause, then came the second intercept. The same two men were talking on the telephone.

You rang?

Yup.

David?

Yup?

What?

Critical.

You're sure?

I'm sure? Jesus, is the Pope Catholic?

So?

Terminal.

Nothing you can do? What about Guthrie?

He's too busy.

The end?

I dunno.

A little later there was a further intercept. By this time the case officer monitoring the tape almost shared the sense of loss.

David? Dead? I'm sorry. You tried so hard.

I liked him.

We all do with playthings.

David was no plaything. David was real.

Course he was real.

He ain't real no more.

What are you going to do now?

I've got to set up Ethel.

Don't like the name Ethel.

OK, we'll call her Rosie.

Background?

Same as David's.

Not quite.

No: Rosie's a woman.

You're not getting carried away, are you?

This thing matters to the Institute. We've got to beat it.

A little later there was a final exchange on the tape. This time it was a monitored telephone call. One of the voices was American.

Hello?

Is that you?

Yes, who's that?

Harper Guthrie.

Where the hell have you been? David died.

I'm sorry, I've been tied up analysing the blood samples.

That's no use to me, nor to David.

I said I was sorry. What happened?

Tried everything. Went back to basics, like you said. Looked at all the vectors. We isolated the gene family which controlled the immune system.

That's where I left you.

Then things changed. New strains, new symptoms. Kept emerging. Mutating. Very rapidly.

That's bad news. That's worrying. When did he die?

Late last night, I guess. I've got Rosie now.

Rosie?

She's coming along fine, but she hasn't had it for long.

How long?

Since David died. I transferred everything over.

That's bad workmanship. You should have started afresh. You may have contaminated . . .

I took every precaution.

OK, tell me about Rosie. What's she showing?

Nothing. Nothing yet.

Talk to you later, then. I may just have something that could help.

The case officer monitoring the intercepts was tired, but he had one more thing to do before he went off duty. He picked up the green telephone on his desk and dialled a number. 'This is G7,' he said softly. 'David's died. Don't know how much that matters. Now they've got Rosie. Is that clear?' He listened, nodded, then put down the phone. Now he could go home.

8

Kisangani, Congo, Thursday 16th June

It was like a blow to the pit of his stomach. On top of all the fuss about the Belgian doctor, an apparently routine message from Boekamper in New York had arrived. It was blunt and to the point: if Clegg Hurley wanted his longterm WHO contract renewed, he would have to agree to stay on in the Congo for another six months. Six more months in this bloody hell-hole. Six more months of this diabolical climate, dealing with incompetent officials and fabricated medical statistics. Six months of ill-disciplined teenage soldiers on the rampage, firing their guns for the hell of it outside his house in the middle of the night; six more months of haggling with shady Arab and Indian traders for the most basic foodstuffs, apart from the everyday burden of keeping statistics on the semi-traumatized victims of starvation and civil war. What the hell did one solitary case of surge fever matter when so many thousands had died in the fighting, not counting the legions of mutilated, the battalions of amputees? Cruelty had always been present in Africa. Every day he saw old men and women with tribal scars cut in their foreheads or their cheeks. That was the old custom. The new generation walked or hobbled around with hands cut off, or legs and feet blown away by the landmines, that crop of the devil. And thinking of the devil, he'd had nightmares about Banquier and his dubious school. Was it just a dream that he had cut people open to see how viruses travelled? 'The end justifies the means, Mr Hurley,' he'd said. That was no dream. It had been spoken like the doctors at Auschwitz.

Hurley was not particularly social, but he longed to have someone intelligent to talk to about it all. He recognized that he was fast growing in on himself. Each day he forced himself to go straight to the office and work long hours, then, when he finished in the evenings, he would return to his house, eat the dinner his cook had prepared for him, and either read or listen to loud classical music, or drink himself to sleep, until the next rotten day. There were a few other whites around, but they were the bleached-out, sweat-stained, longterm hard men, diamond miners mainly, who seemed to thrive on danger. For a while he had got into the habit of talking to a retired African teacher. He had first come across the old man, with his worn-out collar and threadbare tie, as they both waited in a queue to buy some local beer. What type of person would wear a tie in such heat? They started talking. He was an interesting man, a graduate, not only from the university in Kinshasa but also from the Sorbonne. He spoke passable French and English. They'd got on well enough, and Hurley had even invited him round for dinner one night, much to the disapproval of his domestic staff.

Why did he remember the old African now? When they talked together, the man had always watched him intently with his red-veined eyes, as if analysing what the American was thinking as well as saying. When he spoke, the man's cracked lips parted in an almost toothless smile. 'White men have long tried to conquer or patronize Africa, Mr Hurley,' he had argued. 'The one or the other. They manage for a while, through superior strength, or education, or, perhaps, intellect. But in the long run they always fail. There's always something new out of Africa – good, bad, important, trivial. Man, *Homo sapiens*, first evolved in Africa, not far from here, but what exactly does that prove? I can say that but for a white man to do so would be politically incorrect, would it not?' The old man had laughed. 'White men always concentrate on the good and the important. They ignore the detail. As with ants, or bad water, or the tiny mosquito, they take no notice until these apparently trivial things defeat them in the end.'

Shortly afterwards the old man had disappeared and Hurley

had never found anyone else to whom he could relate. He enquired about him, but no one seemed to know where he had gone. Perhaps he had died or been killed. Did it matter? Life moved on. There were other intelligent African civil servants around, holding onto the vestiges of a previous administrative structure, but most of them had gone to seed as well, unpaid for years, often holding onto an office or a title that meant little any more. Here nobody mattered, nothing mattered. Now there were well-founded reports of a new civil war having broken out in the north and east; stories of massacres filtered through from time to time, but it still seemed far enough away. Six more damned months.

Then another list of demands arrived from Boekamper about Banquier and his bloody virus. It meant another long trip to see the Belgian, with his marmoset monkeys, his fat lips, his spooky, white, manicured hands. Boekamper wanted the reply immediately. This time Hurley, his guard and driver, arrived at the school in the midst of a tropical thunderstorm. The rainy season was meant to be long over, but even the climate had gone haywire. Under leaden skies the school looked more abandoned and desolate than ever. He had tried to ring in advance to warn Banquier he was coming, but the phonelines were down again. So what was new?

He found the doctor in more or less the same insanitary condition he had found him in on his first visit. This time he wasn't watching mating monkeys. He was standing at the door of one of the run-down wards, staring through a glass screen at a bed in a side-room, where an African woman patient was lying, obviously in great pain. The Belgian watched and made notes on a clipboard, coldly and clinically, without any sign of compassion. Behind him stood a nervous-looking African nurse with a gauze mask over her face.

'What is it?' called Hurley, keeping well back by the door.

'Just rabies,' said the doctor, shrugging and turning towards him. He was actually smiling, as if it was the most natural thing in the world.

'Just rabies?'

'Just rabies. Too late. She die.'

'Jeez,' said Hurley. God, how he hated this place.

'Come to house,' said Banquier. 'Come, have drink.' He glanced at Hurley, noting the unopened bottle of whisky he was carrying. 'For me?' he asked. His lips again parted in a smile.

'Yes.'

'What you want for it?'

'It's a present.'

'And?'

'A bit more information, please.'

'What information?'

'ZD198 again.'

'I guessed: I isolated it, you know.'

'You what?'

'I isolated it. Tried get to transmit. Couldn't. E'cept once.'

Hurley froze. 'What d'you mean?'

'Lots of blood. An amputee caught it. Dead, too. Not my fault.'

'You never told me. Anyone else who knows about all this?'

'Don't know. Lost touch.'

'Anyone else here we can talk to about how it's caught?'

'Told you before: can't just catch it.'

'Who'd know that?' Hurley repeated.

'Not many. Most are dead.'

'This case in Britain . . .' Hurley began.

'Britain, eh?' The Belgian turned to stare at his visitor. 'Britain?' he repeated, then he smiled. 'Maybe my colonel – how you say, flipped his lid?'

10 Downing Street, London, Thursday 16th June

It was crisis time inside Number Ten. From the outside, politicians, civil servants, the media and the public at large, had no reason to believe that the Prime Minister was not going about his business, looking after the country's interests to the best of his ability. From inside, looking out, it was very different. It was view-from-the-bunker time: bunkering down was always the standard reaction in politics when things were going badly and the world seemed unkind. It was usually the wrong tactic because it was blinkered, because it was those in the bunker who, if they had not caused the problem in the first place, certainly made it worse. In this case, a vengeful nature had played its hand, but then came the cover-up. And cover-ups are more deadly than the event.

The team's ambition was simple, yet it was huge. They had, at times, an incapacitated Peter Morgan, who did not realize, and would not believe, that there was anything wrong with him. Indeed, there was absolutely nothing wrong with him most of the time. He got angry with them; he refused point-blank to have a check up until his routine medical, which was still weeks away. Except for these brief seizures, he worked as hard and behaved as rationally as ever. Even the rash seemed to have temporarily disappeared. His staff never knew when the next fit would come. What if it happened in some public place or at some major event? The media and his many political enemies out there would pretend to be hugely sympathetic. But Rogerson and his ilk would be conspiring behind the scenes in no time. The team had to keep it secret, until they knew for sure what 'it' was.

They trawled their way through all the PM's forthcoming engagements with friends, Cabinet colleagues, senior government officials, business leaders and other public figures who were expecting to come to Number Ten. Daniel Evans's spindoctoring went into overdrive; diversionary tactics were introduced to suggest that the PM was keeping his head down, dealing with a very heavy workload. His diary schedules continued to suggest a constant stream of meetings; the reality was that these were cut back drastically. For those who knew how Number Ten really worked, the message was sharper and more focused. The PM was showing great singleness of purpose: he had insisted on taking quality time to think through a co-ordinated strategy for the future. That line had the advantage of being what Peter Morgan himself believed he was doing. Behind the scenes, his inner sanctum staff concentrated not on 'what shall we do?', but 'what shall we say and how shall we say it?' The packaging of the message, who the messenger was, and what were the camera angles, the media hype, the spin: these were the issues that took up most of the time of Eric Caldwell and Daniel Evans in the press office. Lyle Thane co-ordinated the whole scenario. He knew it couldn't last, time was against them; but they were determined to keep things water-tight, until they got to the heart of the problem. It was a big lie to play.

The press line proved the easy bit. The Prime Minister had resolved to leave day to day matters to ministers, for them to speak for their various departments. Parliament was in Whitsun recess for another few days, so there wasn't the problem of Prime Minster's Question Time to cope with quite yet. At his morning briefings for the lobby correspondents Evans made it clear that the PM was intending to cool it for a bit: no leaping onto public platforms, giving interviews to Radio 4, or to *Newsnight*, or to *Breakfast with Frost*. Not now: later. The facts about the Government's achievements spoke for themselves. This was a good time to think big.

Much effort and guile was used to keep Winston Rogerson at bay. The Prime Minister sent a personal note to him, which Caldwell persuaded him to write, asking the Deputy PM to keep an eye on things. It carried just a hint that Rogerson was being trained for great things. Nobody actually said that Rogerson was the PM's preferred successor, but why not let him believe just that? For Thane it meant a huge amount of extra work. He was at it from early morning until late at night, which hit hard his relationship with Sarah St Just. At a personal level he knew it was dangerous; she was beginning to fret. It was all right being a lady who lunched, but she wanted nights as a lady who partied until two, three, four in the morning, at Tramps, at Annabel's, at the newest, most fashionable nightspots in the city. Then sex.

The indestructible Lyle Thane began to flag, especially with the sex. That was verging on disastrous.

Sir Ian Temple-White, the Director General of MI5, otherwise known as the Secret Service, was one of the last survivors of the old school. But he was no blimp; he was extremely bright, he had a strong belief in himself and his Service, and he knew what they ought jointly to be doing to safeguard the interests of the nation. Sir Ian was an Old Etonian in an age when Old Etonians were decidedly unfashionable. But he had got where he was not via the old school tie network, but by playing a subtler and more cunning game. He would have made a first-class chairman of a City bank, or an Oxbridge professor, or a field marshal, but he would never have made a good politician. He was born to rule. He was an autocrat. He believed that good teamwork was a good team doing what he told them to do. On the surface he was the best kind of secret civil servant: tall, distinguished, immaculately dressed, with impeccable manners and a well-disciplined family that would never get him into trouble in the pages of the tabloids. He was well bred through and through.

Where Sir Ian's tactics became somewhat alien to the niceties of democracy, was when the Service came under threat. He faced this problem from time to time, as politicians of various political persuasions tried to bring MI5 to heel. There was nothing new in all that. Throughout the long decades since the Second World War, not only had MI5 had to defend itself against its sister intelligence agency, MI6, which always considered itself somewhat superior, but increasingly it had been forced to keep the shutters of secrecy closed against the prying eyes, ears, and noses, of various brands of self-seeking politician. They failed to realize that open government was a contradiction in terms. As far back as Harold Wilson's day, the infamous minister without portfolio George Wigg had tried to bring MI5 into the open, and well before that, even the aristocratic Harold MacMillan, another Old Etonian, had never much cared for the underhand methods which the Service was forced to use to protect the State from its enemies. His dismissive handling of their hard-nosed evidence in the Profumo and Vassal cases demonstrated that only too clearly. In the last decade before the millennium, things had got somewhat better and more enlightened. MI5 had become 'declared', with the government of the day not only admitting its existence, but allowing ministers to answer general questions in the House of Commons about its organization, within the limits that the secrecy of some of its operations dictated. This was despite the fact that several of those self-same ministers, including at least one home secretary, had, in their youth, had files kept on them by the very organization they were now answerable for.

Prime Minister Morgan had blandly followed the 'open government' line adopted by some of his recent predecessors, but was privately dismissive of MI5 and much of its work. He'd even publicly suggested amalgamating it with the police, since he felt that, with the end of the Cold War, most of MI5's activities should be aimed at dealing with drug barons, money laundering, Mafia crime and so on. The PM became even more averse to the residual aspects of the Secret Service when he discovered that he too in his student days had been a target of electronic eavesdropping. While he was always polite enough on the surface, deep down the PM was an implacable opponent of much that Sir Ian Temple-White stood for. It was opportune, therefore, that the head of Technical Department at MI5 came straight to see Sir Ian without knocking and without telling anyone else about his strange discovery.

The head of Technical Department was no way apologetic about the partial nature of the intelligence that had been uncovered. The Service often picked up strange information which only made sense much later, when other pieces of the puzzle began to fit together. Clues frequently came to light as the result of someone's out-of-character behaviour, an intercept of an odd telephone call, a sudden large deposit into a particular private bank account, long before any crime itself was known about. The head of Technical Department's remit covered all surveillance aspects that related to the Prime Minister. He was no Old Etonian; he'd been to a local school in Huddersfield, but despite that, he and his chief spoke the same language, shared the same ideals. That was why he was where he was. So when he told his boss that something odd was going on and that there seemed to be a conspiracy of silence among those closest to the Prime Minister about something as yet unknown, which was making them all panic, he correctly guessed what his reaction would be. After a while, Sir Ian turned to face his colleague and smiled. 'I love a good cover-up,' he said. 'They always go wrong. It would be handy, as a first step, to know precisely *what* Mr Thane and his colleagues are trying so desperately to hide. Then we can decide in our own time what we need to do about it.'

It wasn't an order, it wasn't a command, but the head of Technical Department knew precisely what to do next. Anything that threatened the welfare of the Prime Minister was also a threat to national security, and such a threat was the be all and end all of MI5's very existence. What that blinkered, dedicated, tunnel-visioned man did not appreciate however was that he already had the devastating answer to his question in another file in the in-tray on his own desk.

10 Downing Street, London, Friday 17th June

Joe Tinker of ITN was puzzled. He had interviewed the Prime Minister on three or four occasions over the past few years, both in government and in opposition, and it had always been such a glib, boring and inevitable exercise. Peter Morgan had always chosen exactly the right word, the right phrase, the right piece of banality, to dull the interview into unwatchability. The man was all charm, all face, using the right tie, the right expression, the right briefing notes, the right Party line, the right spin, to lull any audience into apathy with his soporific nuances and bland style. Joe Tinker knew about charm and style. He was a man who walked around with a hairbrush in his pocket. He knew about image. He knew that a hair out of place, the wrong knot in the wrong sort of tie, would distract the viewers' attention from the importance of what he was saying. He could put on that studied look – concerned, caring, sad, or excited – to match any occasion. He chose his expressions from the wardrobe of his mind as someone else would choose a suit. Joe Tinker was no modest flower; he held a key place in British society. He was the cream of the cream, the politician's political correspondent.

Tonight, an unbelievable thought welled up in Joe Tinker's mind. He kept it to himself, neither sharing it with his cameraman nor his research assistant, and he certainly made no mention of it to his editor when he got back to the studio. He did not want any gossip traced back to him. He had been entirely on his own after all, chatting to the PM before the interview itself, alone that was except for Daniel the Press Secretary and that oleaginous git, Lyle Thane. The mood was neither happy nor particularly relaxed, yet the thought had arisen in Joe Tinker's mind that the Prime Minister might conceivably, though it was not yet five in the afternoon, be a little bit drunk. It was his unusual inability to marshal the right words in the right order that first alerted Tinker. He remembered how Peter Morgan had mocked John Major for his syntax, disparaging his predecessor for having jumbled his words ungrammatically. Morgan had been quite outspoken. Tinker remembered that quite clearly. He spoke from a position of strength since he was second to none in coming up with the catchphrase of the moment, at the right moment. Devoid of firm ideas or beliefs he might be, but he was superbly able to leap from elegant soundbite to soundbite, using clichés as others used facts. Morgan said things so charmingly, with such a genuine smile, that few took offence. Even when his political opponents did digest and dissect his words and find that there was nothing much there, it did the PM himself no harm whatsoever.

Yet tonight, before the cameras began to roll, Peter Morgan seemed unable to spin the line with his usual flair. Surprisingly, he seemed blissfully unaware of his own difficulty. Tinker threw a quick glance at the other two men in the room, and noted how they sat nervously, on the edges of their chairs, faces tense, staring intently at their boss. Every now and again Evans would throw a quick look in Tinker's direction and flash a well-practised smile, as if to reassure him that all was well. But Tinker sensed that the reverse was true.

When the cameras started running, the interview went well enough, and only one line was fluffed. That was understandable, unexceptional; Tinker faithfully promised Daniel that he would edit it out. Yet, later, when he played the interview back in the studio, there was something about the Prime Minister's voice which, when it was finally screened, was hardly noticeable. But Tinker, who was nothing if not professional, noticed. Had the PM had a slight stroke? No: he answered his own question. No: he was quite certain of that. Believe it or not, the PM had been ever so slightly drunk. So what of that, Tinker thought? Churchill and Thatcher after all, two of the greatest leaders of the last century, had been well known for their liking of strong drink. Had it affected their abilities to control the destiny of the nation? OK, their habits became the subject of media gossip, but which prominent figure in British political life did not have some bad habits? But Peter Morgan, drunk? That was strange, since Joe Tinker could not recall ever seeing the PM with a glass in his hand.

After the interview, Daniel Evans was all smiles. It had gone well, hadn't it, apart from the one understandable fluff? The Prime Minister had said nothing of any significance, and had said it very well indeed. Nobody mentioned anything more and Tinker, hard-hitting man of the world though he was, did not dare to suggest to the PM's acolytes that alcohol might have played its part. So, he dismissed the incident from his mind; except that, deep down, it was filed away in case anything ever arrived to disinter it.

Not so with Daniel Evans and Lyle Thane. When they closeted themselves together that night for a wash-up session, they discussed that insidious mental fog, the grey pallor on the eyes, the skin rash, barely noticeable under the make-up powder but all increasingly revealing themselves. Something was seriously wrong, but still the victim refused to recognize it. They had to play a longer game.

9

They met at the Institute to reassess the situation. General George had died on the thirtieth of May. It had been firmly established that Virus ZD198 was to blame, but it was now eighteen days later and there had been no other outbreak. They had some fragile evidence from the WHO relating to a few other isolated cases over the past few years in a remote part of the eastern Congo. More details of the most recent one were being actively sought via Dr Boekamper in New York. 'Otherwise,' Professor Grant said, as he looked around the room at his colleagues, 'we know of no other confirmed cases in the developed world, except the one in the United States where the patient, a mercenary, had a direct African connection. As the virus seems to act rapidly, we can probably now relax. The case of the general is a complete puzzle: we must list it in medical terms as ideopathic, of unknown provenance and cause. In the circumstances,' Professor Grant smiled, 'we can probably now release Dr Guthrie back to the tender mercies of Professor MacArthur in Edinburgh, though I hope he will agree to keep in touch with Dr Stevenson in case anything new crops up.'

Guthrie nodded politely and said nothing. It was not fear of Professor MacArthur that reduced him to silence, but a nagging doubt that they were all being too complacent too soon.

He was in no hurry to pack his bags and was working quietly in a corner of the lab later that day, checking for any similarities between Virus ZD198 and Marburg disease, which was also known as green monkey disease. The long-tailed African green monkey had been the proven source of serious haemorrhaging and more than one fatality among technicians handling them in a lab in Marburg in Germany, hence the name. But that route of enquiry was put on hold when Dr Stevenson burst in and told him that a prominent British actor, Ralph Rowland, had just been admitted to intensive care at the Brompton Hospital, with some particularly horrible symptoms. The staff there were baffled as to what it was and had rung the Institute for advice. They had also couriered over some blood samples for analysis. Dr Stevenson knew that Professor Grant had been attending a meeting at Imperial College that afternoon and had managed to get a message to him; he was near the Brompton and would look in on the patient on his way back to the Institute.

Less than half an hour later, Grant rang Guthrie in the lab on his mobile phone. 'Cancel Edinburgh,' he barked excitedly. 'Before we've done any tests, my hunch is we've got another definite case. Ralph Rowland's a household name here in Britain, so the press will be on our backs in no time. I can't believe the man will last the night.' Grant paused as he climbed into his car, then continued: 'Can't see any obvious connection, can you, Harper? An actor and a general?'

One further case was listed before Grant managed to reach the Institute. It came, within the hour, via Sir Mark Ivor of all people. His story began two weeks earlier, when he had met up with the daughter of the missing peer, Lord Rumbold, in Edinburgh. She told a scandalous tale: when Rumbold started having odd blackouts, his family had conspired to have the peer sectioned, declared mentally unstable, then had him transferred to a secure private psychiatric clinic near Perth.

Sir Mark had been shocked. 'But this is criminal!' he'd burst out.

'You have to understand,' his daughter argued. 'We were just trying to protect him from himself.'

'I don't believe it,' Sir Mark had stood, as if to bring the meeting to an end. Then the truth came tumbling out.

'My family were terrified he'd do something odd, start changing his will or something,' said his daughter, breaking into floods of tears. 'Huge estates are at stake. Enormous death duties could be payable. We needed time to think.'

'And where exactly d'you think I'd come in?' asked Sir Mark distantly. In no way was he prepared to get involved in anything so suspect.

'We realize we have to come clean,' said the daughter. 'We thought you'd be able to advise us what to do.'

Sir Mark had refused to discuss the matter further but, despite that, Rumbold's daughter had rung him that very morning to admit that, at last, the family doctor and the clinic staff had rebelled. Her father was on the point of death. Her family realized that they'd behaved very foolishly. What should they do? Again Sir Mark refused to have anything to do with it, but later, the daughter phoned again with the news that her father had died. Given his mysterious disappearance, the press would be after the story in a big way. It was all so disgraceful that Sir Mark told her he felt duty-bound to report the whole affair to the appropriate authorities. Deeply shocked both by her father's death and Sir Mark's reaction, the daughter poured out all the details. 'The doctor's deeply worried about the cause of death. He wants to notify the local health board, but the rest of the family won't let him,' she added. Whatever Rumbold had died of, Sir Mark realized it must be something very serious, since she admitted that a total fumigation of his room had been carried out and that the clinic's staff had all been ordered to submit to various blood tests. Sir Mark had heard enough. He put the phone down, then rang a contact of his at the Department of Health, and the news was quickly reported to the Harman Institute's monitoring unit. It led to Professor Grant ringing the Rumbold family doctor direct, and, as a result of the latter's description of the symptoms, Rebecca Stevenson was dispatched to Perth that very afternoon. What she discovered led to many rapid changes in plan, not least the immediate cancellation of the family funeral and the placing of the whole family, the doctor and clinic staff, in the strictest quarantine.

Claythorpe, Essex, Friday 17th June

They now had two new cases of ZD198, one terminal and Ralph Rowland ready to go at any moment. The press had yet to focus on the story, not least because the English soccer team had sacked their manager yet again, and there had been another major earthquake in Central America. The day's news hole was already well filled, and, generally speaking, the unexpected deaths of two men, no matter how famous, are not normally connected. But there were plenty of headlines to come.

A few miles to the east of 10 Downing Street, in rural Essex, behind a high garden wall inside one of the most vulgar, opulent houses in the area, Will Tyndall's henchmen were facing a dilemma not dissimilar to the one with which Lyle Thane and his colleagues were trying to deal. Those closest to him, including Dolly his fourth wife, had noticed his lapses for almost a week, yet, like those around the Prime Minister, nobody dared to mention it. When eventually they did try, when his seizures became more frequent, Tyndall became aggressive, and when Tyndall became aggressive, no one but no one ventured to contradict him. In that, he was far more dangerous than a mere Prime Minister; crossing Tyndall had always been a sure way to the graveyard. That was not where the comparison ended: his cronies, with their scar-faces and prison-sentence CVs, were just as concerned to keep Will Tyndall's ailment a secret as those around the PM. Lyle Thane would have recognized this ballgame. Just as Winston Rogerson was always prowling along the corridors of power, if other criminal overlords got a whiff of a rumour that Will Tyndall was weakening, they would rapidly move in on his territory.

Not since the days of the Kray brothers had there been such a big-time, all-round British-born crook as Will Tyndall. If Britain had a Mafia, Tyndall was its capo. He was into everything: extortion, drug running, blackmail, protection rackets, prostitution, and was rumoured to have more than a few officers in the Met on his payroll. People didn't give evidence against Will Tyndall unless they wanted to end up in a binbag on a skip. The Serious Crime Squad had tried, but no one had been able to pin a murder on him yet, though the gossip on the street said that if he ever slipped, it would only be a matter of time. Tyndall was well known in the East End and certain parts of Essex, but was never mentioned in the crime sections of the tabloid press because even journalists have wives and children to protect. His only current rivals were world-class players; he was said to keep in touch with the big boys from Moscow and to have had meetings with them in their fortified mansions along the Thames Valley over dividing up their European territory. Tyndall kept the big competitors happy – it was safer that way. His British competitors were all little guys and he had nothing to fear from them. Until the day he started slipping.

Tyndall went everywhere with a bodyguard, or more commonly two, carefully picked from his own background, his own part of London, his own street. They were people who knew him, were loyal to him, had known him since they were kids together, when he was gang leader of one of the toughest packs in the whole of the East End. But for some things, bodyguards are useless both to Prime Ministers and gangsters. Guns and bullets and flak jackets are no barriers to infection. When illness first hit Tyndall in the form of short spasms of memory loss, when he started seizing up when normally he would shout and threaten, the guys around him worried a lot but were still so scared of him that they did nothing. Nobody even hinted that they thought he was ill. Nobody dared. In between he was as rational as he had ever been. Only his closest friends, and one or two of the girls who shared his bed usually more than one at a time, noticed the glazed grey film that came over his eyes and the mottled texture which had appeared on his skin. Yet still nothing was said.

Eventually however, the team started to whisper among themselves, choosing who they whispered to in case one of them squealed. They whispered out of loyalty and fear, because the danger was that if Will Tyndall failed, his lucrative drugs and prostitution rackets, his sauna parlours and gaming houses, would be up for the take. In the big wide world of crime, the best time to kick an opponent was when he was going down. Just like politics. Over the last thirty years, Tyndall had built up his empire by making men fear him. Those who had stood in his way had been beaten up, shot down, or disposed of in the slimey marshes of the Thames Estuary. His team had always been good at hiding bodies. It was cleaner that way. They made sure that nobody reported that a victim had disappeared, so there was no crime for the police to investigate. Occasionally they had slipped up; there had been a brief threat of criminal action, but witnesses ran scared when Tyndall's name was mentioned. He had never spent a day in prison in his life.

Big Mac, Will Tyndall's chief henchman, and his long-suffering wife Dolly, agonized over it for a good twenty-four hours, then summoned in the family doctor, Dr Rafiq. He was a pliant and accommodating man who had been most useful to them in the past when they had needed medical help of an untoward nature. What they told the doctor was well beyond Rafiq's experience. He too was scared. He didn't want to put a foot wrong with Tyndall by suggesting to him that something might be the matter. He couldn't, wouldn't, bell the cat. He had once seen Tyndall angry and had had to treat the wound and reset the broken limbs that had resulted from his wrath. Dr Rafiq was not a brave man. He was in a quandary. The trouble was, he explained, he couldn't just go and ask for advice from more expert colleagues, or talk to one of his consultant friends at the Essex Hospital. That wasn't good enough an argument for Big Mac. He was almost as good as his boss at getting what he wanted. Rafiq scuffled off and spoke out of desperation to a consultant who was an expert in nervous diseases. Without mentioning the name of his patient, he explained what the problem was. The specialist raised his eyebrows when Rafiq stammered that even he had not been allowed to examine the patient, then coolly advised that the only thing to do was to whip the patient into hospital for an overall scan. 'That's not possible,' said Rafiq. 'He is much too important.' The specialist knew something of Rafiq's lifestyle and the dubious nature of some of his patients, and was having none of it.

'You know as well as anyone, Rafiq, I can't proffer any advice without knowing more.' The specialist was deliberately distant. When Dr Rafiq returned in fear and trepidation to Big Mac, the latter was surprisingly practical. 'When we need a lawyer,' he said, 'and there ain't no lawyer available, then we pick one up, don't we? That's what we've always done. What we need from you, Rafiq baby, is the name of somebody who can help. Soon and discreet, d'you hear? We'll do the rest.'

Shaking with fear, Dr Rafiq returned to his surgery and made a few calls. His enquiries eventually came up with a name.

The Harman Institute, East London, Friday 17th June

One isolated case had led Professor Grant and his team to a brief, dangerous complacency. They now had two further cases and felt there were bound to be others out there. More to the point, all three cases were household names. When the press made the connection, as they could not fail to do, they would go wild. But the crisis was still containable, thought Professor Grant.

His confidence was soon to be shattered once more.

Even in countries where there are freedom of information acts, governments and their subsidiary departments are seldom forthcoming with the whole truth about serious, unpleasant, or secret issues. They cannot always be blamed for this, except with vengeful hindsight. They hide facts to protect not themselves so much as groups in society which they exist to help. Thus, in the late eighties and early nineties, the British Ministry of Agriculture and a less willing Department of Health, ably but wrongly assisted by Professor Grant, downplayed early scientific worries about the BSE-Creutzfeldt-Jakob disease link. They did not want to harm the British beef industry, or unnecessarily alarm the general public about the emergence of this new and hideous infection. If they had shouted their concerns from the rooftops at that early stage, they would surely have stood accused of scaremongering. It was a no-win situation both ways. Professor Grant had also recently been drawn into the huge, badly informed but very real public outcry over the perceived dangers of genetically modified foods, and had seen how the scientists and the Government had struggled to placate the press and the public with such little success.

Bruised by these past experiences, Professor Grant again found himself in an intolerable quandary. His team had now identified three very high-profile cases of this new virus. If he went public, what could he say? That he didn't know where it had come from? That he had absolutely no idea how it was spread? That he hadn't a clue how it could be treated? Could he admit that he and his experts were totally baffled by its erratic gestation period, which had to mean that there were almost certainly other cases out there waiting to reveal themselves? If he, with the Chief Medical Officer of Health, summoned a press conference and told the media of his suspicions, what would be achieved? Mass hysteria perhaps, and, like the European ban on British beef, perhaps a people ban, the prevention of British citizens travelling abroad, until some of the basic questions about this deadly new virus had been answered? Grant admitted privately to himself that it probably wouldn't be quite as bad as that, but given sufficient tabloid media hype and the fame of the three victims, anything could happen, particularly since there were so many outstanding questions and no solutions on the horizon. Time was desperately needed to think things through.

He need not have relied on that; his hand would be forced before the day was out.

10 Downing Street, London, Friday 17th June

As with scientific secrets, so it is with political secrets. The bigger they are, the more difficult they are to hide. In the recent political histories of the Western democracies, there was a host of cases where a cover-up led to the collapse of a government or the fall of the individuals concerned. The Watergate crisis or President Clinton's affair with the young White House internee, or some of the recent corruption scandals at the European Commission, would have only been a fraction as bad if an early admission of guilt had come from the perpetrators. Crimes are increased a hundredfold by elaborate attempts to hide what actually happened from a wider public.

So it was with the current crisis inside Number Ten. The more they concealed, the more it was necessary to keep concealing. In this case however, there was no crime. All that had happened was that a man had become ill, but this fact was being hidden, not by elected ministers or MPs, but by undemocratically appointed functionaries around Peter Morgan who had not even a civil servant's obligation to keep certain truths about the nation's leader from a wider world. Once that first dissimulation had been made, it was increasingly difficult for Thane and his colleagues to step back from the brink. They might defend themselves for a while yet, saying it was to protect the health of Peter Morgan, or to accede to the wishes of his wife, Janet, but they knew in their heart of hearts that soon all would have to be revealed. Unless, of course, the Prime Minister recovered.

One weakness of their position was that the staffers inside

Number Ten did not fully appreciate the contempt in which they were held by much of the outside world. The senior civil servants in the ministries who had to deal with them, the Cabinet Office staff, and above all members of the Cabinet themselves, hated the control freaks, the spindoctors, the strategy manipulators, who held court there. People like Lyle Thane were known to have far better access to the Prime Minister than his own Cabinet colleagues did. As a result of their desperate policy of hiding Peter Morgan from them, the latter was seen not only as weak, but also for some strange reason, increasingly unavailable. At the last Cabinet meeting for example, Rogerson had taken the chair, which, on the face of it was OK. But it did not make for good governance and the whispers grew ever stronger. Simon Tattersall, the Home Secretary, was openly critical of the Downing Street staff. He called them kindergarten-yuppies who were playing their selfish little games on the nursery slopes of politics. A senior Foreign Office minister, who remembered back to when Bill Clinton first got into the White House, recalled, for some of his closer ministerial friends, that the staffers there had been known as Chelsea Clinton's playmates. Someone overheard the remark and it got into the *Guardian*. The other newspapers picked it up with a certain degree of glee, but all it did was to make the PM's office even more defensive of their position, strengthening them in their resolve to keep the Prime Minister's secret hidden well away from his enemies and detractors.

What those critical outsiders had yet to realize was that it was not some esoteric political strategy which was leading Morgan into becoming 'a semi-detached Prime Minister', as one *Times* leader mockingly called him. The bitter fact was that, hour by hour, he was exhibiting more and more frequent signs of whatever ailment he was suffering from. No one could accuse Caldwell, his private secretary, or indeed his wife and the loyal Dr Taylor, of not doing their best, but when a Prime Minister refuses to believe he is ill, and is rational most of the time, it is difficult to overrule him. When they again tried to broach the subject, he shouted angrily that he didn't know what they were talking about. He would not undergo any urgent medical tests. Why should he? He was very much Prime Minister. They all owed their jobs to him; they could do nothing but go along with him. How different it would have been, Thane speculated with Caldwell, if he'd had a massive stroke or had broken his leg, or had a heart attack. Then there would have been no argument and he would have been rushed into hospital. By contrast, this gradual deterioration was a subtle slide as with the great cover-up of Winston Churchill's Alzheimer's, and the unwillingness yet the authority of the patient determined the outcome. The inside team had been lucky so far. Apart from the brief and hopefully forgotten incident before the interview with Joe Tinker, no single outsider had witnessed his blank spells. But a number of major State engagements were coming up and their luck could not last. The most difficult part was keeping the PM himself under control. He was getting stroppy, questioning why he had been shipped off to Chequers and was being prevented from seeing senior colleagues. The strategy papers kept up the pressure on him, but he had real work to do as well, he insisted. In this conspiracy Dr Taylor proved worse than useless. He had no idea how to handle the PM. He kept muttering about amnesia or the early incidence of ageing, but took refuge in the approach he had resorted to throughout his entire medical career and said, 'We must get him to a specialist.' What specialist? Whom could they approach with discretion? Taylor eventually drew up a list of possible names, among them, Thane spotted, that of Professor Desmond Grant.

As soon as Grant arrived at the Harman Institute that Friday, the phones began ringing. The most important call came from Lyle Thane, of the 10 Downing Street staff. Grant remembered meeting him; he didn't much like what he remembered, but that was beside the point.

'I can't talk about it, professor, but we have a problem. The PM needs your . . .' Thane's voice hesitated. 'Your advice.'

'I have a heavy schedule,' the professor began. 'We have a potentially huge crisis here which I –'

'I appreciate that you have your problems, professor,' Thane cut in. 'But this is more important. This morning, please.'

'I can't possibly get to you this morning,' said Grant, glancing at his watch. He could not conceive of anything more important than the ZD198 outbreak.

'I'm arranging a car and police escort for you right now,' said the cold, implacable voice at the other end of the telephone.

Professor Grant was bewildered, but did what he had been instructed to do. With difficulty, he rearranged the rest of his morning and said nothing about his summons to anyone, including Dr Stevenson. He left a note on her desk which said, 'Called away urgently. Will ring in.' Grant was whipped straight to Downing Street in the relative tranquillity of the rear seat of a black Government Rover. A highly methodical man at the best of times, he was naturally excited at whatever prospect lay ahead of him. But he also felt a huge degree of unreality as the car, proceeded by the police escort, glided through the security gates and up to the door of Number Ten. The policeman on duty outside gave a discreet knock on the door and it swung open immediately to allow Professor Grant inside. He was met by a nervous-looking Lyle Thane, who ushered him straight into his office and closed the door behind him.

As he had waited impatiently for the professor to arrive, Thane had been contemplating his private life, which was rapidly falling to pieces. Sarah had stopped talking to him because he was working so long and late and totally ignoring her, and, understandably, she was threatening to move out. For a moment he fantasized about how much money he could make if he sold the story about the PM to one of the tabloids. It would make him a mint, he could run away with Sarah, but it would break him, politically and socially, for ever. That brief, whimsical course of action was pigeonholed away in the back of his restless mind as the professor arrived and asked him what the problem was.

'He's having brief mental seizures. He goes rigid for some seconds, then comes to and seems perfectly all right.' Thane came straight to the point.

'Has he seen his doctor? Had tests?' The professor asked the obvious questions.

'His doctor's an id— an old friend. Out of his depth. He was given your name.'

The professor looked surprised for a moment, though immediately realizing why the matter was so sensitive. 'I see,' he said.

'He doesn't realize anything's wrong with him. He is still the Prime Minister, after all. What he says goes. He won't countenance a check up. It's most distressing for Mrs Morgan, too,' Thane added.

'Such cases usually are.'

'Such cases don't usually involve a Prime Minister,' said Thane sharply. 'As he doesn't believe there's anything wrong, we've even had to conspire about why you're seeing him this morning. We thought you might like to put forward a case for new funding for your research. I know you've frequently argued the case for that.' He looked enquiringly at the professor, who shook his head.

'Normally I'd be delighted to have the opportunity. But surely the Prime Minister knows this isn't the way things happen?'

'He does. But here, I'm afraid, we've thickened the plot. We've put it to the PM that you'd be an eminently suitable candidate for the chairmanship of his new Medical Research Fund. It's a particular baby of his.'

Professor Grant was totally taken aback, though inwardly pleased. It was the sort of job he would love. 'Is it true?' he asked.

'Could be,' said Thane cautiously. 'You're not supposed to know why the Prime Minister is seeing you and he doesn't know why you're seeing him. Tricky situation.'

It was the understatement of the day. It was not a good

meeting. The PM was in a petulant and ill-tempered mood, seemed annoyed by what was going on, and obviously thought that given the fact that he was meant to be concentrating on long-term strategy, his meeting with Grant was a complete waste of time. Grant felt much the same. Few great figures are heroes in the eyes of their doctors, but even dictators normally listen to them. Those who treated Hitler, Stalin and Mao, gained unique insights into the characters of the tyrants they served. Most of them lived to tell the tale. Even in democracies, leaders generally find in their doctors a trusted confidante who can guide them not only on health matters, but can also tell them the truth about their general popularity as well. It is a matter of record that Presidents Roosevelt and Kennedy, and even Margaret Thatcher, all paid the closest attention to their doctors, realizing that leaders who ignore medical advice do so at their peril. By contrast, Lord Moran, Churchill's doctor, had much of his advice ignored, and Churchill lapsed into depression and Alzheimer's in the end. Was this case so different?

The bedroom farce element of the occasion was reinforced by the fact that Dr Taylor had been hiding in an ante-room, waiting for Professor Grant to emerge. The latter immediately agreed with Thane's assessment: Taylor was totally useless, though he did volunteer to provide Grant with the results of the most recent blood samples of the PM he could find. There was nothing else to go on. During the uneasy meeting, the PM had exhibited no hiatus in his speech nor any other behaviour which might have allowed Grant to come to any more professional judgment. Thane had briefly mentioned the rash around Morgan's neck and cheeks but that had been scarcely noticeable from the distance at which the professor had been sitting. It could have been anything or nothing.

When Taylor had gone, Thane and Caldwell tried to extract a more precise opinion from the professor, but Grant's answers remained blunt: he could not possibly make a diagnosis with so little to go on. He would of course have the blood samples analysed immediately, but they were long out of date, and new ones must be obtained as a matter of the highest priority. Dr Taylor should arrange that, using whatever excuse he could dream up.

As the professor was about to leave and return to the Institute, Janet Morgan burst into Caldwell's office and introduced herself. She looked tired and distraught, and asked Grant straight out: 'So, professor, what the hell's up with my husband?'

'I'm sorry, Mrs Morgan, without a full examination I can't begin to speculate. I see no obvious symptoms to worry about. From what you've described, it could be the early onset of Alzheimer's, it could be a minor stroke, it could be a whole variety of things. I can't give you a view without that full check up. You've got to get him to undergo a full set of blood tests, then I can examine the results.'

'Secrecy is everything,' Thane interrupted. 'Can you imagine the political turmoil if . . .'

'Secrecy is all very well,' said the professor, drily, 'but if you don't act now, it may be too late.'

'He's fretting,' Janet Morgan blurted out. 'He thinks we're conspiring against him, but believes we're trying to stop him getting stressed.'

'Face him,' said Grant. 'You'll regret not . . .'

'I've tried, believe me,' Janet Morgan repeated, tears welling up in her eyes. 'Good God, professor, he doesn't listen! He stares at me as if it is me that's going mad.'

The professor was shown out by Lyle Thane. As he again settled back in the rear seat of the official car, Grant thought about the slight redness he had made out around the PM's neck and chin, but that could just have been a shaving rash. He wasn't familiar enough with the man to know whether his eyes always had that slightly washed-out look. But no: no, that was all absurd. His problems with Virus ZD198 were getting to him. He could easily be forgiven for thinking the unthinkable, but that it could not be.

Late the previous evening, when she called in to say goodnight, Professor Grant had grumbled a bit, but Rebecca Stevenson was determined. Crisis or no crisis, she was not going to work on the Saturday. She had a private life to lead, she had shopping to do, and, above all, since the tenancy agreement on the flat she was renting was about to run out, she had to find somewhere else to live. Saturday was a quality day, a day for herself, to give her time to think. She also needed to relax, and what was more relaxing than to go shopping?

One of her closest friends had once said of her that she had layers like the skins of an onion. Some of her men friends might have defined her in other ways, but one or two of them knew from experience that the more layers they tried to peel away, the more the tears came. She was not easy to get to know. Always stylishly dressed, she was meticulous and disciplined, both in her research and in her private life. To those who tried to get too close to her, this often came across as calculating coldness, while to her work colleagues it was part and parcel of her dedicated scientific approach. To her, each day was an experiment: if she frightened some with her manner and intellectual stamina, that was their loss. Not even her closest family knew of the other facets of her life, other layers of the onion, that lay hidden deep underneath.

Chauvinists suggest that men, unless they are like Lyle Thane, stare into shop windows at the goods on display, while women examine their appearance in the window-glass. Dr Stevenson was, quite decidedly, admiring a smart pair of shoes in a shop window in a narrow road just off Oxford Street, when something caught her eye. It was the reflection of a man standing close behind her. Something about his stance suggested that she was the subject of his interest. She had vaguely noticed him earlier, a short, thick-set thug with a crewcut, dressed in a dark bomber jacket and jeans. She resolved not to turn and look at him, but went into the shop and bought the shoes. When she emerged some time later, he was still there, watching her.

She decided to test her theory as she would some piece of empirical research. Turning down a side-lane into Soho, she quickly doubled back on herself, then walked very rapidly for a minute in the opposite direction. Pausing at the corner of a little square, she turned round. He was still there. Furious, she deliberately began to walk towards him up the lane. She was damned if she was going to be pestered in this way. The man turned away as she approached, and broke into a run. Without a thought, she pursued him. He had a certain agility, but she was faster and quickly caught up with him. He turned, breathless and perspiring, to face her. 'Why the hell are you following me? Damn well leave me alone!' she shouted, a flush of colour spreading across her cheeks. She was standing with her back to the lane while he faced her square on.

'Following no one,' growled the man. For his size he looked surprisingly nervous. He kept glancing from side to side, as if searching for assistance.

'You all right, dear?' A little old lady who was passing stared at Rebecca, a look of concern on her lined face.

'I'm fine,' she replied unwisely. 'Don't worry,' she added. The old lady nodded, smiled, and went on her way.

'What'd you want?' she shouted at the man, her temper rising. He tried to get past her but she moved to block him. 'I want to know why the hell you're following me.'

'Haven't.'

'You have. I've seen you all bloody morning.'

'You flatter yourself.'

'I'm going to call the police unless you explain what you're up to.'

The man suddenly looked relieved. His eyes were focused on something over her shoulder but she didn't want him to escape, so did not turn her head.

'Keeping an eye on you,' the man volunteered unexpectedly.

'Keeping an eye . . . ?' Rebecca Stevenson looked bewildered.

'You're valuable.' The man hesitated. Had she been less angry she might have wondered why he had suddenly become so forthcoming. 'You're someone that people are interested in,' he went on.

'Your mistake. I'm just a research . . .' she began. She failed to finish her sentence as, on an instinct, she turned to see that a large black car had pulled up close behind her. Two men jumped out and advanced towards her. From a distance an observer would have hardly noticed the scuffle, nor heard her muffled shout, since, apart from the little old lady who turned and watched curiously from a distance, that part of the lane was more or less deserted. That same observer might however have seen the woman roughly and unwillingly bundled into the back of the car, the doors slammed shut, and it driving off at high speed.

10

Claythorpe, Essex, Saturday, 18th June

Hot, bewildered and angry, when Rebecca Stevenson pulled herself together she found herself locked in what appeared to be a cellar. Where precisely she was she had no idea, since the rear windows of the car had been covered with blinds for the entire journey. During what she guessed had been a full hour's ride towards the east, despite her loud protestations that she must be the victim of mistaken identity, she was volunteered no information as to why she was being abducted. In an odd way she felt more fury than anxiety. The people in the car were hardly at her intellectual level: indeed two of them, including the man who had been following her, seemed positively Neanderthal. She felt certain that the affair had no sexual motive: they were all too tense and single-minded for that. Her assumption had to be that it was all some bewildering mistake and she kept trying to say so, but when she was abruptly told to shut up by the driver she opted for caution and silence. The basement room to which she had been taken was bare, like a prison cell. There was an air vent but no windows, one simple bed, a table, a chair, and nothing else. Her request to go to the bathroom had been permitted, though they insisted she keep the door half open while she was inside.

'What am I doing here?' As she emerged she attempted to question them once again.

'Told you: shut up. You'll know soon,' hissed one of the men. She had never come across brute physical violence before, so she again forced herself to return peacefully to the cell. Left on her own, she lay down on the bed with her hands cupped behind her head, thinking about her predicament and what could conceivably lie behind it. There was no point in anyone kidnapping her, since neither she nor her family were rich, and no one else would ever consider paying a ransom for her. Such was her mental turmoil that it never once occurred to her that she had been abducted for her professional knowledge.

She pulled herself together and thought about ways to escape. She was resilient, which was why they had recruited her in the first place. She clearly remembered the day she had first been introduced to the awkward world of intelligence. It had been in the best traditions of the Service and she had been hardly aware of it when, shortly after she'd passed her finals at Cambridge, her professor, a dry and humourless figure whom she'd hardly exchanged a word with during her entire university career, invited her to his rooms for a celebratory glass of sherry. She had done well, he said. She showed huge aptitude. He had questioned her about her politics and seemed relieved when she declared herself apolitical. A few weeks after that she had received a rather odd letter: an invitation to an interview in Carlton House Terrace, just off Pall Mall in London. From there she had been subjected to a vigorous process of vetting and scrutiny, and, eventually, had been sent for training to the Special Intelligence Training Centre somewhere near Portsmouth. She had done well and come out top of her intake. She had been offered a full-time job with MI5, but eventually, after much soul-searching, she had turned it down in favour of a life of scientific research. But the Intelligence Community does not like to lose touch with good people. She willingly agreed to act as what they termed a 'sleeper'; she became the SSU's eyes and ears inside the Harman Institute.

What use were these intelligence skills now? The frightening experience she had just undergone reawakened the procedures she had learnt at the Portsmouth centre. Never in her wildest dreams had she believed she would ever be called upon to use them. What was it her long-forgotten instructor, a psychiatrist who had served in the Commandos, had said? 'They will react to force with force. If, for example, terrorists overrun your lab, don't try to be heroic. It won't work. But remember: terrorists or kidnappers are as nervous as their captives. You have to look for their Achilles heel: where they're weakest.' She would set out to identify that.

In the event, her ordeal proved relatively short-lived. It was both more and much less dramatic than she had feared. After about two hours, having been given only a plastic cup of Coca-Cola and a cold Macdonald's hamburger to eat, she was suddenly let out of her basement prison by two of the thugs and led up some stairs to the house above. There, waiting to meet her in a vast living room of expensive but execrable taste, were a blonde, silent woman who had seen better days, a huge bull of a man with a scar across his shaven head, and a small, neat Indian, who introduced himself as 'the family doctor'.

'You are Dr Rebecca Stevenson?' the latter asked, as if interviewing her for a job.

'Yes.'

'Of the Harman Institute? You're a virologist, I think? I was given your name . . .'

'Given? Who by? If you're really a doctor you ought to be struck off,' she said, boiling with suppressed fury.

'Cut the chat. Get on with it, Rafiq,' bellowed the big man. 'We ain't got all day.'

Rafiq looked terrified. His whole body was shaking. 'I'm terribly sorry, Dr Stevenson, but what could I . . .'

'Get on with it, I said!' the big man yelled again.

'Come this way, Dr Stevenson. It's most delicate,' stuttered Dr Rafiq with a despairing shrug.

Followed by the others, he led the way up a wide, purple-carpeted staircase to a huge bedroom where, spread-eagled on the bed, lay a very sick man. Dr Rafiq went up to the bed and stared closely at his patient. The man was unconscious.

Dr Stevenson came up behind him while the huge bald man and the blonde woman hesitated by the doorway.

'Your diagnosis, Dr Stevenson?' asked Rafiq. 'What is the matter with him? It's beyond me. Please, this is a most delicate matter.'

Rebecca Stevenson paused for a moment, then turned away abruptly and moved well back from the bed. 'I'm a medical researcher, not a physician,' she said. Despite her anger, she was shocked by the realization of what this case might be, having so recently seen the dying general. The man's eyes were open but there was that tell-tale grey pallor over the pupils, while the skin on his face was deeply infected with sores, and there were flecks of bloody foam round the edges of his lips. The dreadful possibility that this was another case of ZD198, plus the frightening experience she had just been subjected to, again stirred her instructor's warning: 'They'll react to force with force. Look for their Achilles heel: where they're weakest.' She had the whip hand. It was why they'd kidnapped her and brought her here, after all. Her expertise would win out if she kept cool. She acted with ruthless professionalism. 'Temperature?' she asked. 'No, don't touch him,' she barked, as Rafiq moved towards the bed. He jumped nervously at her shout. 'It is highly infectious,' she added. Had she been forced to lie, it would have been both understandable and believable, but no lies were needed here. 'Normally fatal,' she added, with quiet satisfaction.

'Temperature: 103 degrees,' responded Dr Rafiq, his voice shaking. 'I took it an hour ago.'

'Why isn't he in hospital?' Dr Stevenson demanded.

'None of your bloody business!' shouted Big Mac. He had retreated further and was now standing nervously well outside the door. Rebecca had continued to keep her distance from the bed. She ignored the others completely and addressed Dr Rafiq. 'I'd leave the room immediately,' she said, addressing Dr Rafiq. 'You're even less use to anyone dead,' she added neatly. 'This man is, I suspect, terminally ill. Anyone who's been in recent contact with him is in extreme danger of contamination. I'll get him admitted to an isolation hospital immediately. All of you go with him for blood tests.'

'You're not even going to feel his pulse or something?' asked Big Mac aggressively.

'It's why you brought me here, isn't it? That's my diagnosis. I'm not going anywhere near the body. Nor should anyone else unless they're wearing the right protective clothing.' Suddenly, from where she stood, she smelt the stench of death. Loss of control of bodily functions was but one of the hideous side-effects of the virus.

'Now,' she said coldly, 'out of here. All of you. Wait downstairs and do not move until the experts arrive. On pain of death – like his,' she added, then turned and walked quickly out of the door. No one tried to stop her. She heard the rush as they piled down the stairs close behind her. She went into the hall, found a telephone, and calmly started dialling. Her first call was to Professor Grant. It was late Saturday afternoon and he was at home, sitting in a deep armchair, reading a newspaper. Her call had the touch of the surreal about it.

'You were what?' he asked.

'I suppose I could call it kidnapped,' said Dr Stevenson coldly. 'That's by the by. We need the special team over here right now. Fully protected. We have another case.'

'Where are you?' asked Grant.

'There's a point. Where are we?' Dr Stevenson in turn demanded of Rafiq. She passed on to Grant his hesitant reply. Of Big Mac there was no sign. 'We'll need to isolate the house. Pull in all the patient's contacts. That should be fun,' she added. 'And I need you to check me out as well. I came pretty close to the body too.' When she'd finished with Grant, she picked up the phone again and got through to Duty Control at SSU headquarters. She gave them her personal password to identify herself, then explained briefly what had happened. They went wild.

Kisangani, Congo, Saturday 18th June

Clegg Hurley sat in his air-conditioned study with the windows shut and the temperature control turned as low as it would go, and considered his options. He looked accusingly at a huge hole which had suddenly appeared in the mosquito mesh outside on the verandah. He was always finding holes in mosquito nets: it was probably the young conscripts throwing stones. The early evening rains had passed and it was slightly cooler. He would have gone and sat on the big rattan chair outside but for the huge variety of moths and other insects which somehow had managed to find that solitary hole and were now almost blacking out the electric light on the verandah roof. He stared across the room at the top shelf of his bookcase which was neatly stacked with rows of bottles he had brought out to Africa with him: insect repellents, sting relief, salt and water purification tablets, factor fifteen sun lotions. He looked unhappily down at his ankles, which showed between his stocking tops and the bottoms of his long khaki trousers. The mosquito bites he'd got when he had first arrived had suppurated because he had scratched them so much; now they remained as permanent little scars of Africa. He was wearing sandals, but on the other side of the room were his shoes, shoes that if he didn't keep them in here in the relative cool, would grow green mould overnight. Even the air conditioning could not remove the permanent stench of primitive sanitation that this, the most modern house in the campus, had to endure. God, how he hated it all.

Eventually the hum of the air conditioning got to him. He had to breathe, had to escape. He turned off the light and opened the door from the study that led directly onto the verandah, quickly so that none of the bugs or mosquitoes would get in through the crack and into the room. Out there in the flickering light from the half-obscured bulb above him he stood silently, one hand resting on the verandah rail. He listened to the sounds of the night: the crackling hiss of the crickets, its wave of sound rising and falling, stopping for a moment, then starting up again, like some badly oiled machine. Out there, across the dirt track, beyond the overgrown railway lines that had once led to prosperous copper and diamond mines up country, past the rusted corrugated roofs of the African shanty town huts, beyond the dense wall of lianas and creepers, under the canopy of green that even in the brightest sunlight only let through small flickers of daylight, was the nightlife of Africa. Snakes, monkeys, the larger animals which frightened him less, the termites and other insects, and above all the spiders – he had a deep loathing of spiders. So why the hell was he still here?

As he stood there, he heard, above the cacophony of animal life, the sound of tribal drums. Until recently music had been like music the world over – hot rhythms pounding from every radio and cassette player. But since the collapse of the town's infrastructure and the terminal interruption of its power supplies, and as there were no batteries to be had for love nor money in the market, the Africans had reverted to their traditional music, with ancient stringed instruments and primitive woodwinds dug out of forgotten corners. Above all the tribal drums sounded again across the land. Hurley recalled that the Chinese had used tambourines to ward off war, evil spirits, and plagues. Could he blame anyone for trying: would it be any more futile than prayer? He stood in the darkness for a long time and was still there when a pair of headlights flickered out of the night, tossed by the potholed track. Hurley watched in mild curiosity as an old Volvo pulled up in front of his house. The lights died. He heard the car door creak open, then slam shut. He turned and waited as a man approached uncertainly up the path towards him.

The man paused when he saw the shadowy figure standing in the darkness of the verandah. 'Is that you, Mr Hurley?' he called.

'Yes. Who is it?'

'Thank God. Thank God you're here,' said Dr Banquier. 'I need your help.'

The Harman Institute, East London, Saturday 18th June

That Saturday evening, Grant and Guthrie listened in amazement to Rebecca Stevenson's experience with Tyndall and his thugs, but such was the pressure they were all under that they did not have time to marvel at it for long. She did not volunteer that she knew that the SSU, with the full support of Special Branch and backed by the Serious Crime Squad of the Metropolitan Police, had moved in on Tyndall's house and its operations in a massive way. It was a great excuse.

The Harman team now had four cases, two terminal: Rowland, who was still clinging to life, and Tyndall, who would probably die before the morning. The yawning gap in their understanding was what possible link there could be, or had been, between such different, high-profile victims. A team, under Dr Stevenson, was to be pulled together and their first task was to investigate the detailed backgrounds of all four cases, identifying possible common elements that might link a retired general, a peer of the realm, a famous thespian, and an East End mobster.

Late that night, though now desperately tired, Harper Guthrie was still seated at his computer, the David and Rosie models up on the screen in front of him. He had forced himself back to basics. There *must* be some physical link which they were all missing, unless of course Rebecca Stevenson uncovered some improbable vector contact between the victims. He thought back to research he had carried out some years earlier, when he'd been working on a new variant of the hantavirus, tracing it back to the first known outbreak in an American Indian reservation in May 1993. Working in collaboration with the American Center for Disease Control in Atlanta, Georgia, he had rapidly identified the carriers as American deer and mice, which spread it both through the air and via infected household pets. In that epidemic alone, of the 114 known cases, there had been a fifty per cent mortality rate. He'd recognized at the time, as did the Atlanta Center, that the statistics were probably misleading and that the true figure must have been higher, given that some doctors far removed from the outbreak would have failed to recognize the virus, because so many of its symptoms were like an extreme type of haemorrhagic fever. Flu itself could be deadly enough of course; no one in his profession could forget that over twenty-five million people died of it in the great epidemic of 1918. Even with modern reporting methods, such statistical lapses were widespread. More controversially, he had argued at the time that some doctors had probably been reluctant to test for the hantavirus for the simple reason that a person with it was untreatable. There was no known cure. Most dangerous of all to the statistician was that where an outbreak did occur, the first thing the local authorities did was to try to suppress the news to avoid public panic. They were in the initial stages of the same situation right now. Where and when would the disease strike next?

He went through to the lab kitchen, made himself a sandwich and some coffee, and brought them back to his desk. Vertical transmission was out of the question: Virus ZD198 was obviously not something inherited. It had to be horizontal, and presuming it was not passed on through sexual intercourse, like all other known viruses it must either be transferred through close contact with an infected person, as with the notorious traditional diseases like TB, diptheria or typhoid, or vector-borne, by insects or animals. Though he knew this latter method was also highly unlikely, he accessed the necessary database to remind himself of all the diseases that were normally carried in this way. Insects carried yellow fever, dengue and hepatitis B; other animal species could infect humans with the plague, rabies, or Lassa fever. On the evidence they had accumulated so far, Virus ZD198 did not fit any of these categories.

As he sat there, Guthrie became more and more convinced that once he knew the carrier he would be close to defeating the virus itself. He had closely noted the interesting WHO report which had come in from a Dr Boekamper in New York who, at the Harman Institute's request, had been trying to find out more about the recent outbreak in the Congo. Some doctor out there had reportedly insisted that, 'You can't just pick it up.' This tied in with Guthrie's unvoiced suspicions. He needed to find out, and soon.

He was exhausted. He'd call it a day and return to the agreeable little hotel they'd put him up in right next door to the Institute. How welcome that had been after his experience with Edinburgh's landlady from hell. What a Lady Macbeth she'd have made. Something about that fleeting image of the Shakespearean character, perhaps the thought of her bloody deeds, triggered something at the back of Guthrie's tired mind. He had always had a tendency to arrive at unexpected, intuitive solutions. Afterwards he'd had to work hard to make sure the facts fitted such gut instinct hypotheses. He looked at his watch: it was almost eleven at night. Too bad. With little hesitation he rang Rebecca Stevenson at home. The call woke her but she was soon listening intently. Perhaps the shock of the day with the Tyndall case made her less sceptical than she might otherwise have been when, after the preliminaries, he told her of his suspicions.

'It's provenly difficult to transfer this particular strain,' said Guthrie. 'That doctor in the Congo thinks so too. The people I've contacted in Atlanta tell me they've done it by injecting the virus directly into the brains of rats. They couldn't get it to take in any other way. The virus dies if it is away from the host body for only a few seconds.'

'Broken skin? That's as good as an injection in the right circumstances.' Rebecca Stevenson sat up in bed and stifled a yawn.

'Exactly, but . . .' replied Guthrie, interrupting her. 'I know you're going to think I'm nuts, but I'll say it nonetheless. I've been thinking. Broken skin, plus the live virus, is still not enough. In a lab it has to be transferred deliberately. Supposing therefore that someone has *deliberately* infected the individuals concerned?'

There was a short intake of breath at the other end of the telephone. 'Who in their right minds . . . ?' she responded, her voice reflecting her astonishment. Was he – no, Harper Guthrie was not some low-level American researcher, he had a great track record in the field.

'Not talking about somebody in their right mind,' came the softly spoken reply.

'So?' she prompted.

'So, what we have to establish,' said Guthrie softly, 'is any and all non-medical links between each case we know about.'

'We're already hard at work. But think: a criminal thug dying of it on a bed in the East End of London; at the other end of the probability scale one of Britain's heroic generals. I can't believe . . .' Rebecca hesitated. She no longer felt sleepy.

'My guess? There'll be others,' said Guthrie confidently.

'There will,' she echoed soberly, 'if you're right.'

'We need to get an urgent warning notice to all hospitals,' Guthrie suggested. 'Nothing about its method of transmission, of course.'

'You'll have to get Professor Grant to act. Warnings have to be on his authority,' she said. 'If you're right,' she added softly, 'we're going to have to work very closely on this.' When she put the phone down, she was only a little surprised to find that she was pleased by the prospect.

She got out of bed, slipped on a dressing gown and made a telephone call. 'Duty officer,' someone answered sleepily at the other end of the line. She announced herself, gave her personal password, then said: 'Take this down carefully, will you? We need to act fast.'

Kisangani, Congo, Saturday 18th June

'What's the problem?' asked Clegg Hurley, curious but reluctant to listen to why Dr Banquier had turned up on his doorstep, unannounced, and in such an obvious panic. They were sitting on the verandah, sipping at glasses of cold beer he had poured them both. It was the least he could do. The doctor licked his lips incessantly.

'I no brave, Mr Hurley,' he said. 'I put up too much, long time. These last days much too much. Heavy fighting up country. Place full with rumours. Most my staff have deserted; always sure sign something nasty coming. People say rebel forces less than twenty kilometers away. Now the rains past, they'll want control the town. Yesterday, soldiers stopped outside my school. Left in peace this time, thank God.'

'Government troops or rebels?' Hurley asked. Banquier shook his head. He did not know.

'You're leaving?'

Banquier nodded. 'You organize lift for me?'

'A lift?'

'Plane going out? I want go somewhere.'

'To Belgium?'

Banquier hesitated. 'No, no,' he said quickly. 'Lagos, Accra, Kampala, anywhere, anywhere safe.'

'That's why you came?'

'That not enough?' asked Banquier. He stared at Hurley.

'Of course.' Hurley waited for some moments. 'I don't know of any movements. Maybe later in the week.'

Banquier was still looking at him as if the answer hadn't mattered. 'Something else, too: further outbreak, I think. Soldiers tell me. I scared go look.'

'Outbreak?' Hurley was still thinking of the new fighting up country.

'No. One you ask about. Surge fever. Your people have a number. ZD something.'

'ZD198.'

'That's it. Know what?' he paused, as if tempting Hurley with something special.

'No told no one, never reported, though the colonel and I talked about it . . .'

'The colonel?'

'I tell you later. But this: you know I have marmoset monkeys? Had other breeds, too: baby chimpanzees when the natives brought them in. I see something like surge fever affect them . . .'

Hurley stared at him. 'What d'you mean? You're suggesting it leapt between species?'

'Why not? AIDS did. Marburg fever did.' Banquier shrugged, looked away, then took a gulp of his beer. 'Dunno. No want to stay and find out no more. Been around too long. Civil war and a new plague: good reasons to leave, eh?' He made a sound that might have been a suppressed laugh. Hurley was deeply uneasy. He wished Banquier hadn't come. He wanted to go to bed. He knew what was coming.

'No lift? You put me up a night, then?' asked Banquier, 'Or find somewhere I could bed down . . . ?'

'Sure, sure I could,' said Hurley unwillingly. It was the last thing he wanted, but how could he say no?

'Give us chance to talk.' Banquier smiled helpfully.

'Talk?' said Hurley, hoping it didn't sound ungracious.

'Tell you about the British colonel.'

'Who's he?' Hurley showed his puzzlement.

'May not matter. May fit in,' Banquier added, again looking hard at his host.

Well into the small hours of the next morning, Banquier worked his way steadily through most of a bottle of Hurley's whisky. As he drank he became more and more insistent on telling the story. By three in the morning he was drunk but still remarkably coherent. Hurley had to force himself to keep awake, unable to persuade his unwelcome guest to go to bed. Banquier began by explaining that he had first met the colonel by chance at a WHO sponsored conference in Kinshasa during a brief ceasefire in the civil war. The meeting had been arranged by Hurley's predecessor. At first Banquier had not appreciated that the man, small, dark, with intense staring eyes, was both an army colonel and a doctor. He'd kept very much to himself, but after it was all over he'd offered Banquier a lift back to his hotel. They'd begun chatting, then had dinner together, when they had discovered they were working close to each other near Kisangani.

Banquier was no psychologist, but he'd gradually built up a picture of Colonel Sam Broomfield. The man had so many chips on his shoulders, so many hang-ups, gripes and grievances, about everyone – family, friends, the army, the British Government. All that became strangely focused when he began talking about his secondment to the Congo, in the middle of the civil war. 'This has been my turning point,' the colonel had kept saying. Banquier had chosen to come here, but why the hell should he, Sam Broomfield, have had to serve for so long in such a hellish place? What business was it of the British, whose interests in the Congo were negligible? The Belgians, the French, the Germans, had a huge responsibility for the way the Democratic Republic of Congo, Zaire, call it what they wished, had developed over the years. It was the darkest part of the dark heart of Africa. But now that he was here, he protested, he had worked loyally, without too much complaint, even when confronting the hideous atrocities, the human carcasses in various states of mutilation, which were brought to him daily to amputate, to stitch up, to bury. It was his job; it was his calling. He accepted that. It was a brutal surgery, but he did it to the best of his ability and as humanely as possible, in the appalling conditions that prevailed in his dreadful, so-called field hospital. Hospital? The first thing he had done was to get the men to burn down the existing buildings and set up a field station, under canvas, in the cleanest stretch of open ground he could find nearby. That had been a dedicated action, applauded by all. Once he got going, Colonel Broomfield talked incessantly about himself, the work he was doing, how he felt that they had forgotten all about him back in London. At first he seemed totally uninterested in Banquier's operation. He kept going on about how he and his mixed-race team of medical assistants were doing such a good job. He felt almost proud. Then he'd been sent an unpleasant article about himself that had appeared in a British weekly magazine, after some VIP journalist had briefly turned up to see what he was doing. That had hurt; hurt him badly. But despite all the lies, surely a grateful nation would reward him? No decoration had come, perhaps because of the nasty article. There was no recognition, no letters of appreciation; worse still, there was no onward posting. He was ordered to stay on. Something within the colonel seemed ready to snap.

All this had been going on around the time that Dr Banquier and the colonel had first struck up their relationship. Perhaps it was because they were two of a kind; perhaps it was because there were so few others to whom they could usefully talk; perhaps it was because they both liked to slip down glass after glass of whatever alcohol they could find, late of an evening, particularly at the end of a hard day's sweaty, bloody labour.

Then the colonel began taking more and more of an interest in his new-found colleague and his work. If he was disapproving of some of Dr Banquier's research into the strange, animal-human laboratory which he called his 'School of Tropical Medicine', he did not show it. No one had ever been schooled there to the colonel's knowledge, but what, after all, was medicine but a continuing investigation, a search for the truth? The colonel had been remarkably complimentary about the detached and unemotional way Banquier carried out his investigations into the strange viruses that emerged, with a frightening inevitability, from the jungle of that part of Africa. Some were like those flesh-eating bugs so beloved of tabloid editors, some came as rare spinoff viruses which had no name, then disappeared again without a trace. And then, one day, Colonel Sam Broomfield had upped and gone, disappeared, without a single word of farewell. Banquier had been hurt by that. He'd expected more, particularly since the colonel had taken some things from his lab at the school, some odd items, without asking Banquier if he could. 'Stole them,' added the doctor. 'Yes, stole them.' Which was why, as he told a very sleepy Clegg Hurley, Dr Banquier fully expected that, one day, he would hear from the colonel again.

Ealing, West London, Sunday 19th June

Less than sixteen hours later the very same Colonel Sam Broomfield pushed himself out of a deep armchair, switched off the television, made himself a cup of black coffee, and then, instead of going up to bed, carefully turned out the hall light and let himself through a connecting door from the house into the little garage he'd had constructed up the side of the drive of his suburban semi in Ealing. There were two substantial locks on the door, then, inside, curiously, there was a second door to be negotiated before he could get into the garage itself. He knew his way in the dark and it was only when he was inside and had shut both doors firmly behind him that he switched on a light. Garage it may have appeared to be from the outside, but there was no car parked inside and the double doors to the drive were not only locked, but also welded together on the inside with steel bars, while all the windows were sealed and covered with what looked like sheets of thin, shiny rubber. Along the wall facing the double doors were two large stainless steel refrigerators, while on the long side of the wall, away from the house, a fully equipped laboratory bench had been built, with neat racks above it that held various pieces of complex glass and steel equipment. There were Bunsen burners and a small basin, and various jars of chemicals, all carefully labelled, some of which were stored inside a cabinet to which an exhaust fan had been fitted, to extract any noxious fumes into the London night.

But the dominating smells in the garage came from the opposite corner, from where the squeaks and squeals also came. There, fastened securely to the wall, was a high rack of cages, stacked above one another, with, inside each, a squirming mass of white rats, dozens upon dozens of them. The colonel went towards the racks and the squealing intensified as he carefully poured a measured helping of foodstuff from a bag into each feeding tray. When he had finished, he unhooked a clipboard from a nail on the wall and looked at a shortlist of eight or ten names and addresses he had written on it. As he came to one name he shook his head, as if regretting some act of folly, then went and stared at a calendar on the wall and appeared to be calculating something in his head. He pulled on some rubber gloves, opened one of the steel refrigerators and took out a two-inch-long glass phial, which was hermetically packed in gel inside a transparent plastic bag. He closed the door of the refrigerator, checked the temperature on a thermometer on the outside, switched off the light and returned to the house, locking the double doors carefully behind him.

Millbank, London, Monday 20th June

In an anonymous Millbank office room, a further taped intercept was being painstakingly transcribed. The first voice they now recognized as being that of Harper Guthrie, the other belonged to a male researcher at the Harman Institute.

How's it going?

I've upped the dosage and am waiting to see. It's all I can do.

The vector?

Not a hint on the vector right now. Rebecca's asked me to concentrate on the possible antidote. No joy there, either. Gestation period really puzzles me. It's so erratic.

You're using all my data – every little thing?

Back to basics, like you said. So why the huge difference in the virus showing itself, Harper?

Dunno. Might be genetic. You programmed in David and Rosie's full family history?

Sure. It's standard stuff. Not a trace of anything there.

Their parents?

You know the oldest joke in the life insurance business, Harper?

Not into jokes at the moment.

It goes like this: in any life insurance questionnaire, people are asked what their parents died of. You know what a common answer is?

Tell me.

They write, 'Nothing serious'. Can you believe it?

Really?

Really.

So what did David and Rosie's parents die of?

Nothing serious.

There was a pause.

Thanks. OK. I want you to leave all that for now. Drop it.

Drop it? All this research? I thought . . .

I want you to do something urgently for me. Like right now. I want you to drop everything you're doing and start putting onto your computer every detail we give you on all the four cases we've had so far. We're questioning everyone: doctors, friends, relations, to see if any of them, at any time, have had any contact whatsoever with, or have ever been to, Africa, or if anyone they know has been there in recent times. Is that clear?

That's not medical science, Harper. That's not my field.

It is from now on.

OK, Harper. Just as you wish.

And there the tape ended.

11

Too many uncomfortable things were happening in Lyle Thane's life all at the same time. He had watched more than a few public figures who had easily coped with crises in their business lives, but when those ran in tandem with some tragedy in their private, family circumstances, even the strongest of them had been damaged or destroyed. It was not quite that bad yet, but his private life was intruding too much right now. It was interfering with his work. He sat at his desk trying to think big, and it kept distracting him. His professional problems were not ones he had to solve alone; here he was merely doing his job. The worst that could happen would be that the PM's condition would deteriorate, the news would get out, and his job would be axed. What did that matter in the long run? He was going to have to jump ship some time in any case; there would, he flattered himself, be no shortage of offers. The outside commercial world had one major attraction: it would pay a hell of a lot more than current civil service rates at 10 Downing Street and that would help fund his future political career.

What kept threatening his peace of mind was Sarah St Just. He had just read the Dempster column in that morning's *Mail*. It linked her to a polo-playing scion of a minor titled family. He rang her, woke her up, and she angrily responded that it was all a pack of lies. Didn't he trust her, she asked? But what if she was playing a double game? Did that matter either? There were plenty of other pips in the orange. If she walked out, what would he really miss? Was it the sex? Was she discontented because that wasn't working as well as it should? She didn't seem to mind, but he . . . well, something serious was missing in that department. Would he be hurt if she ditched him? Would he miss being connected to the St Just name? Was it the image of a society wedding in St Margaret's, Westminster? He brooded, trying to isolate his worries, his anger, his physical frustrations, and ended up realizing that there was only one real factor in play: if Sarah abandoned him, there would be wounded pride. If that was all, it was time to find another pip to squeeze. He had to jump before she did.

But not yet. Timing was critical. He pulled out of another official reception, made his excuses with Eric Caldwell, and took Sarah to dinner at the most fashionable of the new Conran restaurants. He pulled strings and got the best table where they could see and be seen. He tipped off a hack who was in Daniel Evans's pocket, and the paparazzi were waiting outside the restaurant when the two of them arrived. The paps for some reason seemed to think – God knows how, he protested – that he was the story rather than her that evening. It was something to do with a rumour that he was the new power behind the PM on his new policy initiative on law and order. The paps shouted questions at him as they went in through the door, arm in arm. Grandly, he refused to comment. Sarah was more impressed than piqued by the fact that, for once, he was getting all the attention.

It set the scene for the evening. He was at his sparkling best. They both drank too much. He boasted about who he'd been meeting and talking to. He'd had a private chat with the Prince of Wales; he'd been advising the PM on the next cabinet reshuffle; he was off to Washington next week for twenty-four hours of meetings on the forthcoming defence review. Sarah was particularly impressed by the Prince Charles bit; she pressed him hard, and, not to put too fine a point on it, he built up a brief, 'Good morning, sir,' into a full-blooded heart-to-heart at St James's Palace.

Later, before they went on to Annabel's, he saw her attention wandering when some ill-shaven pop star and a noisy bunch of his female acolytes hove into the restaurant. Thane brought her back by boasting some more. He consumed a couple of double Scotches on the rocks. He swore her to secrecy, then hinted at a dark and tragic secret that could topple the Government. Sarah St Just wasn't much interested in governments, but later on she remembered enough of what he'd revealed to her about the PM's health when, in his drunken state, he decided that it mattered desperately to keep her interested in him until he was ready to ditch her.

It didn't work. With a lot of Scotch inside him, even cool men like him could lose the plot. Afterwards she point-blank refused to go home with him, and insisted he drop her off at her sister's flat in South Ken. It was bad news; he certainly shouldn't have been driving with all the drink he'd consumed. They had a heated row out in the middle of the street at two in the morning, yelling stupid abuse at each other. Someone opened a window above their heads and shouted at them to shut up or they'd call the police. He left her standing there, outside her sister's door, jumped into his BMW and drove off furiously into the night.

He wasn't clear what he was doing, but he knew he wanted something, something that had been missing in his life. He drove south, unsure, yet sure where he was heading. He crossed the Thames at Vauxhall Bridge, then drove down through Stockwell and Brixton to Clapham Common. He drove slowly the last part of the way, then, when he got there, he drove even slower. He shouldn't have come. What was he thinking of? There was a man, a young man, standing on his own, by a telephone kiosk. He stopped the car and wound down the window. The young man turned, then walked slowly and meaningfully towards him. At the last moment he came to: Christ, what the fuck was he doing? He slammed the car into gear and sped off homewards, leaving the young man standing alone once again by the kiosk. Lyle Thane was cursing to himself: cursing, cursing. What a fool he was; what a fool he'd nearly been.

Lucy Saltmarsh was not a well-known figure in the media world. But she'd had luck in her career so far – luck, plus a few strings pulled by a father who had good contacts in television. One way or another she would have got along on her own, since she was both bright and determined, but her daddy's telephone call to the programme editor certainly helped her move from her local newspaper to a top-level work experience placement with BBC's *Newsnight* team, those pre-eminent deflators of pompous politicians. Lucy was pretty, tough, single-minded and her physical assets were well proportioned. She didn't mind making the tea and coffee and running little errands, but she also knew how to dress to attract the attention of men, so it was not long before some of the key people at *Newsnight* became aware of her presence. Joe Tinker, the most famous face of all, the scourge among scourges, had an eye for a pretty face, and an even more experienced eye for the well-endowed figure of Miss Saltmarsh. He gravitated towards her late one evening after closedown, and began chatting to her without any introduction. Why should he bother? She knew who he was; in due course he would find out all he needed to know about her. He knew a little already: she was young, vulnerable, and on a work experience secondment. He thought he had summed her up as an easy lay. That she proved to be surprisingly difficult to bed was all part of her longterm career strategy: to suggest that she might be available, but get what she wanted first, namely a guaranteed entrée into the big wide world of television. In such negotiations timing is crucial; he thought he had ensnared her while in fact, she had ensnared him.

When the Rumbold story broke, they had still not been to bed together, so Joe Tinker was giving her his fullest attention. She knew a lot about his private life – that he was separated from his wife and that he had a reputation for bedding anything that moved. She wasn't in the business of adding to his score without getting something in return. She flattered him by asking his advice. She told him about projects she would like to develop in the future. What did he think of them, she asked? He put on a pretence but didn't actually listen. 'Let's go find a drink and talk about it,' he said softly. As the two of them left together, the night studio staff watched them go and shared a common thought about what would happen next. It wasn't quite like that. Maybe they did go to bed together, but she got her payback too.

One tiny feather in Lucy Saltmarsh's cap was that she was the young cub reporter on her local paper – a mere three weeks earlier – who had written up the story of Lord Rumbold's strange disappearance, the one which had ended with an odd list of unanswered questions. Which was why she rushed in to see Tinker the next day as soon as the Reuters' story came up on the screens. His more basic motives apart, Tinker was intrigued by just how much she knew about the peer's disappearance. He had forgotten all about Lord Rumbold, and *Newsnight* had not intended to make much out of his death until Lucy started filling some of the gaps. Her unanswered questions were still largely unanswered, so Tinker put her onto coming up with the answers. Later that evening it wasn't the answers that fascinated, it was the remaining outstanding questions. Lucy had been very active and returned with four new puzzles. Why had he been hidden away in a private clinic in Scotland? What was the mystery of his final horrific illness? Why, after all the preparations had been made, had his funeral suddenly been cancelled on the orders of the Chief Medical Officer of Health? Why had a specialist medical team from the Viral Research Facility of the Harman Institute been urgently sent to Scotland to investigate? Lucy Saltmarsh wrote up the story in the context of Lord Lucan and other eminent disappearances of the past. It made sexy television viewing. It caused quite a stir on the night, and much more of one in the days ahead. It also helped to launch Lucy into a glittering career, particularly when, by dint of questioning the family doctor and the staff at the clinic, she was the first to break the news of some new and deadly virus which had caused the peer's death. The next day, when the rest of the British press followed it up, no amount of spinning by the health authorities could stop the story. This one would run and run.

Colonel Sam Broomfield always went to the cinema on a Tuesday evening. The mornings were taken up by a leisurely breakfast and the daily papers. In the afternoon he dozed or worked, but around six on that Tuesday evening he dressed smartly, in a blazer and grey flannels, and went for the five-minute walk to the local cinema. That night it was some stupid American gangster film and only a handful of people were there; it didn't matter much, he always felt refreshed after a visit to the cinema.

It was by pure chance that Eric and Rob, two twelve-year-old budding vandals from the next street, went past the colonel's house that particular Tuesday evening after school. They had stolen some cigarettes from Rob's mother. They had matches. They were on the lookout for a suitably secret hiding place. At the street corner they noticed that a privet hedge ran thickly up beside a garage that had been built onto the side of one of the semis. Between the hedge and the back of the garage there was a splendidly dark and secret place.

It wasn't a great success. The matches were damp and the cigarette, once lit, was a turn-off. It made Eric feel quite sick. He coughed so much that someone somewhere close by opened a door and looked around, wondering what was going on. When that happened, Eric and Rob huddled in silence, excitement and fear, and remained undiscovered.

Now that they had found their den, they were reluctant to leave it. There was a gap between the hedge and the back of the garage; up above them the branches grew strongly, like a roof of African jungle green. Even if it had rained, they would be safe and dry there. But after a while it got a bit boring. They'd come ill-prepared apart from the cigarettes. Next time they'd bring comics, crisps and Coke. But the garage wall was interesting. There was an odd little square panel, right at the bottom corner, which seemed to be part of the structure. Perhaps, because it had been built from a kit, it was where the utilities, electricity and water, were meant to be brought in. But because this garage was tacked onto the house, the panel had not been used. It was quite loose, held on by a couple of rusting screws. Rob had his banned penknife with him so it was the work of only a moment to get the panel off. Sadly it was much too small, about nine inches by nine, for even a twelve-year-old to squeeze through. What was this beyond? Wire mesh and something squeaking? Rob bravely reached his hand in and nervously pulled at some of the mesh. It gave to his efforts, but then something alive started moving about inside. Terrified, he withdrew his hand from the hole. The two boys did not even wait to see the results of what they had done, but in a blind panic they pushed and struggled to escape from their den and then, reaching the road, kept running till they reached home, totally unaware of what exactly had frightened them.

It took some moments before a large and equally terrified white rat appeared at the flap, looking around in bewilderment with its pink eyes at this new environment it had suddenly been released into, then cautiously emerged to explore the natural delights of the roots and branches of the privet hedge.

The Savoy, Central London, Tuesday 21st June

It was the dullest of Cool Britannia receptions. Sir Mark, surveying the throng of young thrusting wannabes struggling for recognition, suppressed a feeling of disdain. The Savoy this evening was very much not his scene. He knew a few people in the room of course, though most of these he would avoid. Over there was the once-great Lord Shand, drooling in a corner over some young woman a third of his age. That old man never learnt. In another corner, Lord Milner was heavily engaged with the Private Secretary to the Chancellor of the Exchequer, so he left them in peace. Sir Mark was still invited to many receptions where the hosts felt that some older grandees might add a certain levity to the New Labour throng, but he didn't often go. A lot of people recognized him, since at one time he'd been a familiar face on television, pontificating about this or that, known as the most brilliant of behind-the-scenes operators. He stood for a moment, chatting in a desultory way with the former leader of the Liberal Democrats, Lord Steel, before deciding that enough was enough and that he would be far better off at his club, the Garrick, where he would find some other like-minded colleagues. Politics bored him now. They lacked style. They lacked depth. He knew he was getting old, getting jaded. He'd seen it all.

As he was about to leave, one of the Young Turks from Number Ten came into the room at a gallop and spotted him. The man's name was forgettable, but Sir Mark did remember he had met him briefly during his last call on the PM. Despite the fact that there were lots of people present whom those of Lyle Thane's ilk would normally stop and talk to, the latter made a beeline for him, and somewhat impertinently steered him into a corner. The man came to the point immediately. 'Sorry to buttonhole you like this, Sir Mark,' he said. 'We've got a problem.'

'We?' prompted Sir Mark, cautiously.

'A few of us at Number Ten. I was sent to find you.'

'I don't hide . . .'

'Sorry, Sir Mark. Didn't mean that. I tracked you here, via your office. I mean we've a real problem.'

'You mean the Prime Minister has?'

'Very delicate, Sir Mark.'

'I've had experience of delicate matters.'

'Sorry. I know that, sir. Just that this is especially tricky.'

'So what's the Prime Minister's problem?'

'The Prime Minister *is* the problem. Can I explain?'

Sir Mark's detached approach to political life was suddenly abandoned. He listened closely to what Lyle Thane was whispering.

The young man had his fullest attention. By eight o'clock that evening, Sir Mark had also abandoned any thought of going to the Garrick. Thane had already left the reception and was waiting for him outside, at the Strand entrance, in the back of an official car. He went out to join him, but before he could sit down behind the driver Sir Mark had to push aside a copy of that morning's *Daily Mail*. It was open at the Dempster column, where a headline read: 'Socialite Sarah jilts PM's Man'. Thane looked embarrassed. 'Me, I'm afraid,' he shrugged. 'Number Ten plays havoc with one's life.' Sir Mark well remembered how the stresses and strains of government work often became unbearable for many politicians and advisers he had worked with in the past. The hours were desperately long, and the availability of enthusiastic young people of the opposite sex was all too present. Work hard, play hard, and burn up early, was an everlasting theme. Ambition was only removed from most politicians' veins by embalming fluid.

When they got to Number Ten and Sir Mark was ushered through the familiar doorway, despite his earlier cynicism he felt more than a little stimulated by the problem he was about to confront. The PM did not realize he needed Sir Mark's services; he was safely ensconced in the private flat, working through Government papers. In the diary, his wife, Janet, was listed as being with a friend; in fact, Thane had whispered, Mrs Morgan had a late-night appointment with a trusted psychiatrist, so stressed was she by what had been going on. They went straight through to the Prime Minister's Private Secretary's office. Sir Mark shook hands with Eric Caldwell, then with Daniel Evans, the Press Secretary. The four men settled down round a table to discuss how they were going to play things.

'What do you suggest?' asked Caldwell.

'Before I answer,' said Sir Mark, 'I need to know everything. No secrets, OK?'

'We've tried to tell him,' Evans interrupted. 'PM refuses to believe anything's wrong.'

'So?' Sir Mark looked round at the three others. 'Why me?'

'You're the spindoctor,' said Caldwell. 'You've got to bell the cat.'

Sir Mark prepared his ground as thoroughly as he had always done. He talked on the telephone to Professor Grant, then questioned the PM's own doctor, Taylor, as to how he might best confront him. Then Caldwell rang the PM's flat and asked if Sir Mark could come up and see him urgently. It was well past nine o'clock in the evening. With Thane lurking nearby, Ivor was ushered into the PM's presence. The ultimate spindoctor had come to deliver a devastating personal message to a man in a position of the greatest power, who not only refused to believe that any problem existed, but would also certainly react very badly indeed to any suggestion that he was not medically fit for the position he held.

The meeting began uneasily. The PM sensed some odd agenda.

'So, Mark,' the PM began, 'what's your problem? And so late at night? Eric said there was some crisis you wanted to discuss urgently. I hope you've got a bloody good excuse.' The PM was both irritable and distracted. He was also puzzled. Usually, when he had meetings with people like Ivor, there were staff around to take notes and progress any future action that might be required.

His visitor decided to take the bull by the horns. 'Prime Minister,' he began, 'I've been delegated to see you, to share a problem with you. You don't realize it, but Janet and a number of your closest advisers believe you should . . . you are . . . you must . . .'

Sir Mark's voice tailed away as he saw what had happened to the PM. He'd taken his eyes off him for only the briefest moment, out of embarrassment. Peter Morgan was sitting in exactly the same position, but his whole body seemed to have locked rigid, while his eyes, which were still wide open, were coated with an unusual film of grey. With equal measures of shock and disbelief, Ivor seized his opportunity. He stood up, rushed to the door and threw it open, calling out loud for Thane and Caldwell.

'OK,' he said, showing the mettle for which he had once been famous, 'no more fooling. His life – as well as the Government's – could be at risk if this continues. Call an ambulance at once. Right now. Get Professor Grant and Dr Taylor here fast. Tell Janet, and get Daniel Evans to draft the press release. I want to see it first. The PM's being admitted to hospital "for tests" – that's all, d'you understand?' Behind him he heard movements coming from the PM's study. He neither turned nor looked back. 'Don't listen to any objections. Neither from him nor anyone, d'you hear? I'll take full responsibility for telling his doctors that Mr Morgan should be sedated if he gives any trouble. For his own good, and, if necessary, by force,' he added. Even then he did not turn round to face the incredulous fury of the man he had just come to see.

12

Ealing, West London, Wednesday 22nd June

Mrs Smith had been deeply saddened when the pigeons began to die. She'd always considered them to be rather like pets, even though they played havoc with her pretty little back garden and defecated all over the flagstones making up the patio. She didn't mind having to wash the area down before she had friends out there for tea, on the occasional day when the sun shone brightly enough for them to sit outside. No, she had been most upset when the pigeons began to die, and speculated which of her neighbours might have been spreading poisoned birdseed around. She had gone to complain to the council, but they, for whatever reason, refused to take any action.

Mrs Smith had once had a furious row with the retired army colonel who lived in the semi-detached house at the corner. He had come out and shouted at her when she appeared on the street to feed them with stale pieces of bread. 'You just cause them to breed, and they become even more of a health hazard!' he had rudely bellowed at her. She had resolutely continued to feed them on a daily basis, and there had been a war of silence ever since. But he'd been an officer in the British Army, so it couldn't be anything to do with him.

And now there was Minnie. Minnie was her cat and she'd watched her days before, prowling around the outside of that garage the colonel had built for himself. Why he had a garage she couldn't understand, since he didn't seem to have a car. She'd called out to Minnie when she saw she was eating something. It was horrible; it looked like the remains of a big white rat. With difficulty she got it away from Minnie, wrapped it in newspaper and threw it in the dustbin.

Two days later Mrs Smith was even sadder when Minnie turned ill. Mrs Smith called the vet when she saw the cat writhing in agony on the carpet. 'I bet it was that rat, or you've been eating one of those dead pigeons, you silly thing,' said Mrs Smith, trying to coax the frantic animal into drinking a little milk. It was obviously in great pain, for it clawed her, scratching her quite severely across the back of her hand. Mrs Smith didn't like that at all. She rang the vet again and told him to hurry, but by the time he arrived, Minnie was dead. The vet looked at the scratches on the back of Mrs Smith's hand and suggested that she should see her doctor and get herself an injection 'just in case'. He listened to what Mrs Smith had said about the white rat and the dead pigeons and took the cat's body away in a box, fully intending to get an animal autopsy done, 'just in case', he repeated. But the vet was particularly busy that week and never actually got around to arranging it. Minnie's body was disposed of rather carelessly by the vet's assistant, and, even now, it was being pulled apart by a marauding fox on the local rubbish tip.

Two days later, Mrs Smith herself began to shiver and shake. She didn't know where she was, and all her joints began to ache in a most distressing way. And all because of Minnie and the big white rat.

The Harman Institute, East London, Wednesday 22nd June

It was devastating: even the preliminary tests indicated that the PM almost certainly had Virus ZD198. The prognosis was bleak. Overnight, both Tyndall and Rowland had died. So far, the press were still concentrating on Lord Rumbold's death, but it would only be a matter of hours. In the event, despite pleas from Thane and Caldwell, the briefing session, which had been called by the Chief Medical Officer of Health in conjunction with the Secretary to the Cabinet to assess the situation prior to an emergency meeting of the whole Cabinet later that evening, was held at the Harman Institute.

Professor Grant was adamant: 'I cannot,' he said, 'begin to explain to everyone what the problem is without you all coming here. I have the data; I can show everyone the photographs. We've carefully plotted the details of each case. It would be impossible in the time available to bring all this material over to Downing Street. Besides, there are serious health and security issues. I don't like taking any of this stuff outside our safe building. If we're to explain fully, I'll also have to have my team along with me.' Professor Grant had continued. 'Dr Rebecca Stevenson is one of the foremost British virologists, while Dr Harper Guthrie, who has written the most advanced research papers on ZD198, is an American from . . .'

'American? We can't have him, professor. This is a highly delicate political matter. We wouldn't want the Americans to –' Thane looked at Caldwell, who nodded his agreement.

'You've heard of medical confidence,' responded Grant, sharply. 'You needn't worry.'

'But I –'

'There's no argument. We work as a team. Dr Guthrie can, like all of us, keep a secret, I can assure you.' Grant stared at the two men until they reluctantly nodded.

When Thane was shown into the Institute, it brought back immediate memories of chemistry lessons at school. Yet it was all so different, so clean, so clinical. Apart from the high security, Number Ten seemed a million miles away. Here was a world of white lab-coats, including the one he himself was instructed to put on, on which was pinned an identity pass with a barcode on it, which allowed him through the fumigation and sterilization chambers into the research laboratory itself. Here were glistening racks stacked with tissue culture flasks, incubation tanks and other hi-tech biotechnology apparatus, which was used to isolate and examine everything from leprosy to legionnaires' disease. Here he heard highly technical talk of transgenic processes, the transfer of human genes to animals, so that by becoming more human, laboratory pigs and chimps could have their body parts more effectively plundered for scientific testing. He was led past lab after sealed lab where small research teams, some in astronaut-style bodysuits, worked under fluorescent light, since the windows were all barred and blanked out by huge refrigeration units which lined every wall. Thane felt out of place in this unfamiliar environment, yet Caldwell and the Secretary to the Cabinet had already decreed that his was to be a critical role as the link between the Institute and the real or unreal world of politics outside.

While he waited for the others to arrive, Dr Stevenson gave Thane a brief tour of the building. 'We study a whole range of pathogens here – sorry, that means any organisms which cause disease,' she explained. 'The histopathology sections monitor the cytopathic effect of various bugs on body tissues. We have other teams working on identifying germs that actually ward off certain viruses. People accuse us of genetic engineering, but that's what nature itself does all the time – developing the body's immune systems. All we do is try and speed up the process.'

They walked together along clinically spotless corridors. To left and right, through triple-glass screens, she pointed to where white-coated scientists, trays of samples in front of them, were monitoring screens, on which, to him, meaningless charts and graphs appeared. 'At the far end,' she pointed, 'one wing of the building houses a team that's working *only* on common cold viruses. I say 'only' but I believe they've identified over two hundred varieties of rhinovirus. That's why a cold's so difficult to treat, since anti-viral agents are highly selective as to what they'll kill. So if a sniffle is that difficult to conquer, you'll see why . . .' She paused.

'Those?' asked Thane, pointing to a sinister-looking stack of black PVC sheets on a trolley outside a barred steel door.

'If you must know, bodybags. That's the door to the morgue and incinerator. If we fail, which sadly we do, the main thing, once we've taken all the samples we can safely handle, is to do our damnedest to make sure no one else gets infected.' Thane gave an involuntary shudder as Dr Stevenson led him past the doors of another high security facility, and stopped outside. 'We have low, medium and high risk areas, depending on what we're researching. Even I'm not allowed into this one without written permission: Lassa fever, hantavirus, Ebola and so on. People in there wear specially designed protective suits with hoods, masks and sealed oxygen cylinders. From that you'll gather we take some viruses very seriously indeed. You don't play games with nature's enemies, particularly those which deliver a one hundred per cent mortality rate.'

By six-thirty that evening, all the key people were seated in a semi-circle in the corner of the main research laboratory. Daniel Evans hadn't come. He was up to his eyes handling the news of the PM's admission to hospital. The press still hadn't linked the other deaths but it was just a matter of time, and after tonight's emergency Cabinet meeting, everything would be up for grabs. Despite her pleas, Janet Morgan had been banned from coming since she would have added a distressingly personal dimension to their discussions.

Professor Grant opened the proceedings by pointing to a rough diagram he had drawn on a flipchart. 'As most of you know by now,' he began, 'this particular bug has the very unsexy name of Virus ZD198. In Africa it's traditionally known as surge fever, and has been around for some years. As far as we know, the most recent cases have all been in the Eastern Congo, which, as anyone who reads the tabloids knows, has been the source of several very nasty diseases over the years. We believe that many of them have jumped species – from monkeys and chimps. It's a process known as zoonosis. We've never got to the bottom of why so many have emerged from that particular location, but that's neither here nor there for the time being.

'Virus ZD198 is particularly puzzling to us because of its highly erratic incubation period. We're sure that a lot of people probably harbour the virus without developing any unpleasant symptoms. In that respect it's like someone being HIV positive without developing full-blown AIDS. To give you another example, a large number of us carry various strains of meningitis in our bodies but, thankfully, few of us actually develop cerebral meningitis as a result. Virus ZD198 is another case in point. Until last night, we believed we'd had only four cases here in Britain. We're urgently working back through the records since there may have been others which were not properly diagnosed. With a virus as rare as this, it's perfectly understandable that doctors are not equipped to recognize it. My research team is, at this very moment, going through the medical records of every major hospital in Great Britain and Northern Ireland, and we've only identified one or two possible outbreaks over the last three years which we are going to follow up.

'The other significant fact is the highly irregular progress of the disease. It can be extremely rapid, and by that I mean from first symptoms through to death in a matter of forty-eight hours, or, as we've seen with the PM and Lord Rumbold, it can develop extremely slowly, beginning with short-term memory lapses through to its aggravated and dreadful final symptoms. The General George case, the first to be identified by us, appeared a mere four weeks ago. Here too it began with short-term memory loss, then it appeared to stabilize for some time, before it accelerated in the final shocking hours. I gather that roughly the same thing happened with Tyndall and Ralph Rowland, so one cannot blame their doctors when at first their patients appeared only to be losing their minds.'

'Other key things we need to know?' Eric Caldwell broke in. He kept glancing nervously at his watch. Halfway through Grant's summary, an assistant had come in with an urgent message from Winston Rogerson, the Deputy Prime Minister. He had heard the news at second hand, and was screaming to see him before the Cabinet meeting.

'Before you go, I'll ask Dr Guthrie to explain one, highly speculative theory of his,' Grant replied. 'I'm far from convinced, but he's the world expert on vector transfers – the way any virus gets carried from one host to another, often leapfrogging over millions of other potential victims in the process.'

Everyone turned to look at Guthrie. He began hesitantly, in his soft American drawl. He did not have their full attention at first, but then, as he developed his argument, they all sat forward in their chairs and listened very intently indeed.

'Let me put my theory to you, ladies and gentlemen,' Guthrie began. 'I have no proof as yet, but we've all been working on it, flat out. To start with, the virus so far can only get into the body through broken skin . . .'

'So far?' asked someone.

'So far. Viruses are clever. They change. They find new ways of travelling. At this point in time, I believe it has to be via broken skin. You're all thinking of AIDS and used hypodermics, but probably everyone round this table has enough of a break in their skin to do the trick: spots, eczema, shaving rash, scalp infections, athlete's foot, haemorrhoids, even – and I've just thought of another, bleeding gums.'

'Bleeding . . . for God's sake!' one of the audience burst out. 'What are you saying, Dr Guthrie?'

'I'm saying that . . . that the infection could get in in a number of different ways . . . If kept active, alive in some way, then it could be *deliberately applied*. You understand what I'm saying?'

There was a long silence, then everyone began talking at once.

White City, West London, Wednesday 22nd June

Some secrets are just too big. The most sensational of them often appear in the press before some of the key players know anything about it. Joe Tinker had picked up rumours of something serious going on, but Daniel Evans was unusually tightlipped, saying very little beyond the fact that the PM had been admitted to hospital 'for tests'. Meanwhile Lucy Saltmarsh had been proving her worth and had uncovered a lot of the horrific detail even before Eric Caldwell got round to briefing Winston Rogerson. There was now no way that Number Ten's attempt to hang onto the 'routine tests' line, until the Prime Minister's condition had been properly assessed, could hold.

As Joe Tinker walked into the *Newsnight* studio late that afternoon, ready to work up the story for the late evening news, he was waylaid by Lucy Saltmarsh. He felt guilty about Lucy. After her Rumbold break he'd picked her up and put her down, and then hoped they could make a clean break. When she accosted him, he was expecting some kind of moral blackmail.

What he did not expect, when he said, 'Hi, Lucy, how's tricks?' was for her to quietly hiss, 'I've got the biggest story you're ever going to have.' He made to pass her, but she moved to block his way, staring fiercely at him with her steel-blue eyes. 'I tell you, Joe, I've got the biggest story ever. Are you going to listen, or am I going to take it elsewhere?'

'OK, OK, come on, sit down. Tell me about it,' said Tinker. He saw he was going to have to let her down gently or she could make trouble for him.

'This is to be *my* story. I want everyone to know it's *my* story,' stressed Lucy Saltmarsh.

'OK, I promise you,' said Tinker indulgently. Who the hell did this chick think she was?

Lucy lowered her voice to a whisper. 'A promise? Right?' Joe Tinker nodded again.

'You remember you told me you thought the PM was drunk the other day – when you interviewed him?'

'Yup. Thought he'd just lost his marbles. And?' He waited for her to go on. He had a lot of other pressing stories to work on.

'It's like this. I've got a new flatmate.'

'So what's new?' Tinker muttered, just managing to control his irritation.

'This girl's called Sarah. Sarah St Just.'

'Lucy, I haven't got time for your life history.'

'You're going to listen?' Lucy Saltmarsh's voice hardened as she stood up. 'I tell you, I can go somewhere else. You're going to look the class one idiot if you don't take this up.'

'Hey, what the hell is this about?' responded Tinker, aggressively. 'Don't you start threatening –'

'Two minutes,' said Lucy, 'or I'll go straight to the editor. I've got it written out here. I'll show it to him and tell him that you didn't see a stunner staring you in the face.'

'I don't like being . . .'

'It's down to one minute,' she hissed.

'OK, OK. Sorry.' Tinker settled back and glanced at his watch. 'So tell me about it.'

'Right. My new flatmate's called Sarah. She's the angry ex-girlfriend of one Lyle Thane, whom you may have met. He's the number two whippet in the PM's office. Know him?'

'Met him.'

'She's just walked out on him. He was working too hard. Ignoring her. Tried to patch it up. Hinted about some great big cover-up to do with the PM's health. He came round to our flat late last night. He was very drunk, very tired. They went to the bedroom. I heard a lot of quarrelling. I heard him talking and shouting, I couldn't help it. The door was half ajar. Did you see last night's news story, from the *Newsnight* crime correspondent, about that Mafia guy – what's he called, Tyndall – who was admitted desperately ill to the East End hospital? He died,' she added.

'I saw something,' Tinker muttered. He wasn't sure where all this was going.

'OK. Tyndall, Lord Rumbold, then, wait for it, you remember that general, Sir George Haycock, who popped off a few weeks ago?'

'Yep. Interviewed him in the past,' said Tinker. 'Gulf War Syndrome stuff, I think. Surely he's –'

'Him too, Joe. But now, guess what? Now there are stories about Ralph Rowland, and to top it all, the Prime Minister himself. Peter Morgan! They're all suspected victims of *the same virus*! They're desperately trying to do a cover-up on the PM's condition. But they can't for long. He's been rushed into an isolation unit: intensive care, the lot. Know why? This bug kills one hundred per cent of its victims.'

There was a long silence. Joe Tinker had turned pale with excitement. He bent over and kissed her passionately. 'Tell me more, Lucy. This is going to make your career,' he said.

10 Downing Street, London, Wednesday 22nd June

Every single member of the Cabinet was present, except for the Prime Minister himself. No one had called off, despite the fact that they had been so hastily summoned. Since then, Daniel Evans had picked up that *Newsnight* were going to lead with the story. The timing was critical. The Cabinet Secretary was the only non-minister seated at the long table, while round the walls sat Thane, the Press Secretary, and a handful of other Downing Street advisers. Thane looked round the room, waiting until the last of the ministers, Winston Rogerson, arrived. The PM's deputy had been fully briefed beforehand by Caldwell, and it had been a stormy meeting. Rogerson had demanded to know why the hell he had not been kept in the picture until now. His furious words, 'Heads are going to roll over this,' had echoed around Number Ten. Caldwell's plea that they had tried to keep it quiet for the sake of the Prime Minister and Mrs Morgan, played no weight at all in the Deputy's judgment. In the event, Rogerson barged into the Cabinet room, sat down at one end of the table and stared angrily round at his colleagues. Normally at Cabinet meetings some members would be alert and vigorous while others always looked half asleep; some had brilliant minds and others were total dullards, typical of any Cabinet at any time in British history. Tonight there were no papers in front of them as there would be for a normal Cabinet meeting, while the number of civil servants in attendance on each minister had been strictly limited, with the exception of a clutch of senior staff with the Home Secretary and the Minister of Health. On them would fall the burden of actioning what happened next.

Rogerson set the tone. 'I'm bloody furious,' he began. 'I gather this has been going on for almost two weeks, and I knew nothing whatsoever about it. There's been a wicked conspiracy of silence about the health of poor Peter. I've heard all the excuses from Caldwell about not wanting to upset Janet, or their hope that it was some minor mental blip that would sort itself out. The blunt fact of the matter is that the PM's doctor is way out of his depth. Then this man, Professor Grant, whom you'll all have heard about, was brought in in secret and very unfairly presented with the problem by these unelected Downing Street staffers.' Rogerson waved in the direction of Caldwell. 'Believe it or not, it was left to that well known figure from the previous government's time, Sir Mark Ivor of all people, to take the bull by the horns and bring everyone to their senses.'

Rogerson again paused and waved in the direction of Caldwell, Thane and his colleagues. 'Whether it was for reasons of their own self-protection,' he went on, 'is a matter for later debate. What we've got now is a desperately sick Prime Minister. The prognosis is very bad indeed. At this moment he's barely conscious and is being held, against his will, in a high-security isolation unit. Daniel Evans has a draft press release of what we intend saying after this meeting. We don't want any panic, and I don't think the Opposition will take too much advantage, given the circumstances. We must tell the truth, that he's suffering from a severe viral infection. No one will make immediate political capital out of that. But now you need to know the real background: it's potentially disastrous. Which is why we're going to bring in Professor Grant, his assistant, Dr Stevenson, and, more unusually at Cabinet, an American research colleague of theirs, a Dr Harper Guthrie, who, I'm told, is an outstanding expert in the field.' Rogerson paused and made a signal to one of the secretaries who went outside and brought in a nervous Professor Grant, followed by his two colleagues.

Grant was immediately invited to begin his briefing. 'Can I begin, ladies and gentlemen, by illustrating our problem in comparison with those meningitis cases we keep reading about?' he said. 'They tend to affect young professional people, at school or university and so on. They occur in clusters, yet even with a huge amount of effort by the doctors involved, it often proves impossible to find out precisely how the outbreak has spread. Yet we've been dealing with meningitis for ages.'

'So no wonder you're lost with ZD198,' Rogerson interrupted. 'That what you're saying?'

Grant paused, nodded and continued. 'Right, minister. Viruses appear very suddenly from nowhere. Some are hardy or mutate quickly in order to survive. Other types, put simply, are pretty stupid. The Ebola virus is one of these. Highly virulent, it kills its host, the victim, before it has time to spread to other people, so it dies out.'

'That's the one the tabloids called the flesh-eating virus, isn't it? I never thought of it as stupid,' remarked one minister.

'Stupid in survival terms,' Grant went on. 'Except that, right now, scientists are waiting for a cleverer strain to emerge, one that gestates more slowly, giving itself time to spread and mature. Like HIV. From an evolutionary point of view, even bugs want to live. Our guess is that another, less virulent strain of Ebola will emerge some day soon, hiding itself, gestating quietly, until it knows it can survive in lots of different hosts. We can only hope we'll be ready for it when it does.'

'We haven't time for an academic lecture, professor,' interrupted Rogerson belligerently.

'You haven't time not to,' Grant retorted with unexpected vigour. 'Either understand the medical background or face the consequences. Can I now ask Dr Guthrie to continue, please?' Rogerson went puce in the face with fury but said nothing.

Guthrie's approach at first seemed even more academic. 'At the time of your Black Death,' he began, 'people thought that infection was spread by smell. Then they wondered if it was the birds. Remember *Ring o' Roses*? Its second verse?' He recited:

> *'The birds upon the steeple,*
> *Sit high above the people.*
> *Atishoo, Atishoo,*
> *We all fall down.'*

He paused and looked around the room. Several members of the Cabinet turned and stared at each other incredulously. Where the hell was all this leading?

'No sneezing symptoms this time, ladies and gentlemen,' Guthrie persevered, unabashed. 'Just erosion of brain cells. Sometimes fast, sometimes slow. We haven't advanced all that much: we don't know the vector this time either – the means of transmission, that is. Mosquitoes could . . .'

'There aren't any carrying mosquitoes in Britain,' Rogerson again interrupted.

'The lessons from trying to control mosquitoes worldwide can help,' Professor Grant stared hard at the politician. 'Please, minister, let Dr Guthrie continue.'

Rogerson again flushed angrily, then nodded.

'OK. Fact number one,' Guthrie went on. 'Since the Second World War, US Defense Department figures show that more American military have died from malaria than from bullets. Malaria is spread . . . you know how. In the forties and fifties, DDT, the new wonder insecticide, almost wiped out both the mosquito population and malaria. Huge amounts of WHO money went on that programme. Malaria was set to become a disease of the past, like the plague or the Black Death. But the bug, which breeds inside the mosquito, fought back, or rather the mosquito did. One female mosquito can produce a thousand offspring. Their life-cycle is very short, so from one insect which finds a way of defending itself against DDT, a million immune ones can spring in a matter of weeks. Frightening, isn't it? Nature's bad for us as well as good. The survival of the fittest, in Darwin's model, doesn't mean the survival of the best, whatever "best" is. Having nearly wiped it out, recent WHO figures show that malaria is as widespread and as fatal to millions as it has ever been.' Guthrie looked around his silent audience. 'All the more so,' he continued, 'because no new variant DDT is on hand to stem this fresh world epidemic, except, very expensively, in certain rich areas like Florida. There, constant spraying of ever stronger insectides by helicopter, something impossible to do on a worldwide basis, keeps things more or less under control. But even then, the very act of killing breeds super-strain survivors which are totally immune to any quinine-based drug. So the battle continues.

'With global warming, which mosquitoes and lots of other bugs seem to love since it encourages them to breed quicker, how long will science stay ahead?' Guthrie paused again, glanced round the room as if to check if he had everyone's attention, then continued. 'Sorry about the medical lecture, ladies and gentlemen, but unless you understand the background you may not fully understand the extent of the threat we're faced with today. It's known as mutation. We've had vast amounts of time to defeat mere malaria, and we've failed. Now we're faced with this Virus ZD198. What we've found strange is the way it's picked its victims. They're all high-profile people, including Tyndall in his own field. In nature, it's difficult to transmit. So we've been forced,' he paused emphatically, to give the fullest momentum to his words, 'to consider that it has been spread *deliberately*.'

A deathly hush fell over the room as Guthrie continued. 'While we're following up that line, we're also looking very urgently for possible antidotes. If we don't catch it quick, find who, or what's spreading it, and wipe it into oblivion *before it finds a way to mutate naturally*, as I believe it will, then the Darwinian order of things may let it, as the fittest, survive. And we mere humans, who take years to change our internal defence mechanisms, could go to the wall.' Guthrie sat down, head bowed slightly, as everyone else in that crowded room stared at him in horrified silence.

'Spread deliberately, Dr Guthrie? You're not for a moment suggesting . . . ? Sort of biological warfare?' asked Rogerson, aggression mixed with disbelief rasping in his voice.

'Not quite that, minister. But specifically, individually, targeted,' responded Professor Grant, quietly.

'Like when the CIA sent Fidel Castro those poisoned cigars?' The note of suspicion in the minister's voice was only too obvious.

'We can't rule out that possibility.' Again Grant was soft-spoken but firm.

'The Armageddon scenario.' Rogerson was getting his catastrophes mixed up.

'Not war, minister. Plague,' said Grant.

It did not go down well.

10 Downing Street, London, Thursday 23rd June

With all that had been going on, Professor Grant and Dr Guthrie had made one serious mistake: they had taken Professor MacArthur, back in Edinburgh, for granted. Rather, they had forgotten all about him, and the one thing the latter hated was to be ignored. He began by being obnoxious, then moved on to becoming a serious thorn in their flesh. It started with a justifiably angry fax accusing Guthrie of walking out on the deal that had been agreed with his American university. Guthrie at once sent back an apologetic reply, saying that he had been summoned to work on a high-priority task to isolate a particular aggressive virus. MacArthur was still understandably upset: Guthrie had neither sought his permission nor told him where he was going. Guthrie had telephoned and half-heartedly tried to explain that he would be back as soon as possible, but the professor put the telephone down on him. Professor Grant's help was enlisted and he too tried to explain the facts to MacArthur, but that just made matters worse. When, finally, the story about ZD198 broke in the newspapers, MacArthur gladly volunteered himself as the rent-a-quote medical expert, guaranteed to belittle any of the theories or statements emanating from the Harman Institute. As usual, the press thrived on the ensuing controversy between so-called specialists. At a further emergency Cabinet meeting held early that Thursday, Rogerson produced a copy of that morning's *Times*, which contained a number of damning quotes from the self-same Professor MacArthur. He pooh-poohed the suggestion of any potential epidemic, accusing Grant of being in conspiracy with Guthrie and of blowing the whole thing up out of all proportion in order to get more funding for their research.

'Who am I to believe when two professors of medicine can't agree?' bellowed Rogerson.

Guthrie, who, with Grant, had again been summoned to the meeting, realized that the latter was only just managing to contain his fury. Rogerson was an illiterate brute but he hoped the professor would react cooly: nothing was to be gained by losing his temper. Guthrie quickly moved to defuse the situation.

'You must judge, minister,' he said in his most reasonable voice. 'But that's just one story in today's paper. Did you notice the other one, the feature article, tucked away on page eight? The two are very similar.'

Rogerson turned angrily in the direction of the American. Medical scientists were bad enough, but an American one . . . 'Well?' he demanded.

'A couple of investigative journalists were sent to test what range of killer germs they could buy on the open market. Their findings are horrifying. There's a research lab out in Indonesia, for example, which, for a few hundred pounds, offered them spores of both anthrax and the plague. Another in Eastern Europe, believe it or not, agreed to sell them mail-order brucellosis and E-coli, which, even in tiny doses, can kill hundreds. That's how countries like Iraq and North Korea have been able to buy what the arms trade call "the poor man's atomic bomb".'

'Sensationalist journalism,' growled the minister. 'Yes, I saw the piece, and I also spoke personally to Professor MacArthur about it this morning. Sensible man. Told me it was a whole load of hyped-up twaddle. Like the recent tabloid rubbish about Arabs bringing anthrax into Britain in bottles of perfume.'

'That story was only too true,' said Professor Grant coldly. 'Ask Sir Ian Temple-White: MI5 asked us to do the analysis. I oversaw it myself.'

There was a long pause, then Rogerson growled, 'OK, so what now?'

Guthrie looked at Grant and Grant nodded, so the American continued. 'We're working on the line that our virus produces symptoms not too different from a toxin-producing organism developed by a veterinary lab near Prague that first gives its victim blurred vision and difficulty in speaking. Paralysis and vomiting follow rapidly, then comes respiratory failure. One in three victims die.'

'We've got the message.' Even Winston Rogerson was less bombastic now. 'So. What d'you want? More money?'

'It's too late for money, minister,' replied Grant drily. 'The Public Health Laboratory here in London and the Ministry of Defence's Biological Research Facility at Porton Down, who are the experts in actual germ warfare, back me up on this. What we need is an urgent directive from HMG that every spare medical resource is harnessed to our efforts to find the antidote. That includes Professor MacArthur and his people in Edinburgh.'

Everyone in the room watched and waited for the minister's reaction. Lyle Thane started to say something in support of Grant, then thought better of it. In the circumstances it might just add fuel to the fire. That was the danger of having mercurial ministers like Winston Rogerson around, who thought they were being decisive and heroic. Mediocre, time-serving politicians, carried to power through a lack of competitive talent, were always best.

'OK. Get on with it. But keep me fully informed. No surprises. Every step of the way, d'you understand?' Winston Rogerson stood up, red-faced and visibly bristling, and stormed from the room. The meeting was at an end.

13

Thane watched and waited while the members of the Cabinet drifted from the room. There was no doubt how shocked most of them had been by the news. Rogerson had taken Professor Grant off with him, while Guthrie was closeted with Caldwell. Chance had always been a great thing in Lyle Thane's life. As one door shut, another always seemed to open up in front of him. That was the crucial skill: keep one jump ahead of the game, both in professional and in private life. With the latter in mind, he'd suddenly noticed a potential new pip for his orange, in the form of Professor Grant's most attractive research assistant, Dr Rebecca Stevenson. There was a real woman. He hadn't heard her say much yet, but she'd been most attentive when she'd shown him around the Institute. There was somebody who, he could see, was his intellectual equal, not some mere sexual plaything. God, but was he not made for bigger prizes than Sarah St Just? Here were the makings of a real partner: a power player in her own right, a proper trophy woman. Maybe that was what had been lacking in his life: some female like Dr Stevenson who would put a stop to him doing anything silly like the other night. Look at the way the Blairs, the Clintons, the Jeffrey Archers, had succeeded, by having wives as bright as themselves alongside. Or brighter. Rebecca Stevenson was still a long way off. He'd only just met her, he knew little about her, but that could all be made to change.

Power was a great aphrodisiac, so he had always believed. He advanced on her just as the last people were leaving and said, in as business-like a manner as he could muster, 'Look, I have to know more about this bug theory. I know what the professor and Dr Guthrie were telling us, but I have to understand how to play it. How to spin the story, how to contain the crisis politically. Know what I mean?' He spoke as if nothing else mattered, as if no other ambition had ever crossed his mind.

They went for a drink together, to a pub just across the road from the Houses of Parliament. It wasn't the best place, but he was playing a multiple game. The pub was crowded but he managed to find a corner table for them, then went to buy her a drink at the bar. He knew she'd notice how many famous MPs and junior ministers came up and spoke to him as he carried their drinks to and from their table, since the news about the PM was the top item in the evening bulletins, and someone from the Prime Minister's personal staff didn't usually venture into a place like this, not at a time like this. It wasn't the most appropriate place to go, but then he was after Rebecca Stevenson as well as her mind.

'So,' he said, sitting back in his chair, 'tell me. Not what Professor Grant, not what Dr Guthrie, thinks. What d'you believe? If it's deliberate, how d'you think the virus was planted?'

'These scare stories about animal transplants,' she began, sipping thoughtfully at her glass.

Thane looked at her, not knowing what she was getting at.

'Thing is,' she went on, 'if you transplant a bodypart from an animal to a human, for example pig hearts, the great worry is that certain bugs or viruses could leap inter-species with the organ. Nasty parasites easily learn how to infect humans. They have to mutate a bit, but it happens all the time.'

'What're you getting at?' asked Thane.

'Most medical scientists now agree that AIDS, for example, came first of all from apes. More precisely, HIV-1 from chimpanzees, and HIV-2 from a breed of monkeys.'

'How?'

'Doesn't bear thinking about. Eating them, probably. Anyway, it leapt. It's known as "zoonosis" – the transmission of infection between humans and animals. Along with famine and war, it's the single greatest threat to world health. Like anthrax: they're particularly deadly because they form spores which retain their power for years. Did you know that anthrax used to be known as "woolsorter's disease"? Handling infected animals, inhaling spores, just wearing infected fur or leather, means that you can catch it.'

'Nasty,' said Thane, watching her closely.

'Science has identified over one hundred and fifty types, like psittacosis, or "parrot fever", which you can pick up by inhaling particles of contaminated bird droppings. Sounds absurd, but can be fatal. Ebola virus, which the tabloids made much of recently, has animal origins as well. The anti-animal transplant lobby have a serious point.'

'Any good news?' asked Thane. 'Another drink, by the way?' He paused and frowned. She looked at him. 'I'd better be getting back to the Institute,' she said.

'If you've a little longer, I'd appreciate it. Come on,' he said, looking at his watch. 'One more drink won't do any harm. Then I'll have to be getting back, too.'

'Sorry,' she said firmly, 'but before we go, you asked about this particular outbreak. Let me tell you: medical science normally tries to control disease.'

Thane paused, an empty glass in each hand. 'What precisely d'you mean by that?' he asked. He'd go hard for her after the crisis was past. She was someone really worth pursuing.

'We have to start looking,' she replied, 'for someone with a lot of medical-scientific knowledge; someone who knows their stuff.'

'No doctors, except his own, have been anywhere near the PM recently,' said Thane.

'We know that. That's the whole problem. But someone in Downing Street may, unwittingly, have helped.'

'In Number Ten? How the hell . . . ?'

'Expert knowledge is needed to know how to keep the virus

alive while it's being transferred. We've been conducting trials and now think ZD198 isn't too tricky on that score: lots of chemical gels and inert agents could store it.'

'So?'

'The broken skin scenario. Did the PM suffer from bleeding gums, spots, anything like that?'

'He had that skin infection.'

'No, no. Well before that.'

'How should I know?'

'Think hard, Lyle,' said Dr Stevenson, standing up to leave. 'It could be the key.'

'Wait a minute. Mr Morgan used to complain that for TV interviews he sometimes had to have make-up put on to hide a nasty shaving rash he got. He found the dusting powder further irritated the skin condition.'

Dr Stevenson turned to stare at Thane. 'Really?' she said. 'OK, look: this trivial thing could be it. Get hold of Dr Taylor, straightaway. Tell him to ring me. Someone's going to have to raid the PM's medicine cupboard. But not, repeat not, till I've briefed a specialist handler from the Institute.'

Central London, Friday 24th June

It was the lead in every national newspaper. Page after page was filled with articles demonstrating varying degrees of medical expertise. The tabloids rapidly christened it the 'nobs' disease', particularly when it was revealed that Britain's most famous actor, Ralph Rowland, had died from it. The news that the PM himself had been struck down and was in intensive care didn't break for another twelve hours, then the story really hit the rooftops. It became a worldwide headline. There had been nothing quite like it since Princess Diana's death. Rogerson, as Acting Prime Minister, issued a rushed statement, backed by the Chief Medical Officer of Health, saying that there was no need for any panic. The media, however, managed to find enough 'experts', including a late convert in Professor MacArthur, to suggest that Virus ZD198 might lie latent in large numbers of people. An apocalypse scenario was rapidly written up by the leader writers which rivalled the early CJD/BSE scares, only a hundred times more alarmist. If a few top people in the country could fall victim to it, what was to stop it spreading throughout society? The great British public rapidly became experts in the disease, the mystery of its erratic gestation period, and how it could possibly have been transmitted to such a select few.

Because of its high-profile victims, the theory that they had been specifically targeted became an obvious subject for press speculation. But what on earth could they possibly have in common? What evil mastermind might be behind it all? Was it an international terrorist plot? Professor Grant and the gangling figure of Dr Harper Guthrie were persuaded to give a news conference. Guthrie became a household name, particularly when it became known that he had once had the nickname 'Bugbuster'. The tabloids especially liked that, it suited their headline writers. He was moved into secure accommodation close to the Harman Institute and was given his own personal bodyguard. His entire past life became public history as he was catapulted into the limelight. His former Edinburgh landlady, Mrs Murray, was interviewed and spoke warmly of the close personal relationship she had had with him. But Professor MacArthur continued to be as difficult as he could. That Friday there was a centre-page spread in the *Telegraph* by him, heavily critical of the way the outbreak had been identified and handled. 'Time will show,' the professor thundered, 'that pure research units like the Harman Institute do not have the leadership, the staff, nor the practical expertise to deal with situations like this.'

It was fuel to the fire as far as Winston Rogerson was concerned. Government policy continued to be entirely directed at avoiding mass hysteria. One bland statement after another was made by the Minister of Health, to the effect that the authorities had everything in hand. This was easily revealed as blatant nonsense when it became widely known that no inoculation against contracting the virus existed. By contrast with the CJD scare, the Government could not offer any practical advice, like avoiding certain meat products, to avoid catching it. This hiatus, this vacuum in medical science's abilities, further fuelled the public outcry. The headlines screamed ever more dire warnings, while editorials searched for people to blame, pontificating as to why the experts had, once again, let the nation down.

The world watched and waited. No known cases had been reported outside Britain apart from that of the ex-African mercenary in the States, and those few unsubstantiated outbreaks that had occurred deep in the jungle of the Eastern Congo.

Millbank, Central London, Friday 24th June

The inevitable side alarms and scares multiplied rapidly. As if to reinforce the views of some experts that the virus must have been deliberately spread, unattributable reports emerged that a blackmail attempt had recently been received by HMG. There was more than a little truth in this, though some threats were immediately dismissed as being the work of deranged hoaxers. Then, that Friday morning, one particular letter was intercepted on its way to Number Ten. It had been typed on an old-fashioned machine on plain paper; it showed a considerable knowledge of the virus; it was unsigned; it was not a blackmail threat since nothing was demanded. It boldly stated that certain additional victims would be picked off in due course. The letter was immediately taken away by MI5 for testing to see what could be discovered about the originator or the machine with which it had been typed. There were no fingerprints on the paper, which was standard issue from WH Smith. There was no way of telling what batch or when the paper had been purchased. The likelihood, in the computer age, of tracking down a manual typewriter was like looking for a needle in a haystack. The letter itself had been posted from Whitehall, but that meant nothing whatsoever.

One complication was that the intelligence system, in the

person of a Mr William Blake, had failed to react to two similar messages which had come in, both anonymous, posted in different places, over the past weeks. Blake was one of MI5's low-level, special case officers. He was a tall, skeletal figure, with the look of a dowdy, retired schoolmaster about him, someone who was cruising gently downhill towards the end of his career. Ambition had deserted him long ago; except, that was, in terms of finding ways of enhancing his final pension. If he was promoted just one more grade, it would make a sizable difference to his eventide years. Blake was more interested in that future than the present. One of his daily tasks was to go through any particularly obnoxious or threatening mail addressed to the Prime Minister and others of his Cabinet colleagues, which Downing Street passed on to the Security Service as a matter of routine. Every prominent figure gets their fair share of obscene mail, cranky mail, self-seeking mail, hate mail. Much of it, often written in multicoloured inks, each word frequently underlined, is of such absurdity or madness as to be immediately consigned to the dustbin by way of a secretarial team which logs each item just in case. But every now and then anonymous, unsigned items, accusing people in power of this or that crime, arrive. They are taken a little more seriously, but only just. Again, there are those, often from the seriously unbalanced, which contain real threats. Where the provenance is known or can be discovered, Special Branch are notified, the sender is tracked down and gets a visit from an officer, and if the subsequent warning is not sufficient, administrative and legal action is taken against the correspondent concerned. Finally, there is yet another category where the degree of threat is perceived to be on an even higher plane. Sometimes these threats come in the form of advance warnings from this or that foreign terrorist organization.

This latest letter, addressed politely enough – 'Dear Prime Minister,' and signed by 'a former loyal servant of the State,' – did not obviously fit into any of the above categories, but rapidly had to be re-codified. It was the old-fashioned type-face that jogged Blake's memory. He recognized the different pressures of the individual letters on the paper. He seemed to remember seeing something rather like it, some time in the previous month. He ran a check; the staff quickly turned up two previous letters; he could see at a glance that all three were a clear match. Blake carefully placed them side by side on the desk in front of him. They had all been typed on the same sort of paper. Both the earlier ones were identically headed and tailed. The key paragraphs contained similar wordings with the second letter, if anything, more threatening than the first:

You don't know me and I don't know you, yet I have served my country as well and for longer than you have. I have served it overseas, without complaint, without regret. I expected recognition in the end: an honour, an award for my selfless service. Now, as I look around me and see who is placed in authority over us in God's scheme of things, I despair. Yet I do not surrender, because I have the means my God has given me, to punish those who do not recognize such unflinching dedication. I will revenge, says my God. Watch out, Prime Minister. I have begun my crusade. You do not know me, but you will one day.

That first letter was imprecise, its threat vague, and Blake felt that, even in retrospect, he had been right merely to have it filed away. The second adopted a somewhat harder, more precise tone:

I wrote to you before. Nothing has changed, but now I have struck at my first victim. Victim? No: it is I who am the victim. He is the criminal. He is suffering. He will pay the price for having tried to crush me. I have others. You will see. I am coming closer, Prime Minister, closer to you. Your bodyguards, your bullet-proof cars, will not protect you. I have the ultimate weapon. You will not know it till it is much too late.

*   *   *

That letter too had been imprecise, but now there was today's: the third. Special Case Officer Blake read the key paragraphs through several times.

So, Prime Minister, now you know what I have done and can do. I am no crank, no boastful madman. I have a mission: I have the means. If you do not recognize this, if this letter does not reach you or if you are already incapable of grasping what I am saying, those closest to you will know, will believe me. And soon there will be more.

In case they have yet to decide, or be certain, that I am responsible, let me, for their benefit, prove that I know what I am writing about. Here is some of the history and the most obvious medical symptoms of surge fever. I know them. I have seen them . . .

Blake's hand was shaking by the time he had read through the paragraphs that followed. They described the horrific spread of a disease, in its incubation periods, its vectors. When he had finished reading, and he did not understand all the medical terms used, he carefully picked up all three letters with the special tongs that were used when further tests on paper correspondence had to be carried out, and quickly left the room.

The SSU rapidly reviewed all three messages and, after consulting Professor Grant's team over some of the technical facts, confirmed that whoever was sending them clearly knew what they were talking about. Dr Stevenson, meanwhile, was pursuing a separate line of investigation: she had questioned Taylor, the PM's doctor, very closely. He reluctantly told her about a very minor condition he had recently treated Peter Morgan for. He also volunteered the name of a man who might be able to help her with her enquiries. As Professor Grant's team agreed that only someone with a high degree of medical knowledge had written the letters, the SSU and MI5 were immediately tasked to interrogate everyone with any medical knowledge whom the victims might have met, known, or come across over the past few months. Guthrie also embarked on a separate investigation; on his own initiative he sent a message to Dr Boekamper in New York, asking him to make enquiries of the New Viruses and Contagious Diseases Division of the WHO for the names of all doctors who had reported on or handled all recent outbreaks. Boekamper rang Guthrie at the Institute within an hour of receiving the message.

'That's a tall order you've sent me,' he said.

Guthrie rapidly explained the background. 'It's crucial,' he said. 'If it's a case of deliberate sabotage it could be devastating.'

Kisangani, Congo, Saturday 25th June

'Urgent call from HQ in New York,' said Clegg Hurley when he returned from his office that afternoon.

'Yes?' said Banquier, hardly stirring from the armchair in which he was seated. Hurley could see he'd been drinking; he'd hardly stopped. It was almost a week since the man had arrived and he'd shown no sign of moving on, even when Hurley had volunteered that there was a spare seat in a Land Rover going across to Brazzaville as part of a military convoy.

'Glad you're still here,' said Hurley.

'Kind of you. Move on soon,' replied Banquier, his words slurring.

'I don't mean . . . I've been asked to ask you . . . They need to know more.' Hurley hated this. Why him? He was a scientist. He worked for the WHO. He wasn't a policeman, or a psychologist.

'Surge fever? Again? I tell them everything I know,' growled Banquier bleakly. Hurley knew that the doctor had showered that day, that his clothes had been newly washed by his domestic staff, but still the man looked unclean. It was something to do with his skin texture and the uneven stubble on his cheeks and chin.

'They're not asking about ZD198 this time. It's different. They want to know whether anyone else might have had access to the trial virus in your lab.'

'Few people. Africans. None know anything. Could not handle it.'

'What about that British colonel? The army doctor you told me about?'

'The colonel? Yes. Him.' Banquier suddenly brightened, sat up and looked much more alert.

'What drove him? What sort of man was he?' asked Clegg Hurley softly. 'I know you talked about him. I didn't listen. I was concentrating on the virus. Tell me. I need to write it all down and send it back.'

'Told you, didn't I? I wait for this, you know,' said Dr Banquier. He was smiling broadly now. 'Somehow, someone, someday, would come ask about the colonel. He that breed of man.'

The Harman Institute, East London, Monday 27th June

As a result of his enquiry, Dr Guthrie received an overnight report from Boekamper, not yet about the British colonel but containing more background information about the mysterious Dr Banquier. He had featured in several reports from the WHO's Congo office over the years. He had once worked in a Belgian government-funded research unit, and, according to their records, had still been there in the early nineties. His principal area of specialization had been in new variant viruses, some of which he claimed to have had identified in Central Africa. On one occasion he had been officially funded by the government to travel there in pursuit of his research. Banquier had had a number of respectable papers published in specialist medical journals. He had been highly regarded for his ability to break down a virus, eliminating some of the worst symptoms it caused, concentrating on ones which first attacked the major functions of the brain.

He'd had some highly developed work in progress when, suddenly, he was caught up in one of the paedophile scandals which had erupted in Belgium over that period. One day he was at the clinic, preparing to give a lecture to his colleagues on his findings. The next day, shortly before the police arrived, he'd apparently received a tip-off and had completely disappeared. In the eyes of his colleagues he became a non-person, but there was no doubt that the Banquier with whom the local WHO representative in the Congo, Clegg Hurley, had been in frequent recent contact, was one and the same person. He was no mere disbarred GP. How, Boekamper wrote, could anyone other than an expert have known what he was looking for, or what he had found?

It is well known in criminal psychology that someone who has committed a crime is often driven to reveal the fact to a family member or a close friend. Many criminals have a deep-seated need to boast about what they have done, whether motivated by a desire for praise, or condemnation, or simply to shock the listener. Acclamation and revulsion are both heady drugs for those who have nurtured some criminal act of vengeance deep within them. But after the third anonymous letter containing the threat to infect others had been intercepted, no further messages came from the sender. It became all the more urgent for the entire resources of Britain's intelligence agencies to track down the writer on the basis of the clues already in their possession. Meanwhile, on the medical front, Dr Guthrie and Professor Grant, backed by substantial additional resources from other scientific research establishments, were devoting maximum time and effort to examining all available medical records for any clues about who had treated the disease elsewhere. MI5, meanwhile, built up a huge database of contacts, friends and acquaintances of all the known victims to see if any common names emerged. Little of any relevance was revealed, particularly as regards the Prime Minister who, in the course of the previous year, had obviously met many thousands of people from all walks of life.

The one or two names which did recur in the course of their investigations – for example the director of the Royal Opera House, whom the Prime Minister, Ralph Rowland, and Lord Rumbold had all met recently – were quickly discounted. Above all else, Rebecca Stevenson's research into the method that had been used to infect the victims continued without a break.

At eight a.m. New York time, one p.m. London time, Harper Guthrie took a telephone call from Boekamper in New York. His researches had come up with a name. He wasn't prepared to give any details over the telephone. It would come through on coded e-mail. A few minutes later, Guthrie stared at the printout in front of him. He now had a man's name and a great deal of background about him. Much of it fitted, yet more of it seemed a million miles away from the sort of person he thought he might have been looking for. It did not make sense. A British colonel, formerly of the Royal Army Medical Corps? It was nonsense. Why should this Colonel Sam Broomfield . . . ? He felt he could not make a judgment about the new information on his own, so he went in rapid search of Rebecca Stevenson.

'I've got a name,' he began excitedly, when he tracked her down in one of the specialist labs.

'Excellent,' she replied, briskly.

As he told her his news he was too full of it to notice her own reaction. 'Just supposing that it is this colonel, and we're some way from establishing that, how could he have targeted his victims so precisely?'

'Can't I . . . ?' she tried to interrupt.

'No, wait. It would be relatively easy to infect someone like Ralph Rowland, though even that must have been very tricky. But, at a guess, thousands of letters, packages and other items must arrive at Number Ten every day. How could this guy, if it is him, select something which would carry the infection, keep the virus alive, that only the Prime Minister would handle?'

'Think of something entirely personal,' said Rebecca, prompting him. 'Toothpaste, deodorant, shampoo,' she added.

'You're joking.'

'I certainly am not,' she said.

'Tell me,' he said, suddenly looking hard at her. 'You've turned up something too? You know who it was: how was it done?'

'We've both found a man,' she replied, a tense smile playing around her lips. 'The same man. But I think I also know who carried the carrier.'

'Who?' Guthrie was puzzled. 'Don't you mean *what*?'

'No, who. He still doesn't realize it, but Dr Harry Taylor himself was the unwitting bearer of the virus to the Prime Minister.'

Millbank, Central London, Monday 27th June

A mere hour and a half later. Many people would have been surprised at those attending the urgent secret meeting which took place in that anonymous Millbank office. Those who thought they knew Dr Harper Guthrie well, with all his little uncertainties and hang-ups, would have been astonished by the vigour and determination with which he conducted himself. Dr Stevenson also seemed surprisingly at home in these highly sensitive surroundings. Lyle Thane, a spectator at the meeting though the instigator of it, was, despite himself, impressed that Sir Ian Temple-White, the head of MI5, seemed to know her so well.

'Are you sure?' asked Sir Ian.

'As certain as we can be. It all fits neatly. He had direct links with at least three of the victims,' said Dr Stevenson quietly. 'We've established how difficult it is to transmit. The colonel seems to have discovered the secret of how it can be done.'

'You're suggesting we actually alert him?' asked Sir Ian. He'd failed to follow her logic.

'Damn sure we do. But gently,' Guthrie broke in. 'He's got access to the deadliest of weapons. We want to know where he's hiding them, how he's storing them, what else he may have. We must try to get him on side until we're ready to act.'

'What d'you suggest?'

'One idea of mine – find what newspaper the man takes in the morning,' said Guthrie.

'Newspaper?' The Director General was a practical man. He didn't like guessing games. He had his lines out all over the place on this crisis and he still wasn't quite sure why this rather eccentric American research professor was here at all. Why d'you want to know what paper he reads?'

'Let me explain, Sir Ian,' said Guthrie. 'We've got an amazing story. We need it to be on the front page of his newspaper.'

West London, Tuesday 28th June

A lot of things happened in the next twelve hours. It took some pressure, even from someone as powerful as the Director General of MI5, to persuade the editor of the *Daily Telegraph* to do what he was asked. A one-off copy, with the special story carefully cut into the front page, was not something any self-respecting editor would normally accede to, particularly as he was losing out on a sensational world exclusive. But the bribe was just that: he would have his exclusive tomorrow. And so one special copy, printed under the highest security conditions, was run off, to be delivered to a modest, semi-detached cornerhouse in Ealing, almost next door to the pigeon-loving Mrs Smith, who, poor lady, had suddenly been taken very poorly indeed. She was currently languishing in a side-ward at the local hospital: the doctors there knew something serious was the matter with her, but they were under-staffed as usual, so her problems would have to wait.

Round about seven o'clock that morning, Taff, a fourteen-year-old newspaper boy, did his rounds as usual. Or almost as usual. There was something odd going on, but he was given an extra couple of quid by his boss at the shop who, for some reason or other, wasn't at the shop that morning but was waiting with another two men, big men in raincoats, at the corner of one of the streets on his route. His newsbag of papers was personally reorganized by his boss, he was handed a special copy of the *Daily Telegraph*, and he was told precisely through which letterbox he had to put it. In everything else he had to behave the same as he did every morning. Was that clear? Taff nodded. He didn't understand what was happening, but he liked the thought of the two extra quid.

About two and a half hours later, the door of the suburban semi opened and a man, wearing a blue raincoat and clutching a battered leather briefcase, hurriedly emerged, locked the door behind him and set off towards the local Underground station. A dozen pairs of eyes watched him as he went. They guessed where he was going.

The story in the *Telegraph* had been totally compelling reading for the colonel. The lead item was about a serious outbreak of Virus ZD198, sometimes colloquially known as surge fever. It reported the fact that Dr Harper Guthrie had discovered not only how the bug could be controlled, but also, more importantly, was close to discovering how it had been transmitted. The paper claimed it had an exclusive interview with Dr Guthrie which just happened to reveal that he was staying at the Ravenscroft Hotel, next door to the Harman Institute. Other readers, though there were none, might have wondered why such detail was reported in a national newspaper, but, in the circumstances, they guessed that Colonel Sam Broomfield would pick up that fact rather than the oddity of its being there at all.

As the victims of gassing in the First World War and the Kurds in modern Iraq discovered to their cost, poison gas knows no boundaries, any more than barbed wire and bullets can stop a germ warfare attack. This was no such warfare, but it had similar elements to it. Those watching, waiting and monitoring the colonel's progress from Ealing to the reception desk of the Ravenscroft Hotel knew what a potentially deadly game they were playing.

Some sixth sense also alerted the colonel to the fact that he could be walking into a trap. He had been playing long-distance games with the establishment for some time now, but the authorities might also be playing games with him. If he managed to meet Dr Guthrie, he resolved not to try to be too clever with him, nor to hint at how much he really knew. He would reveal a little: tell him about his time in the Congo and about having come across case. f surge fever at Dr Banquier's school, just in case they ever tracked him down that way. He would get in first and volunteer his humble services: could he do anything, anything at all to help? He would never admit to knowing the way the virus was transmitted. That would be too risky. If he kept to his plan, they could prove nothing.

Millbank, London, Tuesday 28th June

Within minutes of the colonel leaving, the Director General, and the Secretary to the Cabinet among others, listened to a secret recording of the conversation which took place at the Ravenscroft Hotel. The DG recognized Guthrie's voice as the first to speak.

Everyone will be enormously grateful, colonel. Great news that you have experience of the disease. The Congo, you say?

Yes, the Congo. Very little experience, but I suppose it might help.

You know the symptoms?

Yes: very distressing.

We've found no antidote.

No: nor did we.

It's how it travels, its vector, that's defeated us so far.

I'm not sure I can . . .

We tried all possible means with David.

David?

Yes, David. You want to know about David?

I've never heard of David. Who's David?

We checked it all out with David, colonel.

Is this a guessing game?

No guessing, colonel. David was for real. He died.

I know nothing about that.

No, you wouldn't.

I don't follow.

We built a model on the computer.

You built a model on the computer?

Like I said. We entered all the data we could possibly find on the vector, on the genes, on the gene family structure, on the gestation period of virus ZD198. We put in all the different timings. We monitored its progress. So far we can't understand. In all our tests it kills the victim before it has time to spread. David died.

The tape lapsed into silence for a moment, then:

So your model died?

Yes, but we've got a new one: Rosie.

Rosie? You talk as if it's some sort of game you're playing.

No game, colonel. It's deadly. We've got to wipe it out.

You'll never do that. We never could. It's got a will of its own. It strikes where it wants.

Believe me, colonel, we'll find the key.

14

As soon as the colonel had left, Guthrie returned rapidly to the Institute. Grant, Stevenson and Thane had heard some of the tape by the time he arrived, but they wanted from Guthrie a summary of the conversation and an assessment of the man himself.

'The good news,' Guthrie began, 'was that he'd completely swallowed the bait. He didn't seem at all suspicious. He was slightly nervous at first, but that was entirely understandable in the circumstances. He was self-composed, almost apologetic for disturbing me. He obviously felt safe. Said he'd seen the press report and all that. Then he started bragging, boasting about his experience with the disease. Not many people would have had his experience, he said. Perhaps he could help us in some way? He hadn't recognized the serial number, ZD198, of course, but he'd seen cases of surge fever when he was serving in a hell-hole of some town in the Eastern Congo. It hadn't been the only killer bug to come out of the jungle in the many months he'd been posted there, but it had been far and away the worst. He said he'd been mainly occupied with the results of the civil war: suppurating wounds, deliberate amputations, the remains of people's legs after they'd stepped on a landmine. And, of course, the ever present effects of mass starvation.' Guthrie paused to collect his thoughts. 'I felt sorry for him a bit. No doubt the man went through a lot. He said he wanted to help; he volunteered to assist us in finding how the virus was transmitted.'

'What?' Grant interrupted. They all sat forward in their chairs.

'He got nervous when I started to question him on that. Stared at me as if, suddenly, he suspected something. So I did as I'd been instructed and backed off. Better left to the professional interrogation.'

'Then what?' asked Thane.

'Then . . . ? I wasn't sure I could keep playing the game well enough. I didn't want to frighten him. I thanked him profusely. Said we'd be in touch, that sort of thing. Then he left,' Guthrie added, a little lamely.

'What I still don't understand,' said Grant, 'is why, if we're certain it's him, MI5 didn't just storm the place?'

'If they'd done that,' Thane interjected, 'God knows what might have happened, what might have been set loose.'

'I suppose they're right,' said Grant.

'I'm sure they were,' echoed Guthrie. 'The colonel seemed as rational as you or I, but underneath he's obviously seriously unhinged. We've already made a guess at what extreme measures he might take when he's threatened, so . . .'

'We'll know soon enough,' said Thane, looking at his watch. 'We should be getting some hard action round about now.'

Ealing, West London, Tuesday 28th June

The operation had been meticulously planned. As soon as the colonel had left his house, a small team of professionals, all in special protective clothing, moved in and searched it carefully. At first they found nothing of any significance except for some empty ampoules, thick rubber gloves and a hypodermic syringe. They also discovered a battered typewriter and some A4 paper, which they took away for testing. Then they broke into the garage.

The take-out team had chosen their position carefully. They correctly guessed that the colonel would return by Underground to Ealing after his meeting with Guthrie. They followed him every inch of the way. The walk from the station to his house took between three to four minutes and part of that walk passed close by a children's playground. Had the colonel been more attentive he might have wondered at the lack of any play at that time of day, or of the surprising emptiness of the streets and the absence of other signs of life. But the colonel was a man with a mission. He was running on a single track; he had tunnel vision. He had one solitary objective to achieve that day and he was determined to achieve it.

The men in the strange masks and helmets came at him from all directions. They were all armed. Someone speaking on a loud-hailer ordered him to place his briefcase carefully down on the ground and put up his hands. He hesitated. For a moment he thought he was about to be mugged, then he knew that they'd sprung a trap, that this was it. He had long ago decided what he would do in such circumstances. Instead of putting the briefcase down, slowly and calmly he began to open it in front of them all. He reached inside. Suddenly he had a syringe in one hand; in the other he held an ampoule aloft. He was smiling. They went for him, knowing how fast they must move. They had expected something like this, so, expertly briefed by Grant's technicians, they threw the thick black bodysack over him, enveloping him entirely.

Central London, Tuesday 28th June

When a cell door finally clangs shut, a man becomes nothing. Captivity deliberately and inevitably dehumanizes and degrades. It is an insurmountable part of a nation's system of punishment, particularly for someone from a background of relative wealth, privilege and comfort. In such circumstances, each and every person has a trigger. In the colonel's case it was to be locked up in the special remand centre where, after full medical tests, he was now being held. He had long been living in his own cloistered world of revenge; his sudden arrest pulled the veils aside to reveal the pathetic truth. Here was no vicious enemy, no defiant criminal, no mass murderer; here was a whimpering, broken man, the other side of his split mind at last exposed to the enormity of what he had done. They sat him at a plain wooden table, on a hard chair with a plastic seat. The two professional interrogators, one young, one much older, sat opposite him. To one side, watching him in profile, were the MI5 psychologist and the representative from the Harman Institute, there in case specialist medical terminology needed explaining. They wanted the answers to three specific questions: who else had he infected, how had he infected them, and was there an antidote? They wanted the information fast, but the psychologist advised getting to know more about the colonel's personality first, to avoid tipping him over the edge.

Character and motivation emerged from the tears. Whether they were tears of shame, remorse, horror, or merely fear for himself, his nameless interrogators were yet to discover. The story, horrific in its simplicity, emerged slowly. It began as a rambling justification for playing in areas of medical science that would otherwise have been beyond his reach. He had been a good doctor, but he felt that his reclusive personality had got in the way of his professional career. He nonetheless boasted about his Falklands and Gulf War experiences: they had been successful times for him. His father had still been alive then; he too had been a military doctor who would often reminisce about how, in the Second World War, almost all septic wounds were successfully treatable with penicillin. Now, ninety-five per cent of the infected wounds the colonel had come across, were not. Nature had beaten science; it was doing it all over again with antibiotics. A complacent medical profession had long believed that they would continue to develop new types of drugs which would deal effectively with most things they were faced with. How wrong they had proved to be. New breeds of superbug constantly emerged, triumphantly resistant. When the colonel started mumbling about mankind's oldest battle being between invading organisms and resistant hosts, it seemed to his interrogators as if he was taking the side of the bugs and the viruses. They kept having to force him back to their three basic questions. He kept evading them. They gave him more time. The man from Grant's team took notes as the colonel talked about his time in Africa, about the ongoing civil war, the mass starvation, the malaria, the dengue fever, the mosquitoes, the tsetse flies. He quoted Pliny: 'There's always something new out of Africa.' And so it had been. It took the professional interrogators several hours of intensive questioning before they felt they were getting to the nub of things, before they could start putting the real pressure on the colonel to answer their questions rather than giving them his self-justifying reminiscences. In between sessions, the female MI5 psychologist cautioned that if the colonel was pushed too hard too early, he might crack up. Better, she insisted, to let him ramble on and tell his story at his own pace.

'We don't have the luxury of time,' exploded the younger interrogator. 'We're under huge pressure from the Director General and from Rogerson himself.'

'Rush it and you'll blow it,' the psychologist responded angrily. 'Get a second opinion if you want to.'

'We'll do it your way,' ruled the senior agent. That was why she was there, after all. Digressions and justifications punctuated the entire interrogation. Some of it was fascinating. The colonel described meeting a man, a Dr Wonter Basson, the former head of the South African apartheid regime's chemical warfare programme. He'd been nicknamed Dr Death, since he had experimented with anthrax and mamba venom, while other scientists under his command had attempted to develop bacteria that would attack only black and pigmented peoples by use of a frightening terminator gene that could put an end to the reproduction process.

'What the hell's the difference?' the colonel suddenly erupted. 'Choosing between that and making guns, bombs or landmines? I'd call landmines – and I've treated so many of their mutilated victims – a thousand times worse than biological weapons.'

'That's a damn fool justification,' the younger interrogator retorted angrily. Both his senior colleague and the psychiatrist looked accusingly at him as the colonel stopped talking, then lapsed into mumbling incoherence. He refused to respond to any questions after that, and they decided to leave him and try again later, after he had slept.

Later that day they began again. The younger interrogator had been redeployed to other duties, and MI5's woman psychologist was brought in on the act.

'They must have hurt you badly: your victims, I mean,' she began softly. She had cleverly pulled an emotional trigger and it all came pouring out.

Tears welled up in the colonel's eyes. 'I didn't mean to go so far, not at first,' he said.

'The general?' asked the senior interrogator softly. He was learning fast. 'General George? How did you infect him? He was your first, wasn't he?'

'Did I tell you I sometimes do locum work: standing in at clinics when the doctors go on leave?' asked the colonel, plaintively.

'You did,' said the interrogator briskly. 'How did you . . . ? Look, we really need to know . . .' He felt the psychiatrist's restraining hand on his sleeve. He checked himself.

'I did a stint in an upper-class practice in Kensington. One day, in walked General George – General Sir George bloody Haycock, the man who, more than any, stunted my career, kept sending me to places like the bloody Congo. He was the man who tried to suppress all the findings about Gulf War Syndrome. He was like that, you know.'

The colonel's audience watched and waited.

'One day, what, two months ago now, he walked into the clinic. Just like that. I was on duty. He didn't recognize me, of course: why should he? But I recognized him, all right. Know what the matter with him was? Badly infected hands. He'd been using some specially strong weedkiller in the grounds of his country house, he said. It had burnt his hands. It was the right moment. Broken skin: suppurating; very unpleasant. I should have sent him to the skin clinic at the Western, but I didn't. I gave him a prescription and told him to come back and see me in three days if it didn't clear up. I knew it wouldn't clear up. I had better stuff the second time. I had it in the surgery with me, specially prepared. I knew one thing: it would clear up his hand infection in no time. I knew what I was doing all right.' The colonel laughed, but neither the interrogator nor the psychologist followed suit.

'The others. You want to know why the others?' They looked at the colonel, waiting. The reasons for his selection of his victims could have come later: right now they wanted to know how rather than why. The senior agent wanted to push him on that, force the bastard to reply, but again he opted for caution.

The justification for his choice of his other victims came unasked, in a torrent of recrimination. He had seen himself as an exterminator of his tormentors, seeking justice for so many aspects of his failed life.

'Many dream of such things,' he said. 'God gave me the means. I've always done my best,' the colonel went on. 'Have I not served my country with honour and distinction? I have the Falklands and Gulf War medals, you know. Good staff reports, too. But some people ...' His voice died away for a moment, then, 'It's always been the same. People don't understand. People are cruel. Ralph Rowland bullied me at school, you know. I, we, were at Redlands – used to be one of the best schools. Said he didn't remember it, or me, when I met him a year or so ago, backstage after one of his performances. He didn't remember? He *must* have remembered that I was terrified of the dark, that I suffered from claustrophobia. He was arrogant even then: full of himself, a bully and a bastard. He got pleasure out of beating the younger boys. I tried to stand up to him and he got his own back. He chose his timing well – after chapel on a Sunday when I wouldn't be missed till evening roll-call – nearly seven hours in all. He locked me in a tiny dark cupboard. I couldn't see or breathe. Hell, hell on earth. It took me weeks, months, years; have I ever recovered?'

The colonel paused as if to collect his thoughts. Then he gave a brief, satisfied smile. 'Then that fool, Rumbold. Sweating my guts out in the Congo, I was. He came on a so-called bloody fact-finding mission. I was doing a good job there, in impossible conditions. That shit went home and wrote a mocking article in the *Spectator* about me and what I was doing. "Second-rate Colonel Blimp", he called me. Me, with a hundred civil war wounded a day to amputate, to stitch up, to send to the mortuary. Can you blame me? Can you? Can you?' Eyes blazing, the colonel turned his head to stare at his inquisitors one by one. In the eyes of the woman psychologist at least he saw some sign of understanding, if not of compassion.

No one spoke. The colonel stared down at his hands, which were resting, white-knuckled and shaking, on the table in front of him. 'More. More?' he asked. 'You want to know about the others? Do you? Do you?' he asked, his voice rising in anger. 'Who in a civilized, disciplined, decent world would *not* put down a criminal like Tyndall? How much suffering has he caused? How many deaths from heroin or Ecstasy are due to him? The courts let him off again and again. My sister's boy, Winston's son. Remember the Rogerson boy? It was years ago now. Just another statistic, another death. Tyndall always had enough money to buy bent policemen, to buy alibis. They could never catch him. But I did. Are you going to tell me that the world's not a better place?' He threw a blazing, accusing, pleading look at his audience.

Minutes passed. Neither the senior agent nor the psychologist had picked up on the connection with Winston Rogerson yet. They were interested in the colonel, not coincidental names. The man from the Harman Institute glanced surreptitiously at his watch. This wasn't his scene. He wanted out of this airless room and back to his life with warring bacteria. It was cleaner there.

Suddenly the colonel's expression had a crafty look to it. 'Yes,' he said, 'd'you know that I've got relations in high places? Very high places. Ring him if you don't believe me. He owes me a favour in return for all the good turns I did him. Yes; go on, ring Winston Rogerson. He'll tell you. He'll be on my side. He'll explain.' The colonel stared hard at the shocked people across the table from him, a triumphant look on his face. 'Talk to him and you'll see why I went for Peter Morgan. That's the real reason you're all so upset. But you all know he's a nothing. He's shallow; all window dressing. Everyone knows that.'

The interrogator opened his mouth to say something, then shut it again. He did not believe what he had just heard. Could it possibly be true, the link with Winston Rogerson?

'I'll tell you the real reason why.' The colonel was unstoppable now. 'It's nothing to do with him, nothing personal, that is. But Morgan's a symbol, isn't he? The buck has to stop with him, for the rotten society we live in, where talent, devotion, character, like my brother-in-law's, goes mocked and derided. Shallow, shallow, shallow. Why should he have won out against a real leader like Winston? You call Winston. He'll tell you. He'll tell you I was right to do what I did.'

Beneath his ice-cold, professional exterior, the senior agent was shaking. It if turned out to be true what the colonel was saying, that he was Winston Rogerson's brother-in-law, and he seemed to recall something long past about the Deputy Prime Minister's son and drugs, then this would rival the emergence of the virus in terms of the public impact it would have. God, would it. He stood up and ordered a break. The interrogator couldn't wait to go and pass on what he'd been told. It was too hot to keep. It was sheer dynamite.

They came back in half an hour, gave the colonel a cup of tea and a biscuit, then continued. Before they did so, the Harman representative came over and whispered in the psychiatrist's ear. The latter nodded and began the session with a direct question to the colonel. 'We know why, colonel. We understand you now,' she said gently. 'Please: tell us how, *how* you targeted them so precisely? We need to know how they were infected.'

'The general was easy, he walked straight in.' The colonel's voice was low, his eyes staring blankly into the middle distance. 'I learnt from him. The others . . . more tricky. I should have listened to Banquier: he would have shown me.'

'Who's this Banquier?' asked the interrogator. He got no direct reply. For the next hour the team kept trying to get that one crucial answer out of the colonel. He went off at tangents, either through confusion or because he wanted, deep down, to keep them guessing right up to the end. He'd done what he'd set out to do, he said. The virus had reached and killed his targets; that was an end to the matter. The interrogator, tired himself, broke off and went to ask advice from senior colleagues. Should they use force, or a truth drug? Could a new, tougher, team beat the truth out of him? He needed to know.

10 Downing Street, London, Tuesday 28th June

Winston Rogerson was so buoyed up in his new position as Acting Prime Minister that he felt he could do no wrong. He was in charge: boy, was he in charge. There would be real discipline, real leadership, from now on. That was what the Government, the Party, the country needed. As a first step, he'd decided to sweep out all the yes-men, the cronies, the spindoctors, who had taken over Number Ten, who had tried to keep the PM's secret from him, from the Cabinet, from Parliament itself. They were midgets, schemers, whisperers, media manipulators, enemies of democracy. They had to go. Then, just as he felt that the throne he had always dreamt about was truly his, the rug was pulled out from under him and his ambitions with a cruel and devastating impact.

How could he, Winston Rogerson, ever in his wildest dreams, have dreamt that he was in some way to blame? Later, on lonely and unhappy reflection, Rogerson recognized that his brother-in-law, Sam, had always been far too rigidly fixated in the pursuit of what he perceived to be his duties. They had never been close because of this, because Sam had a singleness of purpose that always infuriated his wife, Tina, and the rest of his family. Sam had been totally dedicated to whatever task he had in hand: nothing could deflect him when he was on some enterprise or other. Consequently, when he retired, the colonel had changed from zealous to zealot. He no longer had a mission in life: the part-time jobs the army had ladled out to him, such as carrying out occasional medical examinations for insurance purposes, gave him no sense of satisfaction. He was too old for the army but not too old to be a doctor; he had put his name on some Health Service list, thus the occasional locum work. When he was questioned about all that later, Rogerson agreed with what Sam said under interrogation: that he had probably done it all in his sister's, Tina's, memory. In practice, Tina had never much cared for her brother; there had been an unpleasant incident in their childhood when he had betrayed her confidence to their autocratic mother, with consequences that only the years had blended into forgetfulness. Following her death, the two men had, naturally, come together for a while, out of a shared grief. In political life, to know one's friends and enemies is a *sine qua non*. Friends can be manipulated and enemies can be avoided or defeated. But, as any politician knows, there are a vast number of people out there in the real world, who have strong views about them, who cannot be clearly identified as either friend or enemy. Ninety-nine times out of a hundred, that does not matter. But there is the hundredth time, where, to have a friend or an enemy that one knows nothing about, can be a singular handicap. Colonel Sam Broomfield's friendship, and the actions he took to augment it, were intended to ensure that Tina's memory was glorified by her husband's success. That dreadful truth was revealed to Winston Rogerson by Sir Ian Temple-White himself.

Rogerson went as pale as if someone had kicked him in the

groin. 'Who . . . ?' he whispered. 'Who? Who did you say was responsible?' Then, 'Oh, my God. Mad, mad, fucking mad,' he said, as he collapsed back in a chair and cupped his head in his hands in total horror and disbelief.

15

Ealing, West London, Early July

Even the most dire events have small, localized beginnings. The trouble with unknown diseases is that they are difficult to control due to the very fact that they are unknown. The medical profession is far from perfect, just as the medical reporting of new or unusual ailments to the central health authorities is highly fallible. What Guthrie, Grant and Stevenson had always feared might happen, happened. The virus went into spinoff: it mutated. Grant and his team were still hard at work looking for a possible antidote when the next stage was reached. At the end of that week, four doctors in one Ealing GPs' practice had met to compare notes on some odd cases of patients who either had become rapidly bedridden or were brought into the surgery by worried relatives, complaining of unusually high fever, aching joints and memory loss. The GPs remarked on the fact that they had not received notification of any special new strain of flu, which was what most of them at first guessed it to be. It took twenty-four hours before the local press ran a story about the mystery illness which was affecting several elderly patients in an old people's home. One of the most obvious symptoms of the disease was a strange grey sheen which spread across the eyes of the victims. Over that weekend, three of these elderly inmates died in considerable pain. Then the balloon went up. They called it Korean flu, but it became obvious even to the GPs that it wasn't flu at all. The Chief Medical Officer of Health was notified and he issued an immediate General Health

Warning via the Department of Health in Whitehall. Only then did an overworked Professor Grant and his staff at the Harman Institute, who were still busy working on the antidote but were also congratulating themselves on having stopped the colonel targeting any more victims, realize what might have occurred.

In fact, it had been heralded in a minor way by Mrs Smith's very unpleasant and painful death. That dreadful event took place only a few days after she had been scratched by her cat, and at first it was not recognized for what it was. It took a further twenty-four hours before it was finally identified as the first of a cluster of self-spreading cases of new variant surge fever, the infection caused by Virus ZD198. When he received her post-mortem test results, Dr Guthrie immediately realized that they could be back at square one. How the colonel had managed to pick off and contaminate his victims became an irrelevance from that very moment. The virus might no longer need help to transmit: tests hurriedly carried out on some dead pigeons and small mammals culled in the Ealing area soon confirmed that they, plus the fleas, lice and other parasites which many of them carried, were now the carriers of ZD198.

Epidemics and plagues strike in the backstreets of Mexico City or in the slums of Karachi or Bombay. They do not happen in the Western World. Britain's emergency services are prepared for all sorts of civil disasters – air or rail crashes, floods or fires. With the help of the army, the police know how to act efficiently in support of the civil power, to contain riots or demonstrations. But epidemics are another matter. In consequence, government civil servants had to dig deep into Cold War archives to search out instructions on what people should do if Britain was attacked with gas or biological weapons. One thing became blindingly obvious from the outset: disease is stopped neither by policemen, nor soldiers with guns.

Over the first week of July things took on a momentum of their own. Even the news of the death of Peter Morgan was quickly passed over in the wake of the epidemic. On the most urgent professional advice of Professor Grant, the Government, under the new Prime Minister, the former Home Secretary Simon Tattersall, issued a draconian Order in Council which was widely and constantly broadcast on radio and television. It banned, with immediate effect, the movement of personnel and vehicles in and out of the London Borough of Ealing. All roads in the area were sealed off by police backed by units of the Territorial Army. All pets and other animals in the district were to be rounded up, taken into strict quarantine, or immediately destroyed. Snipers and sportsmen were called in and a cull of the local bird population was effected immediately. The media went hysterical. They accused all and sundry, but particularly the Government, of a gross lack of preparedness. Where were the antidotes, the inoculations, against such a dreadful disease? Why had the Government been taken unaware? What was the likely fatality rate? Where had the disease come from? Who was to blame? Whose head must roll? Hugely difficult though it proved to be, isolating the streets surrounding that small part of London was enforced by a series of hastily drafted and promulgated Government decrees. It was like the Middle Ages. The entire district was effectively put into quarantine: trains were not permitted to stop at local stations and no commuting was allowed to take place in or out, until clearance was given. Schools were immediately closed, and volunteer medical teams were helicoptered in, equipped with a huge variety of antibiotics and drugs which were widely administered on a trial and error basis in an attempt to limit the spread of the disease.

Civil liberty protest demonstrations were called, but collapsed through lack of any support, particularly when, in the course of five days, the first half-dozen cases had grown to around eighty. Two public buildings in Ealing were requisitioned to serve as temporary isolation hospitals. Around the barriers, there were scenes of mass panic as relatives and friends from outside the controlled area attempted to get in, and those inside, with dear ones in other parts of Britain, made feverish attempts to break free. Troops and police, who had been issued with special overalls and masks, were given strict instructions to prevent, by force if necessary, anyone from passing through the razor-wire barriers which had been hastily erected through parks and gardens and across streets. And all the while, ever more hysterical press headlines screamed with the unanswered questions: what, where, why, didn't the Government do something? The Government could do little other than forcefully try to contain matters until much-needed specialist advice emerged from the newly established Crisis Headquarters at the Harman Institute. The team, under Professor Grant, now also included a group of senior researchers, which, despite Professor MacArthur's protestations, included Dr Euan Davidson from Edinburgh, who had at their beck and call a huge amount of other resources from medical schools and research institutes up and down the country. Lyle Thane, who was again despatched to the Institute by the Secretary to the Cabinet as the official representative of the Government, got the army to bring in enough beds and other necessary provisions to allow the team to eat, live, and sleep on the premises.

Increasingly large areas of West London were barriered off as more cases of new variant surge fever were identified. Vigilante groups were formed and sealed off some streets themselves. People stayed in their houses as much as possible. Specially equipped public health squads were sent in to disinfect the streets with high pressure hoses, and clear away and burn the dead birds and animals that littered the streets and gardens. The law enforcement authorities saw it as their national duty, if not their salvation, to make sure that the *Specified Areas*, as they were now called, were rigorously sealed off by armed troops. Communal and personal suffering went hand in hand, and teams of overworked doctors, still without any effective anti-viral agents to administer, became immune to pity.

South-east England, then Britain itself, became isolated, when a huge public outcry in both the United States and the European Community led to strict immigration controls on all people travelling by air, sea, or through the Channel Tunnel. An almost total ban on all movement was proposed by the Commission in Brussels. It would remain in force until the danger of further infection had been removed or a suitable and proven vaccination became available. A series of Public Health Orders was promulgated, forcing anyone who fell sick to be taken, by force if necessary, to one of the isolation hospitals, with the result that sometimes, when an individual in a family did fall ill, their family hid them lest they should never see their loved ones again. The media doomwatchers predicted that the Apocalypse had arrived, that every facet of modern civilization would become strained to the limit, that charnel houses would become filled to overflowing, and that great pyres would have to be lit to burn the bodies and personal possessions of the many who were sure to perish. That it did not quite come to that was as much due to good fortune as design.

The Harman Institute, East London, Sunday, 3rd July

At the Institute, Dr Stevenson was tiring of always having to explain the scientifically obvious to Lyle Thane. She was also increasingly wary of his motives. He had taken possession of one entire corner of the lab, as if he owned the place. He'd also brought a secretary with him from Number Ten, but she was ensconced in an outer office while he, with three newly installed telephones at his disposal, was seated on their best swivel chair, feet up on the lab bench, from where, like a lot of small yet powerful men, he was trying to run the world.

'The colonel simply didn't realize how clever viruses can be, that this one would soon find a way of transferring itself,' she said wearily, in response to his question.

'But . . .'

'Let me finish, Lyle. I've told you before: medical science is not one step ahead. It's always several steps behind. Malaria is back, TB is back, so is diphtheria. Bilharzia is a major global threat, and a host of others . . .'

'I've heard the lecture.' Thane shrugged.

'Heard, maybe. But have you *understood*?' She stared angrily at him. How different he was from Guthrie. The latter, tall, gangling, stooped, friendly, spoke the same language, was interested in the same things, shared the same intellectual curiosity. But right now he was hardly a bundle of fun. By contrast, Thane, despite his height, was tough, ambitious, uncaring, exuding self-confidence and a brazen love of power which, despite herself, she found almost attractive. Neither man was like the safe, conventional figures she'd had working relationships with in the past. She sensed that, perhaps because of the confined environment and the tension under which they were all working, she was playing one off against the other. She would notice Guthrie looking at her, then he would flash a slow smile at her, rather like a friendly, intelligent Labrador. Thane, by contrast, was a terrier, or perhaps a whippet. Right now he was watching and waiting for her to continue. 'Let me repeat,' she hesitated. 'In ZD198, the colonel picked, by accident or design, a strain of virus he thought he could easily transport and target. He probably tried it out first or saw it tried out.'

'Think so? In Africa?'

'Does that matter now? It's found its own way, horizontally, without help.'

'Think Guthrie's on to some antidote?'

'Sounds hopeful. But that's only with his model. A practical cure could still be a long way off. However, his researches mean that the pharmaceutical labs can start backing him up, working on a range of products, just in case. Try, hope and pray, Lyle.'

'Hey,' said Thane, brightening visibly. 'We've been working so hard. How about you and I taking a few hours off together?'

She looked hard at him and said, 'No way, Lyle. Not now . . . not later, either.'

At that moment, Harper Guthrie walked in, looked hard at both of them as if wondering what was going on, then said, 'I can't delay any longer. I need to talk to the colonel direct. It's the only way to get at the truth. Get the authority, will you, Lyle?' Thane, deeply hurt by Rebecca Stevenson's brusque rejection of his advances, glared at them both, then swung into action.

Since Simon Tattersall had been appointed Prime Minister at emergency sessions of both the Party and the Cabinet, things happened much more decisively. Guthrie's request was approved immediately. In retrospect, everyone realized that they should have brought the American back into play much sooner, but he had been working non-stop at the Institute searching for both carrier and antidote. Now it was agreed that he was much the best man to confront the colonel in his own language, play the one-expert-to-another game, sympathize, empathize, drag out everything he could. Steady resolution replaced the small panics of his life. It was the most difficult and dangerous game Guthrie would ever have to play.

They brought the colonel, under armed guard, from the inter-rogation centre to an MI5 safe house near the Institute. There Guthrie waited for him in a pleasantly-furnished sitting room overlooking well-tended gardens. He was no natural inquisitor, but he was determined to get at the truth. He stood up politely when the colonel was led into the room, and gestured to him to take a seat in a deep chair by the window. He offered him coffee. While he did not relish the role, he made all the running at first, talking about his own past research, describing his little successes, judging how to play the colonel, until he suddenly realized that the only thing that should matter to them both was the virus that had brought them together. He'd already decided to play it long: for the time being he deliberately withheld the information that the virus had mutated. A dozen pairs of ears listened to every word of their subsequent conversation.

How did you get the virus into Britain?

Banquier showed me how to store and transport it. Inert silicon gel. It's easy under the right conditions.

Surely it needs to be kept at a constant temperature – at least most of them do?

Right.

So?

The British Army flew me out to Africa. The US Army flew me home. Kind, eh? I needed to bring home all my special kit with me, didn't I? I didn't need to smuggle anthrax in shampoo bottles as those Kurds did recently. Officialdom did it for me. Controlled temperatures all the way. They even gave me the fridges with the special compartments to keep after I got home. Said they didn't need them. Generous of them, wasn't it?

How did you infect them?

Them?

Them. Your . . . enemies. We tried lots of methods with David. We couldn't find out how you did it.

David? Oh yes, I remember. Your model.

Building models is the only way we have of experimenting.

Why?

Because, unlike you, we can't practise on human beings.

I wasn't practising.

So, how did you transfer it? What carrier did you use?

Two stages. I got the virus into them. It's in a lot of people. Then . . . then I went for the body's immune system. As you know, that's easier. Break that down, then ZD198 goes for you.

I guessed as much, but how?

The virus works itself in.

Not sexually transmitted?

Of course not. What a thought.

Then?

Like a hypodermic. Through the skin. Almost everyone has breaks in their skin somewhere. Spots, rashes, bleeding gums, even athlete's foot. So: put it in toothpaste, deodorant, anti-rash gel . . .

Toothpaste . . .

Anywhere where there's bleeding, like round the gums. There's usually a slight inflammation on the underarm skin, a slight redness – that is enough.

The Prime Minister?

Something like a laugh was caught on tape.

Most people don't set out to harm Prime Ministers, except with harsh words, of course.

So?

So: opportunism. I was presented with an opportunity. A chance to hit back at a rotten, cliquish system, where talent goes down the drain. Peter Morgan was shallow, time-serving, a symbol of all that's the pits in this filthy fucking society. Someone has to make a stand, Dr Guthrie. You, as a doctor, must agree.

It's an unfair world, colonel. So, are you . . . are you all right, colonel?

Yes, yes. I'm fine. Just tired, that's all.

The Prime Minister . . . you were saying?

Winston. Winston Rogerson is my brother-in-law.

You told us.

He had me invited to an official government reception shortly after I got back. It was the only time he had invited me to anything.

And?

He introduced me to a fool of a man, the PM's doctor. 'You two should get on famously,' Winston said grandly. Taylor . . . Yes, that was his name. He couldn't have treated an ingrown toenail, that man. Asked him about his work with the PM. No problems there except for repetitive shaving rash. The PM gets bad shaving rash . . . can you believe it? I laughed, but remembered it later. Later, when I needed to act, I rang Taylor, told him I had just the thing, a super new American anti-bacterial gel. He was very, very grateful.

Shaving rash?

Shaving rash. Like the general: General George. Minor skin complaints. One doesn't need a needle or scalpel to break the skin, Dr Guthrie. You know that.

Then came another *apologia*.

You've no idea how careful I was. I targeted them so carefully, so that no one else would get hurt. I always used a minor variant of ZD198, which Banquier had identified. I didn't want to kill them, you see. Only destroy their brains. How was I to know that it would go on to kill them too? You understand, Dr Guthrie? You understand, don't you? It wasn't really me, it was nature itself.

The voice was wistful, pleading for understanding. There was a long pause.

You were playing God.

Like you were playing with David.

Let me tell you the bad news, colonel.

Bad news?

It's mutated even further. Changed to survive. Gone into spinoff.

Spinoff?

You're slow, colonel. You've seen how quickly viruses adapt.

Yes. But I . . .

They haven't told you. Deliberately. They left it to me to break the news.

What news?

Round where you live in Ealing. We've had to seal off a huge area of West London. Eighty to a hundred confirmed cases. Twelve fatalities already. You'll know as well as I do what their prospects are.

Mutated? I don't believe you. It can't have. Not that quickly.

Listen, colonel. We have a major epidemic on our hands. We've destroyed as much local animal and bird life as we can, since that's how it seems to be travelling. Brussels and Washington have acted harshly and promptly. Britain itself is in quarantine.

It couldn't go into spinoff.

You're repeating yourself, colonel. You must know how it happened.

No.

You did something. D'you know a Mrs Smith?

Smith. No. Should I?

A neighbour. Fed pigeons in the street.

Oh, that Mrs Smith.

Look, colonel. Every single thing at your house has been taken away and analysed. Including some poisoned birdseed. Cross-infected with feed you gave your rats.

Nonsense. That's not a criminal offence, poisoning pigeons.

Some of your rats escaped too.

Vandals broke into my garage. Not my fault.

Nothing's your fault, is it? Look, we know from a local vet that Mrs Smith's cat ate a large white rat and died. And a sick pigeon too, probably.

Whose cat?

Jesus, colonel! I've no idea whether the virus first got out via the birdseed or with the rat. Mrs Smith's cat ate a dead rat and probably had a go at a sick pigeon, then scratched her badly before it died. We have the autopsies.

Autopsies?

Of the pigeons. Of the cat. Of Mrs Smith.

There was another long silence.

She died . . . ? I didn't mean . . .

You didn't mean a lot of things, colonel. But let me tell you one last thing, we're not interested in your confessions any more. We're way beyond that. You're of no more use to anyone now.

So the virus jumped? I . . .

Colonel. It's called zoonosis. Viral agents jumping between species. You know all that.

I . . . yes . . . I know all that. Banquier did a series of experiments: birds, animals, people. Out there, people are cheap.

I'm going to leave you alone now, colonel. Otherwise I might just lose my self-control.

Outside, the listeners had to wait for quite some time. Then they heard the sound of sobbing.

The colonel was left to recover his composure. He had been totally at peace with himself over the deaths he had so carefully orchestrated. But this mutated virus was killing people who were not guilty of anything. They were innocents. He had helped to kill them. He sat in silence and remembered – how he remembered – sitting in an old rattan chair beside the totally emotionless Dr Banquier. He recalled watching, through the glass of an isolation cubicle, an African woman, tied to the bed. She was naked but for a cloth thrown over her middle. She was frothing at the mouth. Her eyes were so filled with pain that it seemed they were trying to pop out of their sockets. Her jaws were stretched wide in a soundless scream. Even if she had screamed, they would not have heard through the panes of glass and above the sounds of an African night. She had lost control of all her bodily functions. It had been a revolting sight. He remembered the strange round wound on her forehead: a witchdoctor's primitive trepanation, Banquier explained; an attempt to release whatever devils her tribesfolk had believed inhabited her head, he had added. Without that means of entry, that horrid cut, the virus would have been rejected and the woman would have survived. Mad, maybe, but she would have lived.

The colonel sat alone with other thoughts of death. He had seen so much. Death, in his experience, need not be horrid. But each man and woman feared the manner of dying. A quick or easy death, preferably anaesthetized by drugs, was always better. That, or the natural anaesthetic that came from Alzheimer's or other decay, killing the brain before the flesh. Nature had other means, temporary means, of coping with too much pain: man was allowed to faint. But what of the continuing, unrelieved pain, the agony of a lingering, ruptured body, the slow, relentless move to physical oblivion, when the mind itself is still sharp and clear? What of the pain that came, as he had often seen it, with a temperature that raged for hours, the body sweating, soaking the sheets, for those who were lucky enough to have sheets? What of searing agony, through limbs and torso, with no respite? The colonel stood and went towards the window.

Alone in the darkening room, many eyes watched and listened unseen. He recalled doctors who did not care, who had neither the competence nor the drugs to cope with pain. He had seen the suffering that was endemic throughout the Third World. He knew that when pain was no longer bearable, delirium took over, when those around the dead or dying were spared the worst excesses of reality because the victim was too weak to scream. Better, he believed, was death that came with the speed of a bullet, the stab of a knife, than from some new dread disease out of Africa.

The colonel suddenly turned and ran towards the locked door. He began frantically to beat on it. 'Ask Banquier. Ask Banquier. Tell him I didn't mean it!' he screamed.

16

He should have taken the day off. This was the Fourth of July, for God's sake! Harper Guthrie should be out waving the stars and stripes, celebrating somewhere. But he wasn't. He was sitting in front of a damned computer screen, getting nowhere. His mood wasn't helped when one of his assistants came up behind him and started chatting as if it was just another ordinary morning.

'That anti-viral agent you asked me to try out on the model?'

'Tell me,' said Guthrie wearily.

'Rosie, the one after David . . .'

'Get on with it.'

'She's surviving. Seems to have slowed its progress at least,' the man said.

'You sure?' Guthrie turned in his chair and showed more interest.

'Want to have a look?'

'I believe you. Get everyone setting up the other tests, then. Tell Zeneca, Bayer, the other pharmaceutical people, what you've found. And –'

'We've already started, Dr Guthrie. Looks promising. But it's still light years away from an antidote. We desperately need another lead.'

Guthrie knew that bitter fact only too well. And they had so little time. The telephone on his desk rang as his assistant left the room. The long-distance voice at the other end sounded peeved.

'You left a message on my answering machine. Know what day this is?' asked Dr Boekamper grumpily. 'It's only eight in the morning, New York time.'

'I know what day it is. It's a working one here,' said Guthrie, 'and I know about East Coast time.'

'So?'

'So I want to speak to this Dr Banquier on the telephone. Urgently. Myself. Direct. No intermediaries. How do I achieve that? Imagine he's buried up country in the Congo somewhere, but –'

'It happens you're in luck. So am I, I can get back to enjoying the holiday. I know exactly where you can get him. Right now,' said the satisfied voice at the other end of the line.

Kisangani, Congo, Monday 4th July

Clegg Hurley was also meant to be taking the day off. It was a holiday even in this bloody hell-hole, but he only had a spooky drunken Belgian doctor for company. He'd stay in his room, reading quietly, for a while yet.

The satellite telephone by his bed rang and kept ringing. It couldn't be New York. This was the Fourth of July after all.

'Yah?' he asked. 'Who? Oh, yes. Yes, he's here. I'll – who exactly did you say was calling?'

Millbank, Central London, Monday 4th July

At MI5, they listened in to the monitored telephone call as a matter of routine.

'Name's Guthrie. Dr Harper Guthrie. Ringing from London, England. Sorry to disturb you. Is this a good moment?'

'Yes?'

'You are Dr Banquier?'

'Why you want?'

'You'll have heard: we've had many cases of ZD – of surge fever, here in London.'

'You speak from London? Goodness . . . Yes: I hear you have had a case.'

'Many cases now. It has spread.'

'Surge fever is difficult to spread.'

'We know that: knew that. It's mutated.'

'The line is bad; what you say?'

'Mutated. It's mutated.'

'So: you have other cases?'

'Close to a hundred.'

'A hundred. Goodness! How . . . ?'

'You know a Colonel Sam Bloomfield?'

'Ah, yes. I remember. You know him? Please send my greetings.'

'He spread the disease.'

'Ah . . . Ah . . . Spread? I see. I thought . . .'

'He is under arrest. He said to talk to you.'

'I sorry. I not know him well. I must go now.'

'No: please, Dr Banquier. Wait. I have to know. He – the colonel – seems to think you might know of an antidote. He asks you to help us.'

'Help? Antidote? I don't . . . Wait. There was something we used out here. On a few cases only. Maybe it work. I do not have good equipment here any more, to test . . .'

'Yes . . . ? Yes . . . ? Hello? Dr Banquier? Are you still there?'

'I still here. Yes. Something you could try. It helps sometimes, with surge fever. Very often. Very good. I will ask Mr Hurley here . . .'

'Who?'

'Mr Hurley of the WHO. I stay with him now.'

'Oh, yes.'

'I ask Mr Hurley to send you detail. The prescription. Yes. *Immédiatement*. Yes. Thank you, sir. Goodbye.'

'No: wait, Dr Banquier. Could the colonel have taken anything, stolen anything else from you, as well as the surge fever virus?'

'I did not say he stole anything . . .'

'We know he stole some ampoules from you.'

'I know nothing.'

'He's confessed.'

'Confessed?'

'Confessed. Yes. What else might he have taken? Hello . . . ? Hello . . . ? Are you still there, Dr Banquier?'

'I'm still here.'

'So? Please.'

'Confessed. I see then . . . Maybe hanta . . . some . . . some Ebola. Smallpox, I not sure . . .'

'Thank you, Dr Banquier.'

'Goodbye.'

And the line went dead.

10 Downing Street, London, Wednesday 6th July

'Can I ask you something?' Lyle Thane spoke with some trepidation. With a new Prime Minister in the chair, he was feeling deeply insecure. They were waiting for the Cabinet to finish their private meeting before the latest statement was given out to the press. The chemists were hard at work with the formulae they'd received, via the WHO, from Banquier. Boekamper was coming up with more details later. Apart from that, nature and the strict public health regime were helping to slow the spread of the disease, and the number of known cases of the virus had stabilized at around one hundred. But it was much too early to start celebrating. Daniel Evans was already in the briefing room, trying to look as optimistic as possible. It was not an easy task.

'Please,' responded Sir Mark Ivor, staring into the middle distance. His summons to see Simon Tattersall had come out of the blue.

'The first time we met?'

'Remind me.'

In other circumstances, Thane would have been riled by such arrogance. This time he shrugged and said, 'Peter Morgan called you in to see him.'

'Of course,' Sir Mark paused reflectively. 'I'd forgotten,' he said. 'Seems a long time ago now, doesn't it?'

'It's only six weeks or so ago. Can you believe that?' asked Thane, turning away reflectively.

'Difficult, I agree.' Sir Mark looked at the younger man as if seeing him for the first time. A buzzer sounded somewhere, and a secretary appeared.

'The PM will see you now, Sir Mark,' she said.

'Before you go.' Thane stared at the minister. 'Can I ask you: in my place, or Caldwell's, or Daniel Evans's, what would you have done differently? Did we handle it so badly?'

'Uncharted waters,' said Sir Mark, moving towards the door.

'You've not answered my question,' said Thane.

Sir Mark Ivor turned and looked at the other man. 'It's a good question, Mr Thane. It deserves a good answer and I haven't got one. You can read that as you will.'

Ivor wheeled into the familiar office. 'Congratulations,' he said to the new incumbent who was sitting behind the great, familiar desk.

'If congratulations are ever due, taking this seat,' said Simon Tattersall.

'You wanted . . . ?' Sir Mark asked.

'Need a new team round me. People I can trust.'

'I'm past it,' Sir Mark said. 'I'm not sure I –'

'Want you to help choose them, Mark. Vet them. Make sure they'll pass the *Sun* test. No nasty scandals hiding in the woodwork.'

'Flattered . . .' Sir Mark responded. 'You ought to start by seizing virtue out of what's happened.'

'Meaning?'

'Grant and his team have achieved a famous victory. It could have been devastating. Salute British medical science at its best.'

'With help from that Guthrie chap?'

'Rewards and praise all round, Prime Minister. A major Government grant to the Harman Institute would go down well.'

'Spinoff from the spinoff?'

'Well put, Prime Minister,' said Sir Mark. He did not smile.

Kisangani, Congo, Wednesday 6th July

Clegg Hurley ran all the way from the office with the piece of paper in his hand. He was out of breath and sweating profusely by the time he reached the verandah. Dr Banquier was asleep in his usual wickerwork chair, an empty whisky bottle and glass on the table beside him. He stirred as Hurley appeared.

'They greatly appreciated your help. They're sending a helicopter for you. I've to fly out with you. Isn't it sensational?' Hurley panted. 'Civilization . . . I can't wait.'

'Sending what?' muttered Banquier, emerging reluctantly from his alcohol-induced sleep. He hadn't shaved in days.

'A helicopter. A British military helicopter. They want to thank you.'

'Flying nowhere,' said Banquier, rising unsteadily to his feet.

'You must,' said Hurley. 'They need you. They want to know about the other things the colonel stole. Ebola, hanta . . .'

'No need me. I told everything. I no be here,' said Banquier with sudden resolution, pulling up his khaki trousers and buttoning his sweat-stained shirt.

'They need you. They need to know more about the antidote.'

'No need me for that,' he responded.

'What?' asked Hurley. The man was drunk again. He hadn't understood him.

'Gave antidote already. You sent it them.' Banquier was staring at him as if he was the stupid one. 'They want more information, tell them: look up '65 outbreak. I just remembered.'

''65 outbreak? Christ! Where was that? ZF 198? Surge fever?'

'Different times; different name. It mutate, probably. 'Course I sure. I know my stuff. They sure know I do. Or no helicopter for me. Tell them look up '65 Zinder outbreak, in Niger. French, Paris, may have records. Colonial Empire. Brussels . . . Atlanta must have, too. Before computers; databases. In a file. Paper file. I was research student then. I help test serum in Belgium. It work then. It work now.'

'Why the hell didn't you say?' asked Hurley, staring forlornly at his houseguest, visions of his release from this hell-hole suddenly dashed. 'Why did you never say?'

'Nobody never asked. I forgot,' replied Banquier, turning his head away. 'No one. Not you, not no one. Not direct. Hey, you.' He paused, then looked hard at Hurley. 'Need jerry cans, for petrol, for Volvo. I buy some here? I guess no drive-in gas stations where I go.'

Central London, Wednesday 6th July

The same key men and women, politicians, civil servants, doctors and scientists, all people who had begun to relax too soon, listened intently to the next cassette tape. Dr Harper Guthrie had been sent on another critical task: to attempt to uncover the colonel's very last secret. The army doctor's voice was at first surprised, then sullen, then determined.

You said you were finished with me, Dr Guthrie.

Things change.

Where's Banquier? Did you find him?

I spoke to him. Now he's gone.

Gone? Gone where? He can't go back to Belgium, you know.

He's disappeared. Vanished.

You'll find him.

With all of Africa to hide in? Anyway, we need you again,

colonel, not Banquier. Yes, I thought you and I were finished, but now I have more to ask you. Banquier never left Africa. You came home. Home with the vials, the samples of surge fever. And something more?

You know?

Yes, we know.

You told me you were not interested in my confessions any more. You said I was of no more use to anyone. Spoke too soon, eh, Dr Guthrie?

I said that, yes, before we knew you had brought more than surge fever into Britain with you. Where are the other things?

There was a long silence.

I hoped it would not come to this, but I had to plan for the eventuality.

What are you saying, colonel? You planned for the eventuality that you'd be caught?

I'm no fool, Dr Guthrie.

So, tell me: where are the other viruses you brought in? Ebola? hanta? Were there others, too?'

Another interminable pause followed.

We've been through everything in that garage. Where have you hidden them? The other ampoules?

There was no response.

Very well, colonel. This time it really is goodbye.

The tape ended there.

Millbank, Central London, Wednesday 6th July

Less than an hour had elapsed. Sir Ian chaired the emergency meeting himself.

'I heard the tape. I know what was said. We'll get the experts working on the colonel. With the right drugs and persuasion, we should eventually break the truth out of him. In the meantime . . .' He growled. 'How serious does the SSU think it is?'

'Bluntly, sir: we can't wait for the colonel to crack. A horrendous time-bomb is ticking away; it must be somewhere in the vicinity of his house in Ealing,' said Dr Stevenson.

'It's sealed off?'

'Of course. Dr Guthrie believes he could have built some sort of delayed action timing device that will release whatever he's got – hanta, Ebola, anthrax – they could start leaking out any time.' Professor Grant looked tired.

'I don't understand: how, even if it – they – are released, how do they get carried to the outside world? Don't they need someone, a person, animal or something, to spread them?' asked Sir Ian.

'Yes. But the colonel's already proved he's not stupid. He could have rigged up some means, quite apart from a booby-trap for anyone trying to find what he's done,' Grant added.

'That too?'

'That too.'

'So? We send in an SSU team to search the house?'

'Plus me. I might spot what they don't,' said Dr Stevenson.

'We can't have . . .'

'Women doing that sort of thing?' Dr Stevenson flushed angrily, but Professor Grant interrupted.

'I agree with Rebecca. Your SSU search people are good, but they're not dealing with killer viruses every day.'

'I'm used to dealing with mere human enemies of the State,' said Sir Ian wearily. 'I take your advice, professor.'

'Targeted by someone like the colonel, what we're looking for is much worse than the most evil terrorist. Microbes, bugs, viruses . . . the most accomplished killers around. If one of these groups of organisms got out, it could cut a horrendous swathe through the population of Britain, and the world.' Grant pressed his point home.

'People used to call epidemics divine retribution. American right-wing fundamentalists called the AIDS epidemic a punishment for the morally corrupt,' Sir Ian briefly philosophized.

For a moment, Rebecca Stevenson wondered whether he

shared that view. 'Think, Sir Ian, if the water supply was contaminated, or the complex drainage system that must run under Ealing, became the escape hatch to hell,' she said.

'You've made your point, Rebecca.'

'One last thing, sir. Dr Guthrie: he should come too.' It was a statement rather than a request.

'He's American. Not his job. Does he want to?'

'He wants to. He knows the colonel's mind better than all of us. Something might just click, and whatever we find,' Dr Stevenson continued, 'we won't be able to risk bringing it out. I'll need his help to destroy it then and there.'

Ealing, West London, Wednesday 6th July

That day Dr Harper Guthrie saw for himself something of the human consequences of what had happened, and was deeply shocked by it. He had, since the beginning of the outbreak, been kept largely cloistered in the lab, and, with the exception of the meetings at Cabinet and his interrogations of the colonel, had not had time to wander the streets of London. He was aware of the sensational way the newspapers and television stations were carrying the story, but he had not been confronted by the basic misery it was causing to so many innocent people. Even as he went about his highly specialized business that evening he could not but witness separate little incidents of a heartrending nature, as, for example, when he stood and watched a weeping mother, a baby in her arms, plead with a stoney-faced soldier to let her out to join her husband. Then there was the furious young man who had to be physically restrained as he demanded to be allowed into the Specified Area to visit his dying mother. Again, he would never forget the sight of a young woman, a small bouquet of white flowers in her hands, standing in floods of tears at the refusal of the authorities to let her join her husband-to-be, today having been planned as the happiest of her life.

The little convoy, a dark official car and a white sealed van preceded by a police motorcycle escort, swept them up to the gates of the Command Centre that had been set up in a school on the edge of Ealing Common. To one side he could see a large notice labelled 'Press', with, beside it, a group of unhappy-looking photographers and TV camera teams. Guthrie had been advised to keep his face hidden. His sudden arrival at the cordoned-off area could, given his high-profile reputation as the 'Bugbuster', easily foment a new panic. Inside, past the armed military guards, he was immediately shown into a room where Rebecca Stevenson was waiting for him. They wasted little time but left by a side entrance that led to the other section of the barbed-wire fence that enclosed the area, where an army Land Rover was waiting to take them to the colonel's house. The white van, loaded with protective clothing and scientific testing equipment, came through a gate behind them along with the volunteer lab technicians.

An extra barrier with red-and-white skull and crossbones signs on it was drawn across the road in front of the house itself. Guthrie and Stevenson climbed out of their vehicle and went across to a large tent that had been set up in the children's playground near to the spot where the colonel had been arrested. Inside, the SSU team leader who had originally searched the house was waiting to give them a detailed briefing of where everything had been found. He stood beside a flipchart on which a rough plan of the house and garage had been drawn. The man explained, somewhat defensively, that they had taken everything as seen, analysed all the chemicals, the contents of the fridges, and had the rats taken away, tested and destroyed. The paperwork had been gone through by another team, while the contents of the house itself had been taken apart with a fine toothcomb by MI5.

'We weren't briefed to go any further,' the man explained. 'We weren't looking for bodies in the garden or anything, so, as far as I know, no one started pulling apart the walls or lifting the floorboards. When we found what we were looking for in the garage, well . . . that was that,' he added lamely.

'Quite right. We thought we had it all, too,' said Dr Stevenson. 'We still don't know what we're looking for, which is why we're here. Your team's prepared?'

'Waiting outside,' said the man. 'Ready when you are.'

'Let's go,' said Guthrie.

A few minutes later, a group of figures dressed like astronauts on a moon walk entered the modest little semi-detached house. All residents within a hundred-yard radius had long since suffered the double misfortune of having been ordered to leave their homes, yet forced to remain within the restricted area, and were now billeted in other parts of Ealing. Guthrie and Dr Stevenson, clumsy in their suits in such a confined area, had to communicate with each other via an inbuilt radio system, or with hand gestures, as, leaving the search of the house to others, they made their way into the empty garage. They had already decided that was where they would concentrate first. Presuming that the colonel had not invented some mechanism for releasing the bugs into the air, and that seemed beyond the bounds of practicality, the water and drainage system seemed the most obvious area for their investigations. They'd already been given a brief lecture on the likely plumbing by the head of the SSU search team. 'One lot of drains will be for basic sewage, while another, as like as not, will run into the street drains to carry the rainwater from the roofs and from the garden ground. Had I been the colonel, that's what I'd have used. Sewage goes off to treatment works; ground water is generally not highly polluted, seeps away all over the place, and is easily accessed by animals, insects, and . . . small children,' he added frighteningly.

And so it proved. Guthrie stood in silence for some time in the middle of the garage, looking around him, trying to think himself into the colonel's mind. How would he have done it? What would he have used? He turned and stared down at the floor, beside where the little sink had once stood until it had been ripped out by the SSU and sent off for checking. The broken wastepipe disappeared into a patch of cemented flooring. Bending down and asking one of the assistants to bring some special lighting and a hammer and chisel, Guthrie peered closely at the cement, then carefully ran a gloved finger along a line close to the garage wall. He paused and turned. 'Can your people dig a trench right round the building? Isolate every single pipe that leads from it, break each one and seal it so that nothing can get out? Meanwhile, can I have someone join me who's good with his hands? There seems to be some sort of trap door, just here, by the wastepipe.' He was facing his colleagues, but with the mask on they could not see how pleased he looked.

Less than an hour later the men outside had completed the sealing of all the outflow pipes. Inside, a technician had levered off the little hatch, which, to their disappointment, revealed an empty hole in the ground with the single wastepipe running through it. Then Guthrie, with that inbuilt attention to small details for which he was known, noticed that the pipe seemed to run in the wrong direction – towards the centre of the garage floor rather than to the drains outside the wall. This quickly led them to the discovery of a large vehicle inspection pit, hidden in the middle of the garage floor. It had obviously never been used, for the cement walls were cobweb-covered but clean. Six feet by four, by four feet deep, it had been floored and cleverly cemented over, thus hiding its existence from the original inspection team. On a stand in the bottom of the pit was a cleverly constructed contraption of pipes and funnels, all connected to the shell of a small household refrigerator that, until the electricity had been cut off by the original team, had been set at a controlled temperature. From this hellish toy, a pipe ran direct to the main drain, while a wire on a pulley led from it to the outside corner of the building and the privet hedge, behind which the two young boys had played those few deadly weeks earlier. Later, tests showed how cleverly this simple device would have worked. One sharp pull of the wire – to a casual observer it looked like some discarded aerial or telephone wire – and that poor-man's nuclear bomb would have been triggered to devastating effect. Individual biodegradable ampoules, containing some of the most deadly viruses known to man, would have been flushed out through the drainpipes into the capital's watertable.

17

Lyle Thane was riding a real high, and he hadn't even reached for the white powder yet. It was great to be on the winning side. He'd recommended Professor Grant for a knighthood, but Guthrie was American so he would have to make do with a citation. Thane had just had a most successful one-to-one with the new PM, Simon Tattersall. That guy was as straight as a die; he wanted everyone cleaner than clean. He'd actually said that he liked Thane: despite his part in the Morgan cover-up, Thane was a safe pair of hands; he could stay on. That was great. Now he would go and celebrate. Celebrate? Celebrate? To hell with Sarah St Just. To hell with Rebecca Stevenson. Nothing could stop him now. He looked at his watch. What was he doing hanging around? It was late, he would go out on the town: alone.

Some uncontrollable longing suddenly gripped him. He needed to escape; he needed excitement; passion; undiscovered, secret, anonymous. Reason deserted him. He went and picked up his BMW from where he had parked it on Horse Guards Parade and went searching. Searching for what?

Drink, then the white powder. What was he doing here? He stared hard and long at his image in the unfamiliar men's room mirror. He'd always had this thing about mirrors. He'd liked their ambiguity. As a child he remembered having looked for hours at his own reflection in his mother's wardrobe mirror, wishing, like Alice, to escape to a happier life through the looking glass. He'd always had a hand-mirror hidden in his desk drawer. Then he'd had that huge one specially hung in the bedroom of his flat. Now, in that disgusting, evil-smelling, white-tiled room, he saw, in the fractured mirror above a row of filthy washbasins, a sudden terrible kaleidoscope of images. Somehow, amid that confusion, he seemed to see a mirror smashed in anger in his childhood, and a horrid reflection of his father's angry face. Testosterone does strange things to powerful men. It was the thrill of danger, of the unknown, of being unknown, with new passions revealed, unhindered, secret, exciting, deadly. He failed to get what he was looking for. Instead of the one young man as arranged, other, older men, with tattoos, bodyrings, shaven heads, came at him. He was tiny; he didn't stand a chance. When he came to, he knew he would never be able to hide what they had done to him. These wounds were for life.

Later, much later. Pieces of expensively capped teeth rasped against road grit and mingled with the unfamiliar taste of blood in his mouth. Other feelings seemed absent, triggering a sudden fear that he might be paralysed. With difficulty he opened one eye; the other was too swollen to do his bidding. The good news was that he still had some sight, though his view was confined to a close-up of wet cobbles and a litter-strewn pavement beyond. Then his sense of smell returned: a repulsive odour of rotting vegetables and canine excrement. By day it was a busy East End streetmarket; by night, street lamps gleamed on pools of dirty rainwater on deserted tarmac outside that notorious public house.

Then came pain: from his head, from his battered kneecaps, from his back. While he was standing at that washroom mirror, did he remember a vicious kidney punch? Thane moved slightly, and immediately a sharp and unusual shock came from his right wrist, signalling that he could have fractured it as he had tried to cushion his fall. Fall? He had been beaten and kicked and pushed and left unconscious. Then came sound. He clearly heard the clip-clop of a woman's high heels on the paving stones, accompanied by the mushing sound made by a pair of trainers. They came close, paused, and he heard indistinct sounds of speech. A high, unwarranted female laugh followed, then both sets of footsteps went on their way. He lay motionless, afraid to move lest some other pain would suddenly assert itself.

Some time elapsed, then he heard a new sound: a distant, then ever closer police siren. From his one good eye, he saw, on the sheen of rainwater, multiple reflections of a blue flashing light as a pair of black official boots hove into sight. They stopped a mere foot away from his face and he sensed authority staring down at him. A firm hand took hold of his wrist as if to feel a pulse. He let rip a scream of agony which, in his condition, was translated into a weak groan. He made out a few recognizable words amid the static and babble of a two-way radio conversation. 'Broken . . . ambulance . . . drunk . . .' Drunk? Was he drunk?

Words dissolved into further action. Another siren. White shoes, green paramedic overalls, then the gentle voice of someone reassuringly whispering, 'You'll be OK, lad,' as he was rolled onto a stretcher. Again his wrist was knocked, again a groan, and he heard the words 'bad fracture all right,' as he passed into blissful darkness.

He came to, to new sights, sounds and the pungent smell of antiseptic, blended with the more comforting aroma of soap and starch from newly laundered uniforms. He was lying on some sort of trolley, head to one side, and so, when he briefly opened his eyes, he saw a dreadful image of himself, staring unrecognizably back at him from the reflection on the side of a stainless steel sterilizing cabinet. Someone was talking to him, asking him for his name, his address, his telephone number. His wallet with all his cards and personal details had gone, of course. Thank God his security pass was safe in his Pimlico flat. Someone came close to him, held him, and he felt and smelt as a pad of surgical spirit was wiped across his upper arm. There was the almost unnoticed prick of a hypodermic, then finally, before he again passed into oblivion, came a fleeting feeling of satisfaction that he had summoned up enough presence of mind from somewhere deep within him not to give his real name, his address, his telephone number, let alone reveal where he worked. That sixth sense, of all his senses, still would not save his day.

Dr Harper Guthrie did not like hospitals; he did not like real patients. He liked germ-free computers, though even they were not safe from hackers' viruses. But Professor Grant had flown to Brussels that very evening, to help the British Minister of Health reassure his European colleagues that the outbreak of ZD198 had now been fully contained, and he had taken Dr Stevenson with him. Thankfully, no word of that other deadly cocktail that had been destroyed a few days earlier would leak out for a long time yet. So Guthrie felt obliged, when the registrar at the hospital rang the Institute, to go himself and examine the test samples taken from a patient who might just have become infected. Once he had confirmed to himself, and the duty medical staff, that their patient was not a victim of ZD198 but was probably suffering from cerebral meningitis, he left to return home. By that time it was almost eleven o'clock at night and, for security reasons, the main doors to the hospital were locked. The exceptions were those at Accident and Emergency. Thus Dr Guthrie, leaving by that exit, happened to notice, lying on a stretcher on a trolley in the corridor waiting to be seen by a house doctor, a young man who looked as if he had been in a road accident, or, perhaps, in a very bloody fight.

Harper Guthrie remembered all too well his own exhausting years as a houseman back in Boston. Would he still have the patience, the humanity, to deal with the self-inflicted injuries of young fools like this? And yet, as he paused abstractly, staring down at the barely conscious young man below him, this one looked different. Guthrie, chaotic figure though he often appeared to be, was, as always, a highly disciplined observer of the little things in life. He noted the well-cut, if bloody, jacket folded over the end of the trolley, and remarked on its Savile Row label. Then he stared at the young man's face. He moved over to look at the identification docket on the trolley that recorded the man's name: a Peter Hutton from some address in Wimbledon. This man was not called Peter Hutton; this man, quite definitely, was . . .

At that moment, Lyle Thane opened his one good eye and groaned. He thought he was hallucinating when he saw Harper Guthrie staring down at him.

'Hey? What happened? Just happened to be passing,' said Guthrie, looking hugely concerned. He knew what he ought to do, but then he paused reflectively. 'This name, Lyle?' Guthrie asked. 'Are you badly . . . ? Look, I'll go get a senior man to look at you immediately. They can't realize who you are and where you come from.'

'No. No. Please. You don't want to know. Go away. I'll be OK. Just leave me,' Thane groaned through broken teeth. 'Name's Hutton. Peter Hutton. They mustn't know who . . . where I work. Please just go away. If this got out . . . Oh, God! It will. It must.'

Scandals were for other people. As Lyle Thane came to much later, he considered his options. He wasn't married. He wasn't newsworthy. Or was he? A moment of temporary insanity, one previous, resigning Cabinet minister had called it. Gay was OK; cruising and getting beaten up in sleazy East London was another. If it became known, he would be out, out of Number Ten. The new PM needed little scandals like this like a hole in the head. Even if Guthrie kept to his Hippocratic oath of silence, others would see his shattered teeth, his broken wrist, the mess his face was in, and would guess, would find out. 'Out' Lyle Thane and he would be out. He would be particularly dead in his own self-esteem, in his belief in his heterosexuality. Could he live with that? He had broached a key fortress of his life. His view of the world had always been less tempered by his own experience of it than by the way the media presented that view. He knew he should never be influenced by what he read in the broadsheets, in the tabloids, or what he saw on television. But he knew he was and always would be. He'd always lived and worked in an environment where perception was the only reality. If newspaper editors went after someone in the public eye, prince or politician, footballer or pop star, they could assassinate them better than any bullet or guillotine. The media made or broke people at whim. They did not like people like him.

Fear is at the heart of every mistake. Thane had a vivid imagination and had seen enough character assassinations to know what his future would be. He thought of trying to cover it up, but given all that had happened recently he knew it would be impossible. It was no simple paranoia. He thought of Sir Mark Ivor's remit to build a Downing Street staff that was whiter than white. He imagined the reactions of Eric Caldwell and the Secretary to the Cabinet. Daniel Evans was used to dealing with media scandals on a daily basis, so he would be more tolerant. But what of Sarah St Just and her glittering friends? What of his still-hoped-for plans to marry at St Margaret's, Westminster? What of his ambitions to pursue the charming Dr Rebecca Stevenson? Above all else, what would his father say? At long last he had won out over that dread figure from his past. He had achieved; he had looked the old man in the face and had laughed, even mocked. But now? He saw only the bottom of a deep black hole, its walls impossible to scale even if he found the will. He could visualize what would happen, so clearly, sometime soon. A *Sun* or *Mirror* journalist would come sidling up to him, smiling, winking, saying they'd heard some nasty little story . . . about to break . . . about to break. No, he suddenly had a vision of extreme clarity: if his entire life had flashed before his eyes right then, there would be so little there. He knew the solution: he would resign, go away, disappear abroad, anywhere; go before he was forced to, since the truth would always out. It was the only way to act in the goldfish bowl that was British public life.

Central London, Friday 8th July

The colonel was clever; clever to the end. Dr Guthrie found it almost impossible to believe him when he said that he had infected himself with Virus ZD198. Even if the man was truly mad, he was also highly intelligent; surely he would not want to die in the same terrible manner he had seen others do? But Professor Grant ruled that they must take no risks. They rushed him off to a specially prepared room in the isolation ward at the Institute. They kept him under armed guard, but armed guards are more relaxed in such circumstances, and, not unnaturally, they also keep their distance in case of cross-infection. A locked and guarded ward contains enough for a clever doctor to do what he wants to do, professionally and painlessly. Later, when they carried out the post-mortem on the colonel, and found that he was not, after all, carrying the virus, Dr Guthrie was not at all surprised.

Central London, Friday 8th July

The *Daily Telegraph* had most of the rest of the story on that morning's front page. On page five they also reported that a fierce fire had swept through a semi-detached house in Ealing which belonged to a retired colonel from the Royal Army Medical Corps. The fire brigade were left wondering at the intensity of the blaze in which everything, including the contents of the attached garage, was completely and utterly destroyed.

But that was a small story on the day of the State funeral in St Paul's Cathedral, when the Queen, members of the Government and Opposition, and all foreign ambassadors kept in the country by the travel ban, attended the funeral of the late Prime Minister, Peter Morgan. It was a tragedy that the re-discovery of a long-hidden antidote for the Virus ZD198 had come too late. It had, however, led to the promise of an early lifting of the ban on travel in and out of Britain.

The addresses from the pulpit given by the Archbishop of Canterbury, by the new Prime Minister, and by the Prince of Wales, brought tears to many an eye. It would take a long time before all the details of the background to the Prime Minister's fatal viral infection, coupled with the reasons for the categorical assurance from the Chief Medical Officer of Health that the epidemic was now fully under control, would come to light. Admittedly a story was circulating among some key journalists, to the effect that the dead colonel had been related by marriage to Winston Rogerson, and that all this had been in some way responsible for the latter's surprise resignation.

Harper Guthrie and Rebecca Stevenson were not at the funeral. They had taken a day off. They were, at that precise moment, having lunch at a corner table in a small café only a stone's throw away from the Harman Institute. Guthrie had, surprisingly nervously given what he had just been through, carefully considered what he was going to say and do. Had he, as a scientist, been studying the female version of some non-human species, and had he noted, circulating around her, a potential male mate, he would doubtless have remarked on its behaviour patterns, and how it set out to attract its chosen target. Throughout the animal kingdom it was a commonplace phenomenon: the human male was no different. Yet his having studied genetics and biology did not make him any more alert to his own behaviour patterns on that special occasion. He thought back over those few short weeks to his first uncertain arrival in Edinburgh on that cold, wet night. He remembered his strangely decisive lunch with Euan Davidson, then his first meeting at the Institute with Rebecca Stevenson. He thought briefly about the injured Lyle Thane, then dismissed that last unpleasant encounter to the back of his mind. He decided to let sleeping dogs lie.

As she sat opposite, talking to him, Rebecca Stevenson felt the skins of that personal onion her friend had once described, being pulled off, one by one. She felt more uncertain, more excited, than she had ever done. She liked Harper Guthrie; in her turn she clearly remembered her first sight of him, tousled and shambling, a battered figure, uncertain and ungainly.

'Our ancestors all used to be members of one small tribe or another. Then came the nation state. Now, I suppose,' Guthrie sat speculating, 'we're tribalized again, not by nationality, nor by race, nor creed, but by profession: scientist shall speak unto scientist; politician unto politician. New bonds, new clans, are created by specialist education; thus computer nerds, car salesmen, diplomats, are the same the world over.'

'A profound thought, Harper.' Rebecca smiled. 'So you and I are of the same new tribe, that's what you're saying?'

'Intellectually, yes. Socially, yes. Genetically, I don't think there would be any danger of in-breeding.'

She looked quickly across at him. 'In-breeding?' she asked. 'We weren't talking about that, were we?'

'Weren't we?' he responded, getting up from the table and, with surprising resolution, taking her by the arm. As he did so, he noted with pleasure how her normally cool cheeks exhibited a sudden high flush.

The Congo-Uganda Border, Saturday 9th July

Braking hard to avoid a huge pothole, Banquier struggled to control the skid, then righted the Volvo and carried on. Another three hours and he would reach the relative safety of the Ugandan border. He had great faith in his ability to talk his way across: he was a doctor and ready to prove it – his stethoscope, the emblem of his trade, lay in easy reach on the dashboard. Less honestly, rolled up on the seat beside him were two purloined items: a blue-and-white United Nations flag, and a Red Cross pennant. In his wallet were three different identity passes; he would decide which one to flash depending on the circumstances.

Dr Banquier had been surprisingly lucky. There had only been one road-block so far, and he had easily talked his way through that. He'd encountered another platoon of soldiers; whose side they were on, he had not even tried to guess. He was far to the east now, and they did not look like Congolese: marauding Hutus more likely, from over the Rwandan border. He'd had the Red Cross flag flying from his radio aerial by then, and that had done the trick. They had waved him on, but he'd watched anxiously in his rear-view mirror until they were well out of sight. A European in a Volvo might make useful target practice. There had been other unpleasant sights en route: burnt-out villages, wrecked buses and lorries, and dead, bloated animals had been commonplace. Once or twice he'd spotted the remains of a human corpse as it lay rotting by the roadside, providing food for both vultures and vermin.

The drive gave him time to think, to survey his life: past, present, future. Had his years at the medical school he had just been forced to abandon been any worse than the ones he would have led, back home in some Belgian prison? Probably not. Had he been sentenced to ten or twelve years with remission for good behaviour, he'd probably be out by now. At least prison would have prevented him becoming the alcoholic he now was. He was non-judgmental: he did not see himself as so badly flawed. At the day of reckoning he could point to some good he had done in life. And the future? He had some money, but not enough. He had skills that would still make him welcome in the more deprived parts of the Third World. He would survive.

Another long stretch of deeply rutted and potholed roadway lay ahead of him. He had hardly passed any other traffic for the past few miles, which he found both frightening and disconcerting. Then, just before a bend, he saw, to his joy, a rusting yellow signpost and an abandoned guard hut, a colonial legacy which announced the border with Uganda. He felt a sudden burst of elation: even if he had another blow-out, with his spare tyre gone already, he could still probably make it on foot to the first Ugandan army post if he had to. Life without fear was at last within his reach.

In that instant he saw the other road-block a hundred metres ahead. It was a far from professional affair but it was manned by half a dozen well-armed soldiers. This was no Ugandan army unit either. At a guess these were also Hutu rebels: the worst. They cocked their weapons and turned menacingly towards him as he brought the Volvo to a stop. He was ordered to get out; as he did so, he automatically raised his hands above his head. In one he waved his stethoscope, with the other he gestured to the Red Cross flag. 'Doctor . . . doctor!' he shouted in French. 'I am a doctor! Please, let me through.'

This time he failed to impress the soldiers, who seemed nervous and ill at ease. They ordered him to move away from the Volvo. Two of them strolled curiously up to the car and he reckoned that its contents would now be looted at the very least. One of the soldiers ordered him over towards the trees, bringing his gun up and aiming at him as he did so. For a moment Banquier felt that his luck had deserted him, that his end had come. It would be pointless trying to make a run for it: the jungle looked totally impenetrable and he would be shot down before he got any distance.

Just then another soldier, with a captain's ranking stars on his epaulettes, appeared from a jungle track at the side of the road. He started shouting at his men, who lowered their guns and backed away.

The captain came up to Banquier. 'You really a doctor?' he demanded in perfect French.

'Of course, captain,' Banquier responded.

'Where from?'

'Kisangani.'

'Where are you going?'

'Uganda. To stock up on some desperately needed drugs and medical equipment,' he lied.

'Red Cross?'

Banquier nodded.

'Come with me. I will show you where medicines are needed.'

The captain turned and, without a further word, moved back

into the bush. With two of the soldiers following close behind him, Banquier walked after the officer along a narrow track through the jungle until, after only a few minutes, they reached a clearing and a huddle of thatched, mud-walled hovels: a bush village.

The captain stopped in his tracks. 'Over there,' he said, pointing. He obviously did not intend going any further. Round the largest of the huts was a small compound, fenced with interwoven sticks and thorns as a protection for the occupants against wild animals. Strange moaning sounds came from within. A rude gate in the fence was half-open. Banquier pushed past it and walked inside.

A horrendous sight greeted him. There, lying on the ground, on mats, on rough palliasses or directly on the naked earth, were eight or ten men and women, all obviously terminally ill. Banquier had seen some vile and shocking medical sights over the years, but this was by far the worst. Each body seemed to rival its neighbour in the number of red and yellow ulcerating sores against black skin, as they cried, writhed, and moaned in their individual agonies. Banquier knew without approaching them that, though their eyes were open and staring, most of them must already be blind, for a dense grey veil seemed to have blanketed each eye.

He moved quickly back to the gate, where the captain was standing staring in equal horror at the scene.

'Aren't you going to help them?' the African asked Banquier.

'You must see they are beyond help.'

'Then?'

Banquier shrugged. 'You and your men have doubtless killed many healthy people,' he said. 'It would be kind to put them out of their misery.'

The captain stared at him in horror. He was deeply shocked. 'I could never do such a thing,' he said. Then, 'Are you truly a doctor?' he asked again. 'Can you really speak like that?'

'Truly, captain, I can. You would also be well advised to shoot any of your men who have been near or touched these people.'

'What? Why? What is it?' The soldier was staring at Banquier, a mixed expression of primitive panic and horror on his face.

'What is it? I think – no, I am confident it is, must be, a variant – a mutated virus of – one that spreads itself, rapidly, cruelly, deadly. There's always something new out of Africa. Have you ever heard of surge fever, captain?'

The captain turned away angrily. 'No,' he said. 'But it's typical. White people like you, from the so-called civilized Western democracies, you turn your backs on all this, our starvation, wars and epidemics . . .'

'I promise you one thing, captain,' Dr Banquier replied, staring coldly back at the soldier. 'The world will not be able to ignore what I have just seen. I promise you faithfully, I will see to that.'

The Osterman Weekend

Robert Ludlum

A VERY 'DIRTY' WEEKEND

John Tanner, network news director, is looking forward to a weekend party with his closest friends – the Ostermans, the Tremaynes and the Cardones. But then the CIA tell him that they are all suspected Soviet agents: fanatical, traitorous killers working for Omega, a massive Communist conspiracy.

From this moment, Tanner and his family are caught up in a nightmare whirlpool of terror, helpless isolation, violence and bloody slaughter. Until the shattering climax, Tanner cannot know who are his friends and who are his implacable, deadly enemies . . .

'Superb . . . pace and tension are stupendous, the solution devastating . . . compulsive entertainment' *Sunday Express*

'Acutely suspenseful . . . nobody is quite what they seem and there is a concussive finish' *Observer*

'Reserve this thriller killer for your next reading weekend and you will take a fresh look at your friends and neighbours' *Sunday Telegraph*

ISBN: 0 586 03743 8

Night Trap

Gordon Kent

This exhilarating tale of modern espionage and breathtaking flying action introduces a major new thriller-writing talent. With its striking authenticity and remarkable psychological depth, *Night Trap* is sure to appeal to the many fans of Tom Clancy, Stephen Coonts and Dale Brown.

Night Trap follows the career of Alan Craik, a young Intelligence officer in the US Navy, whose relentless investigation into the unexpected death of his own father, a legendary naval pilot, sets him on the trail of a father-and-son team of spies within his own ranks – serving members of the US Navy who have been betraying their country for years, and will risk everything not to be discovered.

'Flying, spying and dying – *Night Trap* is the real straight Navy stuff. Better strap yourself to the chair for this one. I loved it.' STEPHEN COONTS, author of *Fortunes of War*

'Here's a thriller that really flies. Gordon Kent knows his subject at first hand and the expertise shows on the page: high stakes, pounding tension and the best dogfights put on paper. A lot of thrillers these days, you come away feeling like you've been in a simulator. In *Night Trap*, Gordon Kent straps you into the real thing. Enjoy the ride!'

IAN RANKIN, author of *Dead Souls*

'*Night Trap* roars along like an F-14 in afterburner, taking the reader on a wild ride of suspense, intrigue, and gripping action. Plug in your G-Suit and get ready for the best military thriller in years.' PATRICK DAVIS, author of *The General*

ISBN 0 00 651009 4

Masquerade

Gayle Lynds

A woman awakes in a room she doesn't recognise, next to a husband she doesn't know, with no memory of her life or her past. She is told she is Liz Sansborough, a top US intelligence agent. But is she? The only thing that is certain is that somebody is trying to kill her. Sent to a CIA camp to regain her expert skills, Liz is given her deadly assignment: she must bring in the world's most lethal international assassin, a man known only by his alias, the Carnivore.

Rapidly entangled in a lethal masquerade, she comes to suspect that she is not Liz Sansborough at all, and that her CIA colleagues are the ones plotting to kill her. As she sets out to determine her true identity, she uncovers a multi-billion-dollar conspiracy that threatens to destroy the financial markets of Europe, and the world.

'Gayle Lynds has proven herself a master of intrigue and adventure. The rush-to-the-next-page excitement never stops. She has a huge talent for gripping descriptions of action.'
CLIVE CUSSLER

'*Masquerad*e is a bravura performance by Gayle Lynds, whose maiden race in the international thriller sweepstakes should make "the boys" turn around and take note. Watch out Robert Ludlum, she's coming up fast on your left!'
SUE GRAFTON

'More chase scenes than a James Bond film . . . Ms Lynds knows how to propel her people into action.' *New York Times*

'Edgy, tricky, very much in the mode of Robert Ludlum – a gloriously paranoid, immensely satisfying international thriller.' *Los Angeles Times*

ISBN 0 00 649770 5